AIKEN-BAMBER
Region

W9-BOT-883

Mrs. Jeffries and the
Best Laid Plans

DISCARD

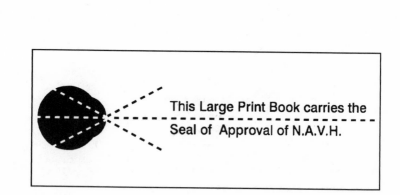

This Large Print Book carries the
Seal of Approval of N.A.V.H.

MRS. JEFFRIES AND THE BEST LAID PLANS

EMILY BRIGHTWELL

WHEELER PUBLISHING
An imprint of Thomson Gale, a part of The Thomson Corporation

Detroit • New York • San Francisco • New Haven, Conn. • Waterville, Maine • London

THOMSON

GALE

Copyright © 2007 by Cheryl Arguile.
A Victorian Mystery.
Wheeler, an imprint of the Gale Group.
Thomson and Star Logo and Wheeler are trademarks and Gale is a registered trademark used herein under license.

ALL RIGHTS RESERVED
This is a work of fiction. Names, characters, places, and incidents either are the product of the author's imagination or are used fictitiously, and any resemblance to actual persons, living or dead, business establishments, events, or locales is entirely coincidental. The publisher does not have any control over and does not assume any responsibility for author or third-party Web sites or their content.
Wheeler Publishing Large Print Cozy Mystery.
The text of this Large Print edition is unabridged.
Other aspects of the book may vary from the original edition.
Set in 16 pt. Plantin.

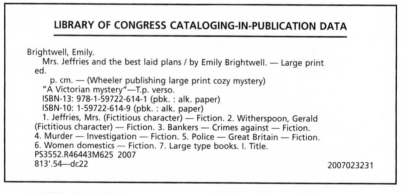

LIBRARY OF CONGRESS CATALOGING-IN-PUBLICATION DATA

Brightwell, Emily.
    Mrs. Jeffries and the best laid plans / by Emily Brightwell. — Large print ed.
        p. cm. — (Wheeler publishing large print cozy mystery)
    "A Victorian mystery"—T.p. verso.
    ISBN-13: 978-1-59722-614-1 (pbk. : alk. paper)
    ISBN-10: 1-59722-614-9 (pbk. : alk. paper)
    1. Jeffries, Mrs. (Fictitious character) — Fiction. 2. Witherspoon, Gerald (Fictitious character) — Fiction. 3. Bankers — Crimes against — Fiction. 4. Murder — Investigation — Fiction. 5. Police — Great Britain — Fiction. 6. Women domestics — Fiction. 7. Large type books. I. Title.
    PS3552.R46443M625 2007
    813'.54—dc22   2007023231

Published in 2007 by arrangement with The Berkley Publishing Group, a member of Penguin Group (USA) Inc.

Printed in the United States of America on permanent paper
10 9 8 7 6 5 4 3 2 1

For Nanette Caldararo, with love and appreciation for all the years of inspiration and support. Thanks, Nanny; you helped me to live my dream.

CHAPTER 1

"I don't think we'll ever get this wedding planned." Betsy sighed and closed the cookbook. "Worrying about all the details has me so muddled that I can't even think of what to serve at the reception."

Mrs. Jeffries, the housekeeper for Inspector Gerald Witherspoon, smiled sympathetically at the pretty blonde-haired maid. "You're doing fine, Betsy. We've still almost a month before the big day. That's plenty of time to decide on the menu."

"It feels like it's happening tomorrow and I'm not near ready. I can't even decide on what kind of dress I want."

"You'll get it all done," said Mrs. Jeffries, glancing at the maid. Betsy was staring morosely at the closed cookbook. The poor girl was going to make herself ill over a few simple wedding plans. This wasn't at all like her. Betsy was normally a strong, rather decisive young woman who could make the

7

hardest decisions, some of them involving life and death, with the greatest of ease. Yet planning her own wedding had turned her into a nervous Nellie of the worst sort. There was nothing that the housekeeper could say that would allay her fears, either. The girl had to fight these demons on her own.

Betsy was afraid she was going to fail, that she was going to embarrass herself or even worse, her fiancé, Smythe, by doing something wrong on the most important day of their lives. She'd come from a poverty stricken family in the East End of London and she'd ended up as a maid here at Upper Edmonton Gardens by collapsing on their doorstep. She was having a proper wedding and an elegant reception. Unfortunately, she had little confidence in her own social skills, and she was terrified that something would go wrong.

"But I don't want to inconvenience Luty, and it's her staff that's doing all the work," Betsy cried. "I'm going to make up my mind. Gracious, it's only a little reception."

"Take your time, child," Mrs. Jeffries said kindly. "Luty won't mind in the least." Luty Belle Crookshank was an American friend of the household. She had insisted on hosting Betsy's wedding reception at her elegant home in Knightsbridge. To anyone outside their immediate circle, it might seem an odd state of affairs for a wealthy woman to host a reception for a poor housemaid. But the bonds between the household of Upper Edmonton Garden and Luty Belle Crookshank were special enough to overcome the rigid class structure of socially conscious London.

"I know she won't mind, but I want to get it done. It's important that everything is planned properly, you know what I mean?" Betsy flipped open the cover of the huge red book. "Mind you, I wish Smythe would tell me what he's got up his sleeve for us. I don't even know where we're going to live."

"Have a little faith, girl," Mrs. Goodge said as she came in from the hallway. The cook had been in the dry larder and she carried a tin of baking powder in one hand and a bag of currants in the other. She was a plump, elderly woman with wire-framed spectacles, white hair tucked under her floppy cooks cap, and a pristine white apron over her pale blue work dress. A big, yellow tabby cat followed at her heels. "Smythe will do right by you. He's got everything arranged."

"Well, it wouldn't hurt him to tell me a few bits and pieces, would it," Betsy declared. "Don't get me wrong; I'm happy to be getting married and I love him with all my heart, but it's going to change things. It's going to change everything, and that scares me a bit. I don't think I'm ready to give it up yet."

"Who says you have to?" Mrs. Jeffries understood exactly what "it" was. "Our investigations are just as important to Smythe as they are to you. I'm sure he's thought of a way for you to live together as man and wife and still work with us. He's not ready to give it all up yet, either."

Hepzibah Jeffries was the widow of a Yorkshire policeman. After her husband's death, she'd sold her property and come to London. She'd intended to spend her days doing charity work, going to museums, and perhaps traveling on the Continent as a companion to a gentlewoman. Instead, she'd seen an advertisement offering a position as a housekeeper for a policeman. She soon found herself working for Inspector Gerald Witherspoon of the Metropolitan Police Force.

Witherspoon had been in charge of the records room, but soon after her arrival in his life, his world had changed when she and the rest of the household had begun investigating the horrible Kensington High Street murders. Naturally, he was unaware of their involvement. By the time the case was solved and he'd caught the killer, he was no longer in charge of the records room. By now, their inspector had solved over twenty homicides and was by far the most famous detective in the city.

"I suppose not." Betsy sighed again. "I just wish he'd tell me. But all he says is that it's a secret and I'll love it."

"Then take him at his word." Mrs. Goodge took off her apron, draped it over the back of the chair, and then sat down. She pushed back from the table and patted her lap. The cat, Samson, jumped up and curled into a ball. After giving the other two women a good glare, he settled down and began to purr. "And quit worryin' so much. It'll all come out in the wash. It's only a simple reception. What could possibly go wrong?"

"What if I serve the wrong thing?" Betsy asked worriedly. "Wedding breakfasts have very strict etiquette."

"Don't be silly. I've cooked in some of the finest houses in this land. Do you think I'd sit idly by and let you serve anything that isn't right?" Mrs. Goodge had had enough of the girl's foolishness. She wasn't going to allow her to ruin the best day of her life by fretting over every little detail.

"Yes, I know," Betsy protested. "But it's not just the food. What if I do something or say something —"

"You'll be just fine," the cook said firmly. "You're an intelligent young woman who knows what's what. Now, take a good gander at that cookbook and decide what you'd like served at the reception. We want to have all the details of your wedding planned just in case we get us another investigation."

"Another murder," Betsy wailed. "Oh dear, I'd not even thought of that." This was an out-and-out lie. She'd thought of nothing else. She'd love to have a good investigation to think about; anything would be better than planning this wedding. Dashing about London talking to shopkeepers and tradespeople would be so much easier than trying to figure out whether to have the reception at eleven or eleven thirty or whether to serve roast beef or chicken cutlets or whether to have pink roses or yellow ones. Or maybe she shouldn't use roses at all; perhaps using flowers as the centerpieces at a wedding reception was completely inappropriate.

She loved Smythe so much, and her dearest wish was for him to be proud of her on that special day. She was so scared she wasn't up to this task. Why couldn't they have just gone off to Gretna Green and gotten married? "For once, I hope that doesn't happen. I couldn't do both."

" 'Course you could," the cook said stoutly. "You're young and spry. You can do anything you set your mind to do." Mrs. Goodge had worked for some of the wealthiest families in England, but there was no household she'd rather be in than this one. When her last employer had let her go, she'd accepted this position thinking she'd taken a step down in the world. She, who had worked for England's oldest, most aristocratic families, had been forced to take a position with a common policeman. But it was the only position she could find. After a lifetime of keeping everyone in their proper place and staying firmly in her own, once she'd come here, the bounds she'd set between herself and others withered and died. These people had become her family. Mrs. Goodge wasn't sure exactly how that had happened. Certainly the murder investigations had helped strengthen the bonds between them all, but it had been more than that. They'd come together because they were each of them alone in the world, and everyday, Mrs. Goodge thanked God he'd guided her here and not to the home of

13

some dissolute baron or count.

Since she'd first walked in the back door of Upper Edmonton Gardens, she'd changed a great deal. Who said you couldn't teach an old dog new tricks? She smiled and stroked Samson's back. She'd certainly learned a few tricks these past years. She'd discovered she could loosen every tongue that passed through this kitchen by plying them with tea and treats.

Mrs. Goodge did all her investigating without ever leaving the comfort of this cozy room. She had a huge network of tradespeople, gas men, delivery boys, street vendors, and old colleagues that she called upon when they had a case. Gossip was her stock and trade, and she'd gotten very good at gleaning every morsel of information there was to be had about a victim or a suspect in one of their murders. But interesting as their investigations might be, she was most proud of the fact that in the twilight of her life, she'd had, through God's grace, the chance to contribute to the cause of justice. Their investigations had brought vicious killers to their just rewards and, more important, had kept the innocent from hanging.

"Mrs. Goodge, are you all right?" Betsy stared at her anxiously.

"Oh, yes, sorry. I was woolgathering. Did you say something?" She shifted in her chair and the movement caused the cat to let out a tiny meow of displeasure. "There, lovey, it's fine," she soothed.

"I asked if you think we ought to have roast chicken or the rolled beef," the maid replied. "What do you think?"

"Have both," the cook replied. "It might be called a wedding breakfast, but it's really more of a luncheon. Your guests will expect a nice feed."

"But I don't want to put Luty's staff to too much trouble," Betsy said. "I don't want to overstep my bounds."

"Don't be silly," the cook replied. "Luty's your friend. She wants to do this for you. You're not taking advantage of her in the least."

"Of course you're not," Mrs. Jeffries added. "Luty and Hatchet are absolutely thrilled to host this for you." Hatchet had also insisted on being a part of the festivities. He was Luty Belle's butler, but from the way the two of them related to one another, he was far more than just a servant. He was Luty's most trusted friend.

The two households had met during the second of the inspector's murder investigations. Luty had been a witness. But though she was elderly, she'd figured out soon enough what they were about, and after that case was solved, she'd then come to them with a problem of her own. She and Hatchet had helped in that investigation, and ever since, they'd insisted on helping with all of them. Their connections had proved very useful as Luty was no stranger to homes of the rich and the powerful. Though Hatchet was a bit reticent about his past, his circle of acquaintances had proved helpful on more than one occasion.

"All right then, we'll have both the roast chicken and the beef. What do you think about the soup?"

"Leek and potato soup is always good," the cook replied. "It's hearty without being overpowering."

"I like leek and potato soup," Wiggins, the footman, declared as he strolled into the room. He was a cheerful lad in his early twenties with a ready smile, rosy round cheeks, and brown hair that had a tendency to curl when he went too long between trips to the barber. He carried a tin of brass polish in his hand. Fred, the household's black-and-brown mongrel dog, trotted at his heels.

Samson took one look at Fred, hissed in his direction, and then leapt off the cook's lap and charged for the sanctuary of Mrs.

Goodge's room. Wiggins laughed. "I'm glad Fred finally learned how to handle your cat, Mrs. Goodge," he said. He knelt down and pulled open the cupboard under the sink and shoved the tin inside.

"It took him long enough," Mrs. Jeffries murmured. Poor Fred had skulked about in fear of Samson for weeks after Wiggins had brought him home. He'd rescued the animal from certain starvation. Samson had been the pet of a murder victim, but he'd such a miserable disposition that he'd have been destroyed if Wiggins hadn't taken pity on him. Samson repaid this kindness by biting and scratching his benefactor and everyone else in the household, especially if they went too near his food dish. Yet the cat had taken one look at the cook, and it had been love at first sight.

"I don't know why everyone thinks Samson is so mean," Mrs. Goodge complained. "He's a sweet old boy if you treat him right."

No one had the heart to argue with her. They all just kept their fingers away from Samson's food dish.

"The brass polish is almost gone," Wiggins said to Mrs. Jeffries. "And I saw Smythe coming down the road. What are we havin' with mornin' tea? Are we 'avin' them little sweet buns you was bakin' yesterday?"

"Those are for supper," Mrs. Goodge replied. "I've got a nice loaf of bread and a plain seed cake for tea. If Smythe is almost here, we can sit down on time for once."

"I'll put the kettle on the boil." Betsy closed the cookbook and got up.

"It's startin' to rain out there," Smythe announced a moment later as he walked into the kitchen. He was a tall, muscular man in his late thirties. He had a headful of black hair, thick eyebrows, and harsh, heavy features. He shrugged out of his jacket and hung it on the coat tree.

"It's been a very wet spring," Mrs. Jeffries commented as she laid a stack of plates in the center of the table.

"I hope it won't rain on our wedding day." Betsy pulled the big brown teapot down off the shelf and reached for the tea tin. "That would really be awful."

Smythe walked over and put his hands on her shoulders. "Now, love, I've told ya a dozen times. Stop frettin' about the wedding. It's all goin' to come right. Even if it rains, the church roof doesn't leak."

"Yes, but I don't want it to rain. It's our wedding, Smythe, and I want everything to be perfect." She looked at him over her shoulder. "Where have you been this morning?"

He laughed and dropped into his chair. "Now that would be tellin', wouldn't it? You'll know soon enough."

Betsy gave him a good glare and then went back to making the tea.

Years ago, Smythe had worked as a coachman for the Inspector's late aunt, Euphemia Witherspoon. Then he'd gone to Australia to seek his fortune. He found the fortune and came home to England. As a courtesy, he stopped in to say hello to his former employer. He discovered her dying and surrounded by a houseful of servants, all of whom were taking terrible advantage of the poor woman. Wiggins, who was really just a lad at the time, was the only one tending to the poor lady's illness.

Smythe had sent the servants packing, called in a decent solicitor to handle the woman's affairs, and then prepared to take his leave. But Euphemia knew she wasn't long for this earth, and she'd begged him to stay on in the house and see her nephew, Gerald Witherspoon, settled in properly. She didn't want people taking advantage of him the way she'd been used. Smythe had come back from Australia as rich as sin, but he did as Euphemia asked and stayed on in the household, telling himself he was simply making sure the newest servants, Mrs.

Jeffries and Mrs. Goodge, were both decent people. Then Betsy had collapsed on their doorstep, so he'd stayed a bit longer, and before you could say "Blast a Spaniard," they were investigating murders and becoming a family. By then, of course, he was madly in love with Betsy.

The problem then became how could he tell them he was rich? People didn't like to think you'd been deliberately trying to fool them, and after so much time had passed, he was afraid that was how they might feel. But Mrs. Jeffries had figured it out on her own, and when he and Betsy had gotten serious, he'd told her. But the others still didn't know his true wealth.

"I wish we 'ad us another murder," Wiggins said as he took his place at the table. "All this wedding plannin' is enough to drive a fellow mad."

"It's got nothing to do with you, lad," Mrs. Goodge chided. "It's us women that are doin' all the work. But that's always the way of the world, isn't it? A woman's work is never done."

"I'm doin' my part." Smythe slipped into his chair. "I went to see the vicar today about the banns."

"That's not exactly hard work," Betsy said.

"It is too 'ard work," the coachman argued. "Fellow likes the sound of his own voice. I spent an hour and a half listening to him go on and on about the need for Portuguese prayer books for the mission in Brazil. I 'ad to given him a couple of shillings to escape when I did."

Lawrence Boyd stepped back from the easel and studied his work critically. The light streaming in from the large windows let him see every imperfect detail of the painting. He frowned, not liking the look of the cat. He'd taken a bit of artistic license here with the color, but so what. That was his right; he was an artist. The color was fine, but there was something about the shape of the head that didn't look right. He could fix that. He laughed to himself as he reached for the tin of turpentine on the little table next to the easel. This was going to be a wonderful day. He reminded himself to periodically check his pocket watch. He wanted to allow plenty of time to get ready for luncheon. But he had a few minutes left before he had to stop.

There was a soft knock on the studio door.

"Come in," he called. He put the turpentine back on the table, leaving it open so he could clean his brushes.

"Sorry to disturb you, sir." James Glover,

his chief clerk, hovered in the doorway of the small studio. "I've brought you the files you asked for, sir."

"Bring them in man. Don't just stand there. I expected you twenty minutes ago."

"The traffic was dreadful, sir." Glover, a fat man of forty with thinning blond hair and a handlebar mustache, stepped into the studio. He wore a dark blue suit, white shirt, and old-fashioned maroon tie. Sweat darkened the hair around his temples, and his face was flushed, as though he'd been running. In his arms, he carried a stack of folders. "There was a terrible accident on the Uxbridge Road. I finally got out of my hansom and walked the half mile."

"Yee Gods, man, you can walk the entire distance in twenty minutes." Boyd waved off his excuses. "Did you bring the Pressley file?"

"Yes, sir." Glover swallowed nervously. "It's right here."

"Put them on the table by the door," he said, staring at Glover. "Good Lord, Glover, you're sweating like a pig. What on earth is wrong with you?"

"I'm fine, sir." Glover smiled weakly. "The rain has made everything a bit sticky. If it's all the same to you, sir, I'll go tidy myself up a bit."

"There's a bathroom off the hall you can use," Boyd replied. "Then I'd like you to peek into the study and check that Miss Clarke is working. Don't let her see you. She seems to know what she's about, but it never hurts to keep an eye on people. Even the most trustworthy staff can disappoint you." He stared hard at Glover as he spoke and was rewarded by seeing the man's cheeks turn deathly pale.

"Yes, sir." Glover's voice was barely audible. He looked as if he were going to be ill. "I'll see you at the luncheon, sir. Thank you very much for inviting me."

"I want to speak to you afterward." Boyd smiled, "Come into my study after the others have left."

"You want to speak to me?" Glover's voice was now a high-pitched squeak. "Really? About what sir?"

"We'll discuss it then," Boyd replied. "Go along, now. I want to work for a little longer"

"Yes, sir." Glover backed up toward the door as he spoke, then whirled about and hurried out.

Boyd watched him through the small window that overlooked the back garden. Glover's head was bowed and his shoulders slumped as he trudged across the wet lawn to the main house.

"You've reason to look worried," Boyd muttered. But he was determined not to let the ugliness of what was coming ruin his perfect day. He could deal with Glover after the luncheon, after Gibbons made everything nice and official. He picked up his cigar from the ashtray on the small table, struck a match, and lit the end. He turned back to the painting and studied it as he smoked. It was very good, but there was a detail or two that he still thought could use a bit more work.

He put the cigar down and picked up his brush. He had enough time to correct the shape of the cat's head. For the next twenty minutes, he concentrated on making the delicate brush strokes that would perfect the painting. He heard the door open again, but he didn't bother looking away from his work. "I told you I'd see you after luncheon, Glover. Now take yourself out of here and leave me in peace. I've got another ten minutes more work to do."

But there was no reply, merely the sound of footsteps crossing the hard wood floor. Alarmed now, Boyd tore his gaze away from the painting and whirled around. His eyes widened in surprise and his mouth gaped open in shock. But before he could speak, something hard and heavy crashed into the side of his head. Moaning, he slumped to his knees. The assailant raised his hands and hit him again, this time harder, landing the blow smack in the back of his victim's skull.

Boyd swayed to one side, but his attacker grabbed him by the back of his smock just as he toppled to the floor and maneuvered him toward the settee. Working swiftly, the killer managed to shove, push, and pull Boyd until he was lying on the settee with his feet hanging over the end and his head at the other end, battered side down.

Working quickly, the assailant checked for a heartbeat, but there was nothing. Lawrence Boyd was well and truly dead.

The murderer stood up and grabbed the tin of turpentine off the table, pausing for a brief moment to look at the painting before continuing on with the grim task of pouring the paint remover on the dead man. It was important to make sure it soaked Boyd's smock and the settee. The tin was almost full, so the liquid splashed everywhere as it dispersed, dousing the muslin table runner, the floor, and the bottom of the easel.

Then the assailant picked up the cigar and tucked it neatly between Boyd's now lifeless fingers, reached for the matches, struck one, and tossed it at the muslin runner.

The killer tossed the remainder of the turpentine about the room, soaking the old carpet remnant by the side table and splattering the limp curtains on the little window by the door. The killer struck another match, and within moments, the curtains were blazing and the carpet smoking.

The killer moved to the doorway, took one last look around, and smiled in satisfaction before opening the door and stepping outside. By the time help arrived, it would be too late; the entire studio would be up in flames and with it, the evidence that murder had been done. This would simply be an unfortunate accident.

That was exactly the way the murderer had planned it.

"Oh dear, the guests should be arriving any moment now. I suppose the luncheon will have to be cancelled." Leeson, the butler to Lawrence Boyd, looked anxiously toward the main house. He was standing on the gravel pathway leading to the studio. A fireman stood at the front door and another two were on the roof of the small building, checking that the fire hadn't spread to the rafters. Tendrils of smoke drifted on the wind and the air smelled like burning wood, but the fire itself had been put out before it could do too much damage.

Leeson sighed and wished he didn't have to deal with this mess. It simply wasn't fair. He was a butler, for goodness sake. Now he was going to have to go and tell the guests that Mr. Boyd was dead and the luncheon cancelled. He wondered if he ought to invite them to eat before they left. What did etiquette dictate in these circumstances? They had been invited and there was plenty of food. Perhaps Mrs. Rothwell would know what they ought to do. After all, she wasn't just the housekeeper; she was a distant relation to Mr. Boyd. Yes, that's what he'd do. He'd let her make the decision.

He breathed easier and turned his attention to the clump of people standing on the small terrace by the back door of the main house. Miss Clarke, the typewriter girl, was speaking to one of the maids, and Mrs. Rothwell was standing next to the cook. Leeson moved toward the fireman standing by the studio door.

"We're almost finished here," the fireman said as he approached.

"Poor Mr. Boyd. What a terrible thing to have happened, but I suppose if Miss Clarke hadn't seen the smoke and raised the alarm, it might have been much worse. We were all gone."

"If she'd not raised the alarm, the building would have been completely burned." The fireman adjusted the chin strap to his helmet. He glanced through the open door of the studio to the body lying on the settee. "But before you do anything else, you'd best get a policeman here and be quick about it."

"A policeman?" Leeson was dreadfully confused. "But you said the fire was out. Why do we need a policeman?"

"Because your Mr. Boyd is dead, but it wasn't the fire that killed him."

"At least this one is in your district, sir," Constable Barnes said to Inspector Gerald Witherspoon as their hansom cab headed for Bayswater. Barnes was a smart old copper with steely gray hair, a ruddy complexion, and weak knees. He'd been on the force for more years than he cared to recall but now found himself in the enviable position of working almost exclusively with Inspector Gerald Witherspoon. "That's a bit of a relief."

Witherspoon had a pale, bony face, thinning brown hair, and deep-set blue eyes. He pushed his spectacles up his long nose and looked at Barnes. "Why is it a relief? Is there something about this case that I ought to be concerned about?"

Barnes tried to think of a diplomatic way of putting the situation. "Well, sir, I only meant that Inspector Nivens can't grouse that you've stolen this one from him. It's in your division, sir, so by rights you should be the one to take it."

"He'll still complain." Witherspoon shrugged philosophically. "But there's nothing I can do about that."

Barnes grabbed the handhold as the cab lurched forward. "You can get there first, sir. I know you don't like running to the chief inspector and telling tales, but you could let him know that Nivens has threatened to ruin you. If you get that established right away and make sure a formal complaint is lodged in his record, it might make Nivens think twice before he tries making any mischief."

Witherspoon waved his hand impatiently. "We mustn't blow it out of proportion, Constable. He was very upset about the Odell matter and if you look at it from his point of view, we did interfere in the case."

"We kept an innocent man from hanging," Barnes protested.

"Of course we did and we acted properly in doing so, but our proving Odell innocent meant that Inspector Nivens lost his only homicide conviction."

Barnes realized that being diplomatic wasn't going to be very useful. "He's out for blood, sir. Take my word for it; Nivens is going to do everything he can to ruin you and your reputation. You must take care."

The inspector said nothing for a moment. "I appreciate your concern, Constable, but I won't complain against the man. Not until he actually does something to me."

"By then it might be too late, sir," Barnes said earnestly. He had to get Witherspoon to understand how much damage Nivens could and would do.

"We've no time to worry about Inspector Nivens at the moment. Tell me what you know about *this* murder." The inspector was tired of both his constable and even his household constantly warning him about Nivens. Why just this morning his housekeeper had mentioned watching out for the fellow. Honestly, they were all making far too much of a few idle threats made in the heat of the moment.

Barnes knew when to shut up. He whipped out his little brown notebook and flipped it open. "The name of the victim is Lawrence Boyd. He's a banker."

"How was he killed?"

"The report didn't say. It only gave his

name and address: 14 Laurel Road, Bays-water." Barnes looked out the window. "This is a posh neighborhood, so I expect he's someone with either money or connections, probably both. Oh good, we're almost there. We've turned onto his street."

Lawrence Boyd lived in a large four-story house made of white stone and red brick. There was no fencing between the house and the road, merely a strip of lawn with newly dug flower beds at each corner. On each side of the black doorway, there was a large brass lamp. A police constable stood guard by the front door. He hurried toward them as they climbed out of the hansom.

"I can see why they called us in so quickly," Barnes muttered. "Rich people hate murder. It's so very inconvenient for them."

"Yes, I daresay, you're right," Witherspoon murmured. Murder amongst the wealthy was always very tiresome. It had been his experience that the more money people had, the less inclined they were to cooperate with the police.

"Good day, sir." The constable directed his remark to the inspector and then nodded respectfully at Constable Barnes. "I'm Constable Tucker. We're very glad you've arrived. If you'll come this way, I'll take you around to the body." He started toward the side of the house.

"I'm Inspector Witherspoon and this is Constable Barnes," the inspector said as they trailed after the constable.

"I know who you are, sir, and in keeping with your methods, Constable Maxton and I have made sure that nothing has been touched," Tucker said eagerly. "Once we got here and saw the body, we didn't even let the fire brigade muck about any more than was necessary to insure the fire was out. But actually, they had the fire already out, so it wasn't so much a matter of them mucking about as it was picking up their equipment and leaving. But we made sure they were careful not to move things about any more than they had to, sir." Tucker smiled proudly at the inspector.

"Er, yes, that was very good thinking on your part," Witherspoon murmured. By now, they had rounded the building and come to the back garden. By London standards, it was huge. The lawn was ringed by flowers beds and thick bushes, behind which was a wood fence that stood at least eight feet high. At the far end of the garden was a small wooden structure that was larger than a shed but smaller than a conservatory. Two policemen were standing by the open door.

Tendrils of smoke drifted up from the small open window. Witherspoon wrinkled his nose as an ugly, burning scent assaulted his nostrils.

"Ugh, that's not very pleasant." Barnes made a face. "It smells like burning carpet mixed with roasted pig."

"It could have been a lot worse, sir," said Constable Tucker as they continued across the garden. "If the body had been burnt, it would really stink the place up to high heaven. That's what the fire captain told us."

"You were called here by the fire brigade?" Witherspoon asked.

"Yes, sir. As soon as they saw the body, they sent for us straightaway."

They reached the structure, and Witherspoon nodded at the two constables.

"The body is just in here, sir," one of the lads said helpfully. "We've not touched anything."

Witherspoon hesitated. There was still smoke rising from the roof, and now that he was this close, he could see scorch marks on the door and window. "Is it safe?"

"Oh, yes, sir," Constable Tucker said eagerly. "The fire brigade assured us the fire is completely out. It'll smoke for awhile, but it's quite safe to go inside."

Witherspoon nodded dully. "Uh, is the

body badly burnt?" He swallowed heavily, telling himself he must do his duty. He mustn't be so squeamish. Looking at corpses was part and parcel of his position.

"No, sir. It's hardly been touched. Which is a bit of a luck if you ask me," Tucker replied. "See for yourself, sir."

Barnes stepped through the door. Witherspoon steeled himself and followed.

Once inside, they stopped and gaped in amazement. On the right side of the room, most of the wall had been removed and the wood replaced with three very large windows. At the far end of the room behind the settee, there was a row of built-in cupboards. The body was on the settee, looking for all the world like a man asleep.

Witherspoon crossed over to the table on the far end of the settee and looked at the painting on the easel. It was singed a bit about the edges, but otherwise it appeared intact. Near the door, there was an old faded carpet remnant, now badly burnt and soaked with water, and beyond the rug, another smaller table with what looked like files piled atop it. He was surprised at how nothing appeared to be badly damaged. If it wasn't for the water soaking everything, one would not even notice there'd been a fire.

Witherspoon stiffened his spine and turned to the body. He stood looking at for a long moment. "The body's hardly been touched."

Barnes eased in on the other side of the settee, directly across from the inspector. He reached down and grasped Boyd's chin, gently turning the head to afford a better view of the back of the skull. "I can see why they called us so quickly, sir. His head's been bashed in. That's probably what killed him."

Witherspoon swallowed the bile that rose in his throat. He took a deep breath and then wished he hadn't as his nostrils filled with air smelling of harsh chemicals, smoke, and now, blood. He knew he was being fanciful; it was far too soon for the corpse to begin to smell, but nonetheless, he was certain he could sense it. He sniffed again, this time concentrating and trying separate out the different scents. "Do you smell that, Barnes?"

"Smell what?" Barnes sucked up air through his nose and then shook his head, his expression rueful. "I can't smell much of anything, sir. I never could. The missus claims I couldn't smell a dead skunk if it was lying two feet from my big toe."

"It's a chemical smell." The inspector

frowned. "You know, like creosote or lime water."

Barnes noticed the tin of turpentine lying on the floor beneath the small window. "It's turpentine." He pointed at the tin as he came out from behind the settee. "The cap is off, sir."

Witherspoon glanced around the room and spotted the cap on the table. "Someone deliberately took the lid off and spilled it about the room," he concluded. "That tin didn't fly from the table to the floor on its own. I expect the killer used the turpentine to try and spread the fire. Perhaps even cover up that the poor fellow had been murdered."

"Surely no one could think this would be thought of as an accident?" Barnes said. "The poor man's head has been bashed all to bits."

Witherspoon thought for a moment. "Yet why bash his head in and then try to make it look like an accident? Why start a fire at all? No, the killer either started a fire to draw attention to the body, which I highly doubt as most people tend to want to avoid drawing attention to people they've just murdered, or the murderer wanted to cover up the fact that it was murder. If the fire had spread and the walls had collapsed, then the entire ceiling would have caved in. In which case, there wouldn't have been enough of the victim left to give us any indication of how he'd really died."

Barnes wasn't so sure, but he said nothing. He didn't have any better ideas himself.

Witherspoon moved over to the small window and turned to survey the room. He noted the position of the corpse, and on the floor, just below where the man's fingers rested, he saw the burnt remains of a cigar. "And in case the roof didn't cave in and only the interior of the room and the body were burned, the murderer tried to make it appear as if Mr. Boyd had fallen asleep while he was smoking," he said, speculating. "That's what the killer wanted us to think."

"If the killer was trying to make it look like an accident, he botched it badly." Barnes pointed at the burnt cigar stub. "The first thing that would burn in a fire is that bit there. There'd have been nothing there but ash."

"True." Witherspoon turned his head and glanced out the small window. Constable Tucker was trudging across the lawn. He carried a pair of scissors and a ball of twine and had a roll of brown paper tucked under his arm. "What's more, people are afraid of fire. When they see smoke, they call the fire brigade. Surely the murderer must have known someone would get help and the ruse would be discovered."

Constable Tucker popped his head into the studio. "May I come in, sir? I'd like to wrap up the evidence and take it down to the station." He waved the roll of brown paper and grinned triumphantly. "I know all about your methods, sir, so I said to myself, 'Tucker, what would the inspector do?' So I marched right into the kitchen and asked the cook if I could borrow a few things. She was quite happy to oblige, sir."

Witherspoon wasn't sure what Constable Tucker wanted to do, but he didn't wish to discourage the young man. "Certainly, Constable, come right on in. We're almost through here."

Tucker dashed across the wet floor, almost slipped, and then righted himself.

"Take care, Constable," Witherspoon warned. His gaze shifted to the floor. Most of the water had seeped through the floorboards, leaving bright puddles and splashes of color, especially under the easel. "We don't want you breaking a leg." He turned back to Barnes and left Tucker to his evidence gathering, which looked to consist mostly of wrapping up Boyd's painting.

Witherspoon didn't particularly see that as any sort of evidence. It wasn't as if the man had written the name of the killer on the painting, but he didn't wish to make Tucker feel like his efforts were unappreciated.

"Er, excuse me, Inspector, may I have a word with you?" The voice came from the open window.

Witherspoon turned and peered out between the remnants of the burnt curtains. A tall, gaunt-faced man dressed in an old-fashioned butler's uniform stared back at him. "I take it you're the butler," he said.

"Yes, sir, I'm Leeson. I'm sorry to bother you, but the guests were wondering if they might leave. They've been here for several hours now and they want to go home." Leeson struggled to keep his gaze on the Inspector and not the body lying on the settee.

"Guests? Mr. Boyd was having guests today?"

"Yes, sir, I tried to get word to all of them that the luncheon was cancelled, but they all arrived just as the fire brigade was leaving and then insisted on staying until they heard what had happened. But now they'd like to leave. Especially Mr. Glover. He'd like to go back to the office and let the others know about Mr. Boyd's death."

"No, I'm afraid the guests can't leave," Witherspoon said quickly. "Tell them we'll be up directly to have a word with them."

"But they weren't even here when the fire started," the butler protested. He knew that none of the guests were going to take kindly to being trapped here any longer. Besides, if they stayed much longer, they'd want tea and cook was already in a horrid mood. "No one was here but Miss Clarke and Mr. Glover."

"What about the servants?" Barnes walked over to stand beside the inspector. "Weren't they here when the fire started?"

"We were all at a funeral," Leeson explained. "One of the housemaids died of pneumonia. Everyone except Mr. Boyd went to the funeral. The fire brigade was here when we got back."

"But you were having guests for luncheon today?" Barnes pressed. "Who was doing the cooking?"

"It was already prepared," Leeson explained. He looked nervously over his shoulder at the house, as though he were expecting a horde of angry guests to come streaming out the back door, demanding to be either fed or let go. "Mr. Boyd knew the staff wanted to go to Helen's service, so he told cook to prepare a cold luncheon.

Everything else was done; the table was set and the serving trolleys at the ready, so all we had to do was serve."

"What about this Miss Clarke and Mr. Grover?" Witherspoon interjected. "Why didn't they go to the funeral?"

"They're not part of the household. Miss Clarke is a typist. She's from one of those agencies. She came along to help Mr. Boyd catch up on his work. Mr. Glover brought some files over from Mr. Boyd's office. Please, sir, can I go back to the house and tell the guests that they've got to stay for awhile longer? I do believe that some of them are going to leave with or without your permission."

Witherspoon glanced at Barnes. "Constable, can you go along with Leeson and insure that no one leaves just yet. I'll be in as soon as I've given the police constables their instructions."

Barnes grinned broadly. "Certainly, sir. Come along, Leeson. Let's go and take care of your guests."

As soon as the two men had gone, Witherspoon forced himself to go back to the body. Tucker was putting another sheet of brown paper around the painting, but he stopped what he was doing and watched the inspector.

Witherspoon went behind the settee and gazed down at the back of the skull. He wasn't sure what he was looking for, but he knew it was important to absorb as much detail as possible. Unfortunately, the ugly mangle of matted hair, blood, and bone told him only that the poor fellow had been hit with something very hard.

"Excuse me, sir, but what are you looking for?" Tucker asked.

"Anything that may help us solve the crime," he explained. "I think our victim was hit with something very hard, something that killed him very quickly and that might become important evidence."

Tucker reached for the ball of twine. "I don't see anything in here that could be a murder weapon."

"Let's have a good look at the place before we make any assertions, Constable." He surveyed the small room again. "The weapon would have to be something heavy, something that could be easily lifted by the killer and used to hit hard enough to break through hair and bone."

"Right, sir." Tucker wound the ball of twine around the painting. "There's no metal doorstops or big brass candlesticks."

"Let's have a look at what's in the cup-boards." Witherspoon opened the one nearest him and looked inside. The cupboard was wide and deep with two shelves. On the top shelf there were two fat sketchbooks and a box of charcoal. On the bottom shelf were three canvases stored sideways. Witherspoon pulled one out and saw that it was simply a painting of the sea.

"Did you find anything, sir?" Tucker asked eagerly.

"No, just art supplies and more paintings." He shoved the last one back into the cupboard and continued his search. In the other cupboards, he found more paints and another tin of turpentine. But he found nothing that could be used as a weapon. "I'm afraid, Constable, that the murder weapon isn't here. That's going to make finding the killer much more difficult."

"Not to worry, sir. You'll catch the murderer." Tucker lifted the painting off the easel. "You always do."

Witherspoon wasn't so sure. He was beginning to think that living up to his own reputation was becoming harder with each and every case.

CHAPTER 2

"How much longer are we going to be kept waiting?" Walter Gibbons demanded. He glared at Constable Barnes, who stood solidly by the drawing room door, making sure that none of them actually managed to leave.

"I'm sure the inspector will be here shortly, sir," Barnes replied easily. He stared at Gibbons curiously. He wasn't an old man; judging from the smooth skin on his face, the constable would put his age in the mid-forties. Yet Gibbons's hair was completely white.

"This is outrageous." Gibbons, his hands behind his back, stomped back and forth in front of the fireplace and glared at Barnes. "Utterly absurd. You've no right to restrain any of us from leaving. I shall speak to your superiors; you can rest assured about that."

"The constable was acting upon my instructions." Witherspoon strode into the room. "So kindly direct your comments to me. If you'd like to lodge a complaint, the name of my superior is Chief Inspector Barrows. His office is at New Scotland Yard."

"Humph," Gibbons snorted. "Rest assured that I shall. Now, may I go?"

"No, I'm sorry, but you may not." The inspector surveyed the small group of people in the drawing room. A well-dressed couple was sitting on the settee, and a lone young woman wearing a long-sleeved white blouse and a dark green skirt was standing by the window. A heavyset fellow was sitting next to a small table by the door at the other end of the drawing room, staring morosely at the floor. He had barely looked up when the inspector had come into the room. Witherspoon wondered if these were the only guests that had been invited for lunch or if some of the others had managed to slip away.

"I'm Inspector Witherspoon," he said. "I'm sorry to have inconvenienced you, but we do have some questions for all of you."

"Questions?" The man who'd been sitting on the settee rose to his feet. "What kind of questions? We had nothing to do with the fire, so I don't see how we can be of any use to you, sir. When my wife and I arrived, the fire brigade was already here." He was of medium height with brown hair, a square jaw, small gray eyes, and a stocky build. He wore a dark gray suit with a maroon waistcoat and a black-and-white striped cravat.

"It's not about the fire," Witherspoon said softly. He glanced at Barnes, who gave a barely perceptible nod. The constable hadn't told them there was a murder. "Mr. Boyd's death wasn't an accident. It was murder."

"Murder?" the woman on the settee gasped.

"That's ridiculous," Gibbons snapped. "The butler said he died in a fire."

"Oh dear," the fellow sitting at the table murmured.

The young woman by the window simply sighed.

"Please explain yourself, sir." Gibbons stomped over and stood directly in front of Witherspoon.

The inspector briefly wondered how much clearer he could be, but he'd give it another try. "I know this must be a shock to all of you, but as I said, Mr. Boyd didn't die as a result of the fire. He was murdered. Now, I'd like to ask you a few questions and then you can be on your way. But before you go, can any of you tell me if you were the only guests that came here today?"

For a moment, no one spoke, then Gibbons said, "Yes, it was just myself and the Sapingtons."

"Uh, I was invited as well," the chubby fellow said. His voice was so low it was barely audible. "Mr. Boyd invited me this morning."

"So it was just the four guests." The inspector scanned their faces. "No one else, no one who might have slipped off before making a statement?"

"I've no idea if Boyd invited anyone else," Gibbons snapped. "And I've no idea why he thought he had the right to invite anyone else. This was an official luncheon of the Bankers Benevolent Society. That's the only reason that I'm here. I had business to conduct with Lawrence Boyd. Now, can we please get on with your questions. I'm a busy man."

"Constable Barnes, please take this gentleman," Witherspoon nodded toward Gibbons, "into the reception room next door and get his statement."

"This way, sir." Barnes pulled open the door and stepped into the hall. Gibbons looked as if he wanted to argue, but he clamped his mouth shut and followed the constable.

Witherspoon trailed after the two men, stuck his head into the hallway, and called out, "Constable Tucker, can you step in here, please?"

Tucker, who'd been at the front door ensuring that no one left, hurried toward Witherspoon. "Yes, sir," he said.

"Can you please take this gentleman," the inspector said, nodding at the man sitting at the table.

"My name is Glover," the fellow said glumly.

"And this lady," Witherspoon continued, indicating the young woman by the window.

"I'm Eva Clarke," she said.

"Thank you, that helps a great deal," Witherspoon said. He turned back to the constable and wished this wasn't so difficult. Egads, simply getting people apart long enough to take their statements was an ordeal, let alone trying to find out how many of them were actually supposed to have been having lunch with the dead man. But perhaps it was his fault. He really ought to have asked them to introduce themselves as soon as he'd come into the drawing room. "Can you please take Mr. Glover and Miss Clarke out to the hallway? Ask Constable Maxton to take Mr. Glover into the dining room to get his statement, and you take Miss Clarke into the study for hers, please."

"Yes, sir." Tucker beamed proudly and scurried for the door, glancing over his shoulder to make sure his charges were following after him. He ushered them out into the hall and shut the door softly.

Witherspoon turned to the two people left in the room. "May I ask your names?"

"I'm Arnold Sapington and this is my wife, Maud," the man replied. "But I don't think we'll be of much help to you. As I've already said, the fire brigade was here when we arrived for luncheon."

Maud Sapington smiled slightly at the introduction. She was a dark-haired woman with a jawline almost as sharp as her husband's, a wide mouth, and blue eyes. She wore a high-collared pink dress overlaid with a plum-colored vest trimmed in pink piping and a pair of cream-colored gloves. She carried a matching pink-and-plum striped parasol with a pink-frilled edge. On her head was a plum-colored bonnet with small cream and pink feathers on the side.

"What time was that, sir?" Witherspoon asked. He wondered if it would be uncivil of him to sit down. His knee was bothering him again.

"One o'clock," Sapington replied.

"But we were a few minutes early," his wife supplied. "It was ten to one when we knocked on the door."

"Who answered?" Witherspoon thought it might be useful to establish who was actually here at what time. He edged closer to an uncomfortable looking chair next to the settee.

"The housekeeper," Sapington said.

"That's not quite true," Mrs. Sapington interjected. "Mr. Glover actually answered our knock.

Arnold Sapington gave his wife an irritated glare. "For goodness sake, Maud, Mrs. Rothwell was right behind the fellow."

"Sorry, dear," Mrs. Sapington murmured.

Sapington sighed. "Mr. Glover answered the door, but only because he appeared to be leaving just as we arrived. The housekeeper was right behind him."

"Mr. Glover was leaving?" Witherspoon pressed. That was very interesting.

"Well, he said he really ought to get back to the office, but then he was prevailed upon to stay," Sapington replied.

"Are you his employer, sir?" Witherspoon asked.

"No, he's employed by Mr. Boyd."

"So he stayed at your request?" The inspector wanted to make sure he understood every single detail.

"Not really. It was Miss Clarke who suggested he might want to stay," Sapington replied. "By that time Walter Gibbons had arrived, so he put his briefcase down and came into the drawing room with us."

Witherspoon made a mental note to ask Miss Clarke why she suggested Glover stay at the house. "Er, Mr. Sapington, I got the impression from the other gentleman that today's luncheon was some sort of official function for this society he mentioned. Is that correct?"

"I don't know that it was all *that* official," Sapington replied. "It was just a luncheon."

"That's not quite true, dear," Mrs. Sapington said. "We expected Walter to tell us who was going to be this year's chairman of the Bankers Benevolent Society." She smiled broadly at the inspector. "It was going to be either Lawrence or my husband." She looked at her husband. "I suppose now it'll go to you by default."

"Maud, I don't think it's appropriate to comment on such matters with poor Lawrence dead." He pursed his lips in disapproval and then turned his attention back to Witherspoon. "The luncheon was Lawrence's idea. He thought it would be amusing and I agreed. The chairmanship is a friendly sort of rivalry. But I'm sure you're not interested in that. No doubt you'd like a few more details about today. My wife and I arrived at about ten to one. When the hansom let us off, we noticed the fire wagon out front, and of course, we were concerned. When Mrs. Rothwell told us what had happened, that there had been a fire and Mr. Boyd was dead, we were shocked."

"So it was Mrs. Rothwell who gave you the news?"

"That's correct," he continued. "We came in here with the others, as I said. By that time, Walter had arrived. A few minutes later, a constable stuck his head in and asked us to wait. That was hours ago, sir, and frankly, that's really all I can tell you."

Witherspoon wasn't going to keep them any longer. He had no grounds for holding people against their will, and all in all, they'd been fairly cooperative by waiting as long as they had. "If you'll leave me your address, sir, you and your wife are free to go. I might have more questions for you as the investigation progresses."

Sapington nodded. "We live at number 34 Parrington Street in Mayfair." He extended a hand to his wife and helped her to her feet. They walked to the door. Sapington looked back at the inspector. "You're sure it was murder?"

"Oh, yes, there's no doubt about that. Uh,

before you go, I do have one more question. How well acquainted with Mr. Boyd were you or your wife?"

"We're business acquaintances." Sapington reached for the doorknob and pulled the door open. "I'm the managing director of Reese and Cutlip on Broad Street."

"You could say they were competitors." Maud Sapington smiled at her husband. "But only in the most gentlemanly sort of way."

In the room next door, Constable Barnes wasn't having much luck getting information out of Walter Gibbons. "I've already told you," Gibbons said as he began to pace again. "I arrived right after the Sapingtons. Mr. Glover and Miss Clarke were already here."

"And you were invited to luncheon, sir?" Barnes probed.

"Yes, luncheon was to be at one o'clock," Gibbons said impatiently. "I've already told you all this."

"From your earlier comment, Mr. Gibbons, I take it you and Mr. Boyd weren't friends." Barnes watched him carefully as he asked the question. But Gibbons didn't so much as bat an eyelash or do anything else to indicate he might be uncomfortable.

"Hardly. As I said before, I'd have never

set foot in the man's house if I hadn't had to come here in my official capacity as the president of the Bankers Benevolent Society."

"And the reason you had to come, sir?" Barnes pressed.

"Because Boyd sweet-talked our board into making him this year's honorary chairman — a most presitigous position, I might add. Boyd and Sapington were our two final candidates for the honor, and this luncheon was to officially let Boyd know he'd got the prize. Poor Sapington. He's worked very hard for the society, but that didn't seem to make any difference to the board. All they could see was the huge donation that Boyd was prepared to make. Sapington can't or couldn't compete with that sort of thing. He's quite willing to work for charity, but he doesn't give much in the way of actual cash."

"Did Mr. Sapington know that he wasn't going to get the chairmanship?" Barnes wondered if these sort of people ever did any work.

"I don't see how he could." Gibbons sighed. "The board only made their final decision yesterday, and the luncheon's been planned for a long time."

"When you arrived, did you notice anything unusual — I mean, other than the fire wagon?"

Gibbons shook his head. "Just the fire brigade."

"Who told you Mr. Boyd was dead?"

"Mrs. Rothwell, the housekeeper. She said luncheon was cancelled and that there had been a terrible accident."

"Then why didn't you leave immediately?" Barnes asked.

"Because by then the police had arrived, and before we could go, a constable had sent the butler in to ask us all to remain."

"So you sat in the drawing room waiting?"

"Oh, no, Mrs. Rothwell insisted we eat. After all, luncheon was already prepared, so it was a shame to let the food go to waste."

"The inspector's late this evening," Mrs. Jeffries said to no one in particular as they milled about in the cozy kitchen.

"Not to worry," Mrs. Goodge said. "His supper is staying nice and warm in the oven. The longer it sits, the better a beef stew tastes, that's what I always say."

"It tasted good tonight." Smythe sank into his seat and reached for Betsy's hand under the table. They'd had their supper earlier and even done the clearing up.

Mrs. Jeffries frowned. "It's past seven.

55

He's always home by now unless he's on a case."

"Maybe he's got a murder," Wiggins said eagerly.

Under the table, Smythe squeezed Betsy's hand. She smiled at him, trying to let him know without words that she trusted him to find a way for them to continue their investigations. She wasn't worried about their future together. They could have their marriage and their home, and do the work that was so important to both of them. She trusted he had a plan.

Mrs. Jeffries glanced at Betsy and noted with some relief that the girl didn't look as if the idea of a murder was going to cause her a flurry of nerves. The wedding was taking a lot of planning time, but the housekeeper was sure the lass could cope. Betsy was strong. She looked up at the clock again and told herself not to jump to conclusions; there were many reasons why the inspector might be late getting home.

Fred, who'd been sleeping peacefully on the rug near the cooker, suddenly shot to his feet and charged for the back stairs. "That'll be the inspector," Wiggins muttered. He looked morosely in the direction the dog had disappeared. Fred had gotten a tad more attached to the inspector since

Mrs. Goodge's Samson had taken over below stairs, so to speak, and the footman's feelings were a bit raw on the subject. But he didn't begrudge the inspector; no, he wasn't the sort to act like a jealous old tabby. He cast a quick glare at Samson, who was curled up on a little stool near the cook's chair. Samson twitched his tail and glared right back.

Mrs. Jeffries was already on her feet and moving to the back stairs, not quite as fast as Fred, but hurrying none the less.

Fred bounced wildly up and down as the front door opened and the inspector stepped inside. "Gracious, old fellow, don't make such a fuss," the inspector said, but he was beaming broadly as he spoke. Fred's tail wagged madly and he tried, unsuccessfully, to lick the inspector's face.

"Good evening, Inspector," Mrs. Jeffries said. "Fred, get down now so the inspector can take off his hat and coat."

The dog settled immediately, and Witherspoon took the opportunity to slip off his coat. "It's nice to be so warmly greeted, especially after the day I've had."

"Tiring was it, sir?" she held her breath, hoping that she wasn't wrong; then she immediately felt guilty. If there was a murder, it meant some poor soul had died. Really, she mustn't allow herself to be so hopeful about such wickedness.

"Exhausting." He handed her his bowler hat. "I got called out for a murder at a house in Bayswater. I don't suppose we've received any word from Lady Cannonberry?"

Ruth Cannonberry was their neighbor and a special friend of the inspector's. But their relationship was having a difficult time making any progress as Ruth kept getting called out of town to play nursemaid to her late husband's relations, most of whom seemed afflicted with one ailment after the other, both real and imaginary. This time she'd had to go all the way to Northumberland to stay with her sister-in-law.

"Nothing yet, sir, but she only left yesterday morning. You'll probably get a letter tomorrow." She took his hat and hung it up next to his coat. "I'm sorry your day was so awful, sir. No wonder you're home so late." She was thoroughly ashamed of herself for the feeling of elation that swept through her. "Who was murdered?"

"Fellow by the name of Lawrence Boyd. He's a banker." Witherspoon sighed. "I don't wish to inconvenience the household, but do you think Mrs. Goodge would be put out if I had a sherry before dinner."

"Not to worry, sir." Mrs. Jeffries started

down the hall toward the drawing room. "The household won't mind in the least. Mrs. Goodge has laid on a nice beef stew. It's in the oven and I'll serve it whenever you're ready."

She was so very grateful that the inspector hadn't been raised with servants. He'd never learned to treat them as objects for his own convenience.

She swept into the drawing room and headed for the sideboard. Opening the lower cupboard, she pulled out a bottle of Harvey's and then reached for the glasses. The inspector, now minus Fred, who'd wandered back downstairs, sank into his favorite chair.

"I've so looked forward to this," he admitted as she handed him a glass of sherry. "It's been a very busy day. Do pour one for yourself."

"Thank you, sir," she replied. She took her drink and sat down in the chair opposite him. "What happened, sir?"

"Well, I was working away at Ladbroke Grove station, and we were getting ready to go have lunch when the duty officer came in and said they'd had reports of a murder at number 14 Laurel Road in Bayswater. As it was in my district, I was up for it, of course."

Mrs. Jeffries had no doubt that even if he hadn't been the detective on duty, they'd have sent for him anyway, but she said nothing.

"Constable Barnes and I took a hansom, and we were there very quickly. It's amazing how fast one can travel about London these days, isn't it." He took a quick gulp of his drink. "Apparently, Mr. Boyd, the victim, was in the studio behind his house working on a painting when his assailant murdered him. The killer then set the place on fire, probably trying to hide the fact that a murder had taken place at all."

She forced herself to give him an encouraging nod instead of blurting out one of the many questions that had sprang into her mind.

"Luckily for us, there was a young woman on the premises who saw the smoke and took immediate action. The fire brigade got there very quickly and put the fire out."

"So the body wasn't burnt?" she ventured.

"Oh, no, though there was enough turpentine splashed about the room that it should have gone up quickly, but I suspect the wet weather we've had recently worked to our advantage. Even wood doesn't burn very quickly when it's so damp out."

"How was Mr. Boyd actually murdered?"

"He was bashed on the back of the head with something very heavy," Witherspoon replied. "There was nothing in the studio that looked as if it could be used as a weapon, so I had the police constables do a thorough search of the grounds and the house. We found nothing, so I've expanded the search to the neighborhood around the home, not that I think we'll have much luck."

"Had the servants seen anything?" she took a sip of her drink.

"No, they weren't there." He frowned. "It was the oddest situation, Mrs. Jeffries. Apparently, they were all at a funeral when the fire started. If it hadn't been for Mr. Boyd's typewriter girl — or are they called Remington Girls? I can never remember which it is, but that's not really pertinent. What is pertinent is that other than Miss Clarke, the house was empty. Except, of course, for Mr. Glover, who I believe brought along some files and then stayed as he'd been invited to luncheon."

"He was invited to the luncheon as well?" she queried. She wanted to keep all the facts straight.

"Yes, but I gather it was a last minute invitation."

"I'm not sure I understand," Mrs. Jeffries

61

murmured. "How could there be a luncheon planned if there were no servants?" She knew that if the house was in Bayswater and the victim a banker, it probably meant the household was wealthy. In her experience, the rich rarely served themselves.

"It was a cold luncheon," Witherspoon replied. "Everything was laid out and ready for when the guests were to arrive. Of course, when the servants got home, they found the fire brigade there and the master of the house dead." He finished off his sherry and got to his feet. "I better not keep Mrs. Goodge's dinner waiting any longer."

Mrs. Jeffries finished her own drink and stood up as well. "I'll serve you, sir. Do go into the dining room and make yourself comfortable. I'll be right up with your supper."

"That sounds wonderful. What does Mrs. Goodge have for pudding?"

"Apple tart with custard," Mrs. Jeffries replied. The inspector did enjoy his sweets. "It's especially good this evening." She hurried out and flew down the hall to the back stairs. The only thing that kept her from a flat out run was fear that she'd fall and break a bone.

The others were still in the kitchen. Mrs. Goodge had put the inspector's supper on a large wooden tray.

"Don't any of you go to bed." The housekeeper grabbed the tray and hoisted it effortlessly. "We've got a murder. As soon as the inspector finishes his meal, I'll be down to tell you everything."

"Learn as much as you can," the cook said bluntly. "If he got it today, we're already behind."

On several of their last few cases, Witherspoon had been summoned from home instead of the station. The household had gotten quite used to starting their investigations almost from the moment the inspector began working.

Mrs. Jeffries disappeared down the hall with the inspector's dinner. They rest of them kept busy by doing small chores to pass the time. Betsy filled the sink with soapy water, Wiggins topped up the fuel in the cooker, Smythe moved some provisions off the top shelf in the dry larder into the kitchen cupboards, and Mrs. Goodge wrote up a list of provisions. Finally, after what seemed hours but was in reality less than thirty minutes, they heard Mrs. Jeffries footsteps coming down the backstairs. Betsy leapt to her feet. "I'll go clear up the dining room."

"No need." The housekeeper swept into

the kitchen carrying a tray piled high with dirty dishes, a wrinkled serviette, and an empty water glass. "I've got it all. If there's any crumbs left on the dining table, we'll get them tomorrow morning before the inspector eats his breakfast." She handed the tray to Betsy, who took it over to the sink and began putting the crockery in the pan of soapy water.

"The inspector is going directly up to his room," she continued. "He's very tired. I told him that Wiggins would take care of giving Fred his walk."

" 'Course I will," Wiggins said. Fred, hearing his name, rose from his spot near the cooker and came over to the footman. "You 'eard the word, didn't ya, old boy? Well, you've got to wait till we 'ave our meetin', then we'll go out."

Ten minutes later they had the last of the dishes washed and were taking their usual spots at the dining table. Mrs. Jeffries had slipped upstairs and made sure the inspector had actually retired for the night. It wouldn't do to have him coming down while they were in the midst of talking about his latest murder.

"Who was murdered?" Mrs. Goodge asked bluntly.

"A banker by the name of Lawrence

Boyd," the housekeeper replied. "He lives in Bayswater. He was murdered in the studio behind his house while he was painting a picture." She repeated the details she'd learned from the inspector, taking care to stress the circumstances and making sure she didn't forget anything. "Boyd was the general manager of Boyd, Stanford, and Sawyer, Merchant Bankers."

"I've heard of them," Mrs. Goodge muttered. She was somewhat relieved. The further up the social ladder a murder victim was, the easier it was for her find out what she needed to know. There was generally far more gossip to be had about the rich and the famous than there was about the poor and obscure. "They've offices just off Chancery Lane."

"That's good," the housekeeper said. "I've a feeling this case is going to be very odd, and it's going to take all our resources to get to the bottom of it."

"Seems to me the inspector's cases are always strange," Wiggins muttered. "But this one takes the cake. Imagine trying to kill someone by burnin' down a building."

"Actually, when you think about it, it was quite clever," Betsy replied thoughtfully. "I mean, if the killer knew the victim was going to be alone, then a fire might have destroyed the evidence of murder and everyone would think it an accident."

"But Mr. Boyd wasn't on his own," Wiggins pointed out. "There was the typewriter lady and that fellow from his office."

"But the murderer probably didn't know that," Smythe interjected. He agreed with Betsy's assessment. "Look at it this way: if the killer wanted to do this Mr. Boyd in and he heard that all the Boyd servants were going off that morning, then he probably thought he could get away with it."

"We're getting very much ahead of ourselves," Mrs. Jeffries interrupted. "Until we know more facts, this sort of speculation is very dangerous. I suggest we proceed as we usually do and see what we can learn."

"That's too bad. I was quite enjoyin' myself." Smythe grinned broadly.

"Me, too." Betsy laughed. "But Mrs. Jeffries is right. We'd best find out a few facts before we come up with any ideas. We know how easy it is to make a mistake when you let your imagination run wild. I'll start with the local shopkeepers tomorrow and see what kind of gossip I can find about our poor Mr. Boyd."

The housekeeper nodded in agreement and turned to Wiggins. "I'd like you to find someone from the Boyd household and see what you can learn. Find out how long the servants had known they would be going to a funeral that morning."

"Surely it couldn't have been too far in advance." Mrs. Goodge pursed her lips disapprovingly "According to the inspector, the girl's death wasn't unexpected, but no one could have known for certain when she was actually going to die."

"But you have to give the undertaker and the priest a bit of notice," Wiggins pointed out. "You can't just show up at the church with the body and 'ave a funeral. You've got to talk to the vicar, and that's got to take a day or two."

"Maybe the killer didn't need much time," Smythe suggested. "Besides, I thought we agreed we'd not do anymore speculatin'. Just get us some facts, lad."

Wiggins didn't take offense at the gentle chiding. "I'll do my best," he promised. "If I don't 'ave any luck with the Boyd servants, I'll try and chat with a servant from one of the neighbors' houses."

"Excellent idea." Mrs. Jeffries beamed approvingly. She was so proud of them all. They certainly didn't need to be told what to do.

"I'll get up extra early and get the baking done," the cook said. "The laundry is going be picked up at nine, and Mr. Miller is coming by at ten to repair the shelves in the wet larder." Mrs. Goodge mentally began to calculate how many people were going to be in and out of her kitchen tomorrow. After a moment, she realized it wasn't near enough. "I'd best send out an invitation or two," she said. "Surely one of my old colleagues will know something about someone involved with this case."

"Speaking of which, what about the others that came to the house that day? The luncheon guests and the typewriter girl," Betsy asked. "Shouldn't we look at them as well?"

Mrs. Jeffries thought for a moment. "The guests supposedly got there after the fire and the murder had already happened. But as they're the only names we've got so far, we might as well see what we can learn about them."

"What were their names again?" Mrs. Goodge asked. "I know the typewriter girl was a Miss Eva Clarke."

"Arnold and Maud Sapington." Mrs. Jeffries tried her best to recall everything the inspector had said. "I believe the inspector said Mr. Sapington is also a banker, but I don't think he mentioned the name of any bank. A gentleman named Walter Gibbons was present, and of course, Mr. Glover, the chief clerk from Boyd's office. Mind you, I've no idea where any of these people might live. But when Constable Barnes comes by tomorrow morning to fetch the inspector, I'll have a quick word with him and see if he has any further details."

Barnes was one of the few people who knew what the household did for the inspector. It had taken him a goodly number of cases before he'd put it together, but once he had, he'd made sure to let Mrs. Jeffries know he approved.

"What about Luty and Hatchet?" Smythe asked. "We'd best include them right from the start. They missed the last one."

"Oh dear, you're right." Mrs. Jeffries agreed. "We must include them."

"It's not that late. Why don't I go along to Knightsbridge and tell them what's what," Wiggins suggested. "Then they can be here for our morning meetin'. I can take Fred with me . . ."

Mrs. Jeffries interrupted him. "That's a very good idea, but you must take a hansom cab. Otherwise you'll be gone all night." She wasn't an unduly cautious person, but she did realize that they worked for the famous Inspector Gerald Witherspoon who had sent over twenty murderers to the gallows and not everyone in London appreciated his efforts. Mrs. Jeffries was fairly sure there wasn't any immediate danger, but it paid to be careful. "Don't worry about the cost. I've household money set aside for situations like this."

Wiggins looked doubtful. "Will the driver let Fred ride in the cab?"

"He will if you give 'im this." Smythe handed the lad a sixpence and two farthings. "Just be sure to tell 'im that Fred's a good dog and you'll not let him climb on the seats."

"Cor blimey, this is workin' out well. I'll nip upstairs and get my jacket. Betsy, can you put Fred's lead on 'im. This is goin' to be a right old adventure."

Luty Belle Crookshank's Knightsbridge home was ablaze with light from top to bottom. Even from the pavement, Wiggins could hear the tinkle of glasses and the sound of laughter. He looked down at Fred. "Cor blimey, Fred, what should we do? Luty's 'aving some sort of fancy do. Listen, you can even 'ear music."

Fred plopped down on his hindquarters and began scratching his ear.

"But if we don't tell 'em, they'll be upset, especially Luty. Come on, Fred, whatever's goin' on, we'll just 'ave to interrupt." He tugged gently on Fred's lead, and together they bounded up the short walkway to the front door. He knew better than to go to the servants' entry because the one time he'd done that, Luty had given him a stern lecture. She had told him he was a friend and she didn't want him or anyone else, even her own servants, to use that entrance. The servants door was to be used only for deliveries and then only because it made life easier for the delivery lads. Luty had some very strange ideas, but that was to be expected. After all, she was an American.

Keeping a firm hold on Fred's lead, he raised the heavy brass door knocker and let it drop. A moment later, the door opened and Hatchet, Luty's white-haired butler, appeared. He smiled broadly. "This is a very pleasant surprise. Do come in Wiggins."

"Let me tie Fred's lead to the fence," Wiggins replied.

"No, no, bring him inside. His manners are probably better than most of madam's guests." Hatchet opened the door wider and motioned them inside. "I'll tell madam you're here."

Wiggins began to have second thoughts. Maybe this could wait for tomorrow. Maybe he should just leave word with Hatchet and get back home. The place was filled with people. "Cor blimey, do you think I should? It sounds like you've got a 'ouseful."

"Of course we do," Hatchet replied cheerfully. "But that doesn't matter. It's only one of madam's charity functions."

Wiggins hesitated. He really did feel odd about interrupting a big do like this. But Fred had no such qualms; his tail wagging wildly, he strained forward and butted his nose against Hatchet's hand.

"Oh, come on, lad." Hatchet reached across the threshold and pulled Wiggins inside. He petted Fred and then shoved them gently in the direction of the library. "I do hope you're here because of that murdered banker, and believe me, if you think the madam wouldn't throw the whole lot of them out the front door so she could hear what you've got to say, you're sadly mistaken." He jerked his head toward the sound of the festivities. "Now get into the study lad. I'll send Julie in with some food and drink for you and the pup. It might be a few minutes before madam can extricate herself from Lord Dinsworthy. He does rather love the sound of his own voice."

Wiggins laughed and started down the hall. "Right then, I can always eat."

The house was elegantly furnished and

very beautiful. In the foyer, a huge Chinese ceramic vase containing an artistic display of fresh flowers stood on a round mahogany claw-foot table. The hallway was lined with ornately framed portraits, pastoral scenes, and seascapes. Gas lamps in polished brass sconces blazed brightly, showing off the pale cream walls and intricately detailed white molding on the high ceiling.

He stepped through the big double oak doors and into the library. As always, he stood for a moment staring at the huge room with its wall-to-ceiling bookcases. Wiggins loved to read. "Cor blimey, Fred, I'd not mind being stuck in here for a few days." It wasn't the first time he'd been in the room, and Luty had always told him to come along and borrow any book he wanted. But he was still a bit too shy to do such a thing. Besides, the lending library near Upper Edmonton Gardens was perfectly fine for his needs. But this was a treasure trove. He dropped Fred's lead and wandered over to the nearest shelf. He spotted a copy of Mark Twain's novel, *Tom Sawyer*. It was one of his favorite books. He pulled it out, flipped open the cover, and began to read. Within moments, he was so engrossed in the story he didn't even hear the door open.

"Get off, you silly pup," Julie said with mock severity. "You're going to make me drop your treat."

Wiggins turned. "Hello, Miss Julie. Fred, leave off. She's got her hands full." The young, dark-haired maid was carrying a tray with two plates piled high with food and a glass of lemonade. She put the tray down on the top of a small end table.

"The pup's no trouble." Julie reached down and stroked Fred's back. "He just gets a bit excited. Madam will be here in just a moment. Last I saw of her, she was trying to get away from Lady Dinsworthy."

"I thought she'd been trapped by Lord Dinsworthy." Wiggins put the Twain book back in its place and moved toward the food.

"It's both of them." Julie laughed. "Even madam has a hard time outtalking those two, but I've no doubt she'll do it. She's a very determined —" Julie broke off just as the double doors opened and Luty Belle Crookshank flew into the room.

Luty was wearing a bright red taffeta evening gown with a high lace collar and long sleeves. It rustled as she charged across the room. A concoction of feathers and ribbons were wound in her gray hair, and there was a sparkling diamond necklace around her neck. Matching earrings dangled from her ears.

"Did the inspector get it?" Luty asked. "And don't pretend you don't know what I'm talking about, boy."

Wiggins glanced at the clock, noted the time, and decided he'd better eat while he had the chance. He reached for a slice of roast beef. "He got it all right. The victim was a banker named —"

"Lawrence Boyd," Luty interrupted. "I know. I've already got my feelers out asking about him. Go on and tell me the rest of it."

"Mrs. Jeffries wants you to come to the morning meeting," Wiggins said around a mouthful of succulent beef. "There's all sorts of bits and pieces you need to know." He didn't want to stay too much longer.

"Don't you worry; we'll be there. But I've got half of London in my parlor" — she jerked her thumb toward the double doors — "and I ain't missing this chance to ask a few questions. Come on, give me a few facts, something I can inquire about. Everyone's already heard the news, and they're jawin' about it something fierce. There are more bankers in my parlor than there are fleas on a barnyard cat."

Wiggins understood her point. "I'll tell

you what I know. Boyd was bashed in the 'ead, and the killer tried to make it look like an accident by settin' the place on fire, but it didn't work."

"Who else was there?"

Wiggins took another bite and tried to recall all the names. "Uh," he swallowed, "I believe one of them was named Arnold Sapington. He and his wife Maud were both there."

"Don't eat so fast, lad, you're going to choke to death. Give Fred a few bites; he's hungry, too," Luty admonished.

Julie snickered. "I'll feed Fred."

"I can't stay too long. The women'll 'ave my 'ead if I'm too late. You know 'ow they worry," he protested.

Luty waved her hand dismissively. "Don't be daft. The carriage is right outside. I'll send you home in that. Now, who else was at Boyd's house."

Wiggins tried to remember. "The typewriter lady was there. Her name is Eva Clarke. She's the one that called for help. The household was out at a funeral, and so none of the servants were about the place. There was another man there, too. I think his name was Walter Gibbons."

"Good, good." Luty nodded encouragingly. "Go on. What else can you recall?"

"The inspector said they didn't see any-thing in the studio that could 'ave been used as the murder weapon. No brass candle-sticks or doorstops or anything like that. He's got police constables searching the Boyd house and the neighborhood for the weapon."

Luty snorted. "He'll not have much luck finding it, not unless the killer's a real fool. Most likely the murder weapon is at the bot-tom of the Thames."

Hatchet stuck his head into the room. "Madam, your guests are asking for you. Your absence has become quite noticeable. Miss Teasdale and Lord Dinsworthy are making quite a fuss."

Luty's eyes narrowed suspiciously. "How long have you been listening at the door?"

Luty and Hatchet were very competitive when they were on one of the inspector's cases. Wiggins picked up the glass and took a drink of the lemonade. He might as well enjoy himself a bit. These two could squabble worse than Samson and Fred as they vied for clues and the upper hand.

Hatchet contrived to look offended. "Really, madam, that is an outrageous slander. I'm hardly in the habit of eaves-dropping." As he had been listening at the door, that was also an outrageous lie, but he didn't care in the least. Madam would pretend to tell him all the details she'd learned from Wiggins, but he knew that she was quite capable of leaving one or two pertinent facts out of her recitation. And she wasn't the only one with sources here tonight.

"Slander my foot," Luty snorted. "You just don't want me gettin' the drop on you."

"I've no idea what you're talking about." He turned his head and looked down the hall. "Lord Dinsworthy is coming this way, madam. I suggest you come out and meet him." Hatchet smiled wickedly. "I'll be happy to take your place and get the rest of the details from Wiggins."

From outside the room, they heard a voice bellow, "Luty, where the deuce are you?"

"Blast." Luty stamped her foot and headed for the door. She glared at Hatchet as she swept out into the hall. "I know you told him where I was," she hissed.

As he had, Hatchet didn't bother to deny it. He simply came into the library and smiled at Wiggins. "Now, what else is there to hear?"

CHAPTER 3

The next morning, Luty and Hatchet arrived at the back door of Upper Edmonton Gardens at almost the same time the inspector and Constable Barnes were leaving by the front door. "We're here," Luty announced as they came into the kitchen. "And I for one am rarin' to go. I found out some good bits last night."

"Really, madam, do contain your enthusiasm. You've no idea if what you learned is going to be useful or not," Hatchet sniffed disapprovingly. Despite his best efforts, he'd not been able to get her to say a word on the way over here.

"I'm sure you'll both have much to contribute in the coming days," Mrs. Jeffries said quickly. "Do take a seat and we'll get started." She slipped into her chair at the head of the table. "I think we've quite a bit of ground to cover this morning."

"Why don't you give us a brief summary

of what you know thus far," Hatchet suggested. "Wiggins told us a few details, but I'm sure there's more." He was also sure she'd managed to have a quick word with Constable Barnes this morning, which meant there might be even more information to be had.

"And we've got some bits to tell," Luty declared as she smiled wickedly at Hatchet. "The murder was all people could talk about last night, and I got an earful."

"As you know, the victim was a banker named Lawrence Boyd," Mrs. Jeffries began. "The presumed cause of death is multiple blows to the head, and the killer or killers then set the room on fire. But luckily, the fire didn't spread."

"Killer musta been a fool," Luty muttered. "This is the wettest spring we've had for years."

Mrs. Jeffries nodded and continued on with her recitation. She went over the facts they had thus far and even added an idea Constable Barnes had shared with her earlier. "The guests don't appear to be overly fond of Boyd, so we must have a good look at them as well." The inspector hadn't been clear about that point last night, and she was glad she'd had the chance to talk to Barnes.

"But the guests came after the fire was started," Mrs. Goodge mused. "So I expect we'd best try to find out where they were that morning, see if any of them can account for their whereabouts during the time the murder was happening."

"That's a very good idea," Mrs. Jeffries agreed.

"And I think it's tellin' that the killer tried to make it look like an accident," Wiggins said. "Means whoever did it might 'ave planned it out in advance."

"Boyd was supposedly alone in the house?" Luty asked.

"That's right." Mrs. Jeffries picked up her tea cup. "The servants were at a funeral. Boyd had taken the day away from his office to work on a painting. Constable Barnes told me Boyd was quite an accomplished amateur artist. He always entered a painting for the summer exhibit at the Royal Academy."

"But there was the typewriter girl there, a Miss Clarke," Hatchet mused. "I wonder how many people knew she was going to be in the house."

"And that Mr. Glover was there as well," Wiggins added. "He brought Mr. Boyd some files from his office."

"I think the question is whether or not the

killer thought Boyd was on 'is own," Smythe said. "But we'd best not get too far ahead of ourselves. We've come a cropper a time or two with speculatin' too early in a case on what was what."

"That's certainly true." Betsy nodded in agreement.

"What did you hear last night?" Mrs. Jeffries looked toward Luty and Hatchet, who were sitting next to one another.

Luty spoke first. "The gossip I heard was that Boyd was a pretty ruthless character. He had a mean streak, and considerin' I heard this from a banker, then Boyd musta been pretty bad. Them money men usually hang together."

"Was he ever married?" Betsy asked.

"I didn't hear anyone mention a wife," Luty replied. "But then again, all they could talk about was who mighta wanted him dead. Apparently, it's a pretty long list. He's sacked a few clerks and called in a fair number of loans in his time. As it's a merchant bank, when he called a note, lots of people might have lost their jobs."

"Why is that?" Wiggins asked. He wasn't sure what the difference was between a merchant bank and an ordinary one.

"Because merchant banks lend money to businesses, not individuals," Luty explained.

"So when Boyd called in a loan on a business, he'd probably force it to close, and if there were employees, they'd be out of a job." Since her husband's death many years earlier, Luty had managed her own business affairs. She knew more about banking and money than most men.

"Boyd was also considered a very competitive individual," Hatchet added. He'd picked up a tidbit or two of information, but he was saving them until later. Truth was, some of what he'd heard didn't make much sense at this point. But he'd learned to be patient. One never knew when a stray fact or two might become very relevant.

"I expect bein' competitive would be useful if you were a banker," Mrs. Goodge commented. She looked at Luty. "Do you remember which of your guests seemed to know the most about Boyd?"

"Oh, everyone had heard of him." Luty grinned. "He's got his fingers in a lot of pies, not just banking. He's on the board of half a dozen charities, serves on a couple of local political committees, and he has the ear of the chancellor of the exchequer."

"So he's quite well known," Mrs. Jeffries murmured. Drat, that might make things difficult for Inspector Witherspoon. If their inspector didn't get results quickly, she had no doubt that Inspector Nigel Nivens would try to horn in on the case.

Nivens was politically well connected and ethically underhanded; in short he was a boot licking dog. He was desperate to rise in rank, and he let nothing, including justice, stand in his way. He loathed Witherspoon and would do everything in his power to ruin him. Nivens was a worry, but she couldn't think what to do about him.

Hatchet, not wanting to be outdone by Luty, blurted out a few of the tidbits he'd been saving. "I overheard Lord Dinsworthy comment that Boyd's paintings were considered top quality, but he never sold them."

Luty grinned slyly. She knew it was just killing Hatchet that she had found out more than him. " 'Course he didn't sell 'em. He gave 'em away to charities and institutions. Lady Dinsworthy claimed that was how he got on so many prestigious boards."

Mrs. Jeffries forced her concern about Inspector Nivens to the back of her mind. She needed to concentrate on the task at hand. "Did you hear anything else?"

"Not really, just people jawin' over the murder," Luty replied. "Oh, I did hear Eudora Higgleston makin' some comment about who would get Boyd's paintings. But when I pressed her on the matter, she didn't really know anything."

"His paintings are that good?" Smythe asked. "I mean, good enough that people are already speculating on who will inherit them?"

"Sounds like it." Luty shrugged. "He's exhibited at the Royal Academy, and from what I hear, every amateur in England would sell their grandmothers for a chance to have their work hanging on those walls. But like I say, there was a lot of talk last night and it's hard to tell what's true and what ain't. You know how people are: everyone wants to pretend they know more than they do."

"That's certainly true," Hatchet said with a sideways glance at Luty. "I, on the other hand, only repeat information I know to be factual."

Luty grinned at her butler but didn't rise to the bait. She turned her attention to Mrs. Jeffries. "I thought that if it was all the same to you, I'd see what my sources in the city have to say about Boyd."

"That's an excellent idea," Mrs. Jeffries replied. Luty's access to the financial community in London was unsurpassed.

Hatchet leaned forward and said, "I've a number of sources in the art community that I can tap for information, if, of course, you think that line of inquiry would be useful."

"At this point, all lines of inquiry are useful," Mrs. Jeffries replied. "And if his work is as good as we've heard, perhaps his death is connected to his painting."

"But that was just a hobby," Mrs. Goodge protested. The one area she was sadly lacking in sources was the art community. None of her previous positions had been with anyone connected with the creative world. She'd mainly worked for aristocrats or the wealthy, and none of that lot was remotely artistic. "Surely no one would go to the trouble of murdering someone over a painting!"

"But we don't know that," Betsy said. "And according to what we do know, he was in his studio working on a painting when he was killed."

"That's true." The cook frowned. "I wonder what happened to the painting. I mean, maybe the fire was set to destroy it, not hide the fact Boyd had been murdered."

They all stared at her. Finally, after a long moment or two, Mrs. Jeffries said, "That's a very interesting idea, Mrs. Goodge. We really must find out. I'll ask the inspector tonight. But really, we mustn't get ahead of ourselves. We've much to learn, and I've a feeling we'd best learn it as quickly as possible."

"What's wrong?" Smythe asked. "Why do we have to be quick about this? It's not like our last case. No one's life is at stake."

"No, but the victim was apparently a very prominent person, which means the Home Office will be watching it closely and pressing the police for results." Mrs. Jeffries sighed heavily. "I suspect that Nigel Nivens will do everything he can to get the case taken away from our inspector, especially after what happened with Tommy Odell."

"Nivens won't forgive or forget the fact that our inspector overturned his one and only murder conviction," Wiggins muttered. " 'E'll be out for our inspector's blood. We'd best be on our toes on this one."

"I say we'd best watch our backs as well," Smythe warned. "I wouldn't put it past the fellow to sneak about and try to suss out what our inspector is doin'."

"Surely he'd not go that far," Betsy said.

"Nivens was willing to let an innocent man hang," Luty exclaimed. "So I'd not put anything sneaky or underhanded past him. Smythe is right; we'd best all watch our backs."

"And what do we do if we see somethin' odd?" Wiggins looked at the housekeeper.

He'd not wanted to say anything, but last night when he'd come home in Luty's carriage, he thought he'd felt someone leap off the back just as the carriage pulled up and stopped. But street urchins sometimes hitched a ride by leaping on the back of a carriage, so he'd put it out of his mind. He'd even done it a time or two when he was younger and more willing to risk breaking a leg or getting a thrashing from an irate coachman.

"I'm not sure," she mused, "but rest assured, we'll do something. I thought I'd go see Dr. Bosworth today."

"Going to see if he can get a copy of the postmortem report?" Betsy asked.

Mrs. Jeffries nodded. "Yes, he might have some idea of what the murder weapon might have been. I think that information would be very useful."

"Maybe the inspector or one of his lads will discover something," Wiggins suggested. "I mean, they didn't find the murder weapon, so the killer must 'ave took it with 'im. Seems to me, carryin' something covered in blood about London is a bit risky. I'll see if I can find a scullery maid or a tweeny who's heard something."

"But they weren't there," Betsy pointed out. "They were at a funeral."

"True, but they might still know something. If the killer used an object from the 'ouse to bash Mr. Boyd's 'ead in, it would 'ave to be cleaned off before it could be put back. Someone might 'ave noticed something out of place or wet, and I'll see what else I can learn as well."

There was a knock on the back door just as the clock struck the hour. "That'll be the grocer's lad." Mrs. Goodge got to her feet. "I doubt he knows anything, but he might." She looked pointedly at the others. They quickly got out of their chairs.

"We'll meet here this afternoon around half past four," Mrs. Jeffries said as she headed for the coat tree to get her hat and spring jacket.

Smythe grabbed Betsy's hand. "Walk me to the back door, love."

"I've got to get my hat and gloves," she protested. "I want to get out and about as well. There are shopkeepers out there with all sorts of useful information."

"Here's your bonnet." Mrs. Goodge handed the pale gray hat to the maid. "And your gloves are tucked neatly inside. Now be off with all of you. I need this kitchen for my sources."

"May we speak to Miss Clarke, please?"

Witherspoon smiled at the young maid who answered the door of the small lodging house. "She's expecting us."

"Miss Clarke's in the sitting room." The maid opened the door wider and pointed at a door just off the small foyer. "It's just through there."

Eva Clarke nodded politely as the two men stepped into the small room. She was seated on a maroon sofa. "Hello, Inspector, Constable. I appreciate your punctuality. I've an interview for another position later today and I shouldn't like to be late. Please sit down." She gestured toward two matching horsehair chairs opposite the couch.

Witherspoon took off his bowler and Barnes whipped out his notebook as they took their seats. She sank back to her spot on the settee. Eva Clarke was an attractive young woman with red-gold hair, a porcelain complexion, and brown eyes. She wore a gray skirt and a crisp white blouse with a high neck and long, narrow sleeves. Lying next to her on the settee was a plain gray jacket, black gloves, and a sensible gray hat decorated with a small, wispy veil on the crown.

"We'll try to be as brief as possible," the inspector said. "First of all, can you tell us what time you arrived at Mr. Boyd's home?"

"Ten o'clock," she replied. "Mr. Boyd had sent a messenger to the agency that morning, requesting my services. Luckily, the agency is just around the corner from here, so they contacted me immediately and I went straightaway."

"What's the name of the agency?" The inspector shifted slightly. The seat of the chair was quite rough, and he could almost feel the horsehairs poking through his trousers.

"Croxley and Gills," she replied. "They're a secretarial agency."

"What the address, please?" the constable asked.

"They're at number 54 Potter Road," she replied. "As I said, they're just around the corner."

"Mr. Boyd requested you specifically?" Barnes looked up from his notebook.

"Yes, I'd worked for him on several previous occasions. Usually I worked at his office, but this time he specifically requested I come to his home."

"You were comfortable doing that?" Barnes asked.

"Oh, yes." She smiled easily. "I'd been there before, and I knew Mr. Boyd had a full staff. Mind you, I didn't realize none of them would be there yesterday. I was a bit concerned when he answered the door instead of the housekeeper, but I needn't have been worried. Mr. Boyd simply gave me my instructions and then went off to paint in his studio."

"Yes, I see." Witherspoon understood what she meant. A young woman alone in a man's home could easily be a cause of concern.

"I'd never have taken the assignment if I'd known he was there alone," she explained. "But once I got there, it seemed silly to make a fuss, especially with Mr. Boyd. He's only interested in how fast I could get the work done."

"You operated a typewriter." Witherspoon looked at her curiously. He'd seen typewriters, of course. They had several of them at the Yard, and some of the younger lads claimed they were exceedingly useful in writing reports. But the actual operation of one seemed like magic. Why, one's fingers seemed to be actually operating independently of one's eyes.

"That's correct." She smiled brightly. "I went to business college in the United States, in Chicago. Typewriting is a most useful skill to acquire. Take my word for it, Inspector, within a few years, all offices will use typewriters. They are so much more efficient than writing by hand."

"Yes, I'm sure you're right," Witherspoon replied. "How did you come to be acquainted with Mr. Boyd?" He'd no idea why he asked that question, but it had popped into his head so he supposed it must be important. He'd learned to trust his "inner voice." As Mrs. Jeffries always told him, that "inner voice" of his had led to success in numerous cases.

"Through the secretarial agency." She smiled again. "Mr. Boyd acquired a typewriter for this bank, and then he realized there was no one who knew how to operate it properly. So he contacted the secretarial agency, and they asked if he would consider a woman. He said he would. He never offered me a permanent position, but he'd call me in whenever he wanted typewriting done."

"I see." Witherspoon wanted to ensure that Miss Clarke's relationship to the victim was a business one and not personal. Miss Clarke looked like a perfectly nice young woman, but he'd seen other perfectly nice-looking young ladies turn out to be ruthless killers, especially in matters of the heart. Just to be on the safe side, he'd have a chat with the servants at the Boyd household and see just how well Miss Clarke and victim were acquainted. He'd also have a word with the secretarial agency. "So you went there yesterday morning and he gave you your assignment. I take it he had his own typewriting machine?"

She frowned thoughtfully. "I'm not sure. I think whenever he wanted personal typewriting done, he brought the one from the bank home. But I can't be certain. Remingtons all look alike."

"You weren't doing work for the bank?" the inspector asked.

"Oh, no, I was typing his acceptance speech." She grinned. "It took quite awhile. He'd written it out in longhand, and deciphering his scribbling wasn't the easiest task I've ever had. But I managed. I did feel a bit of sympathy for the poor souls who were going to be at the Bankers Benevolent Society dinner; it's a very long speech." She sobered. "But I suppose now, no one will hear it. That's very sad. Mr. Boyd was always nice to me."

Witherspoon nodded. "You worked in Mr. Boyd's study at the back of the house, correct?"

"That's right. As I said, it wasn't easy to decipher his handwriting, so actually typing the speech took longer than I'd originally thought it would. As a matter of fact, I was quite surprised when I finished and realized how late it had gotten."

"Was that when you saw the smoke?" Barnes glanced up from his notebook again.

"Yes, I wanted Mr. Boyd to know that I was done. I was going to take him the pages, but then I looked out the study window and I saw smoke coming from the studio. I ran out to the hallway, toward the back of the house, and raised the alarm. You know the rest."

"Did you actually go to the studio and see the fire?" Witherspoon asked.

She shook her head. "Oh, no. Mr. Glover, who I didn't even know was in the house, came rushing out as well. I must have made some sound of alarm when I saw the smoke. He's the one who ran to the studio. He shouted for me to get the fire brigade."

Witherspoon gave an encouraging nod. "And is that what you did?"

"Yes, there's a fire station two streets over from the Boyd house, so I ran as fast as I could to fetch them. They came straight-away," she replied. "When I got back, Mr. Glover was beating at the flames with a rug through the open door, but as the fire brigade was right on my heels, they pushed him aside and took over."

"Could you see flames when you returned?" Barnes asked. "Or just smoke?"

She thought for a moment. "Now that I think about it, it was mainly smoke billowing out of the building, but I do recall seeing fire through that little front window. It was very frightening."

"You weren't aware that Mr. Glover was in the house." Witherspoon looked at her curiously. "Isn't that a bit odd?"

"I suppose it must seem so." She smiled hesitantly and shrugged. "I did ask him about it. He said he'd come by at Mr. Boyd's request to bring him some files and that he'd been invited to stay to luncheon."

"Where was he waiting?" Witherspoon asked.

"In the drawing room," she replied. "He said he was waiting for everyone to arrive. Then he heard me cry out and came running down the hall, when I saw smoke. He said that's when he knew something was wrong."

Witherspoon looked doubtful. "So that means you hadn't let him into the house earlier and that you had no idea he was in the house at all?"

"That's correct." She frowned. "That is very curious, isn't it? I guess this is the first time I've thought about it with any clarity. If Mr. Glover had come to the front door and knocked, I'd have had to have been the one to let him into the house. The servants were all gone and I was there alone." Her brow furrowed as she looked at the inspector. "I wonder how he got in."

That was precisely what Witherspoon intended to find out.

Wiggins surveyed his surroundings with care as he walked down Laurel Road. There was a very good chance the inspector might be about the area. Wiggins had overheard him telling Mrs. Jeffries they still had to interview the servants, and the house-to-house task of looking for witnesses wasn't finished as yet either, so he kept a sharp eye out.

The street was quite lively. Farther up the road, he could see a woman wearing a brown housekeeper's dress sweeping the front steps of a huge, elegant house, and coming around the corner was a lad pushing a grocer's delivery cart. On the far side of the street was a laundry wagon making the morning stops. He came abreast of number fourteen and stopped, dropped to his knees, and pretended to tie his shoes. Cor blimey, this was going to be his lucky day: the woman was sweeping the steps of the Boyd house.

He cast a quick glance in her direction, trying to decide how best to approach her. She was a middle-aged woman with brown hair tucked under a black cap, a pale complexion, and a thin, disapproving mouth. Wiggins could see her quite clearly as she had turned and was staring straight at him. She didn't appear to like what she saw. "What do you want, boy?" she said harshly.

"Beggin' your pardon, ma'am," he said, "but I was just tyin' my shoe."

"Then move along and tie it elsewhere." She glared at him. "Go on, get off with you, boy, before I set the law on you."

As this was precisely the sort of reception Wiggins hadn't been expecting and certainly didn't want, all he could think to do was stumble to his feet. "Sorry, ma'am, I didn't mean to cause any offense." He wondered why on earth the woman was in such a foul temper. But before he could say another word, she'd turned her back on him and resumed her sweeping. He watched her covertly as he walked away, noting that she appeared to be moving the broom back and forth in the same spot over and over. He reckoned if she kept that up much longer, she'd be taking the paint off the steps.

Wiggins went up the road and around the corner. He spotted a café and decided to have a cup of tea. He went inside. It was a very small room with a counter and three tiny tables, all of which were empty. The only person in the place was a young girl standing behind the counter with her back to him. She turned as he stepped through the door. "Good morning," she said. "What can I get you?"

"Tea, please," he replied.

"Would you like a bun as well?" she asked. She was about his age, with dark hair, thick eyebrows, blue eyes, and a tiny rosebud of a mouth.

"No thanks, just the tea. You're not very busy, are you?"

"Not now." She grinned and picked up a huge brown teapot. "We were earlier, of course. We're always busy early in the morning, but then it dies down until midmorning when people start drifting in for a cuppa." She poured his tea into a tall gray mug and added milk. "Sugar?"

"Yes, please," he replied. He decided to try his luck here; at least she seemed like a talker. "I hear there was a murder around here yesterday." That was always good to get a conversation started.

Her eyes widened in surprise. "Really?"

"You mean you haven't 'eard?" he said. "There was a fellow that was bashed in the 'ead just up the road." He gestured in the direction of the Boyd house. "He died. Surely you've 'eard about it."

She stared at him blankly. "Was it in the newspapers?"

Wiggin's heart sank to his toes. His day just kept getting worse and worse.

Lawrence Boyd had worked at Boyd, Stanford, and Sawyer on Blakely Street near Chancery Lane. The bank took up the street floor of an old, two-story redbrick building.

Witherspoon and Barnes walked through the door and into a large room. Wooden shelves filled with ledgers lined three of the walls, and two doors, both of them open to reveal private offices, were on the fourth wall. A small wooden divider ran down the length of the room, behind which half a dozen men sat working at desks.

"We'd like to speak to Mr. James Glover," Witherspoon told the clerk closest to them. He was a young man with ginger hair and freckles. He'd risen to his feet when they'd entered and was now staring at them with his mouth slightly open, as though he'd never seen a policeman before. "I'll go get him," he said as he turned and hurried toward one of the private offices. "He's in Mr. Boyd's office."

"This doesn't look like any bank I've ever seen," Barnes muttered. "But then, it's not for people, is it. It's for businesses and that sort of thing. There's nothing here but desks and clerks."

Witherspoon wasn't really sure, but he didn't want to admit to his ignorance. "I believe you're correct. I don't think merchant banks cater to the general public." He noticed that on each desk there were ledgers and files. Everyone had stopped working and the room was deadly quiet. Every clerk in the room was staring at them openly.

"I don't see a typewriter anywhere, sir," Barnes muttered.

The door to an office opened and the ginger-haired clerk stuck his head out. "Mr. Glover will see you now." He waved the two policemen over.

James Glover was sitting behind a large desk. "You may go back to your post, Watkins," he said to the ginger-haired clerk before turning his attention to the two men.

The clerk scurried out, taking care to close the door behind him.

Glover stared at them for a moment. "What do you want, Inspector? I've already made a statement."

"We need to ask you some questions," Witherspoon said politely. He was a bit irritated. There were two perfectly good chairs in front of the desk; the man could ask them to sit down.

"As I said, Inspector, I've already made a statement and I think that ought to suffice." He started to get up.

"It won't suffice, sir," Barnes said harshly. "Your statement doesn't quite match what we've heard from other witnesses, so we'll either ask you a few questions here or we can do it down at the station. It's your choice, sir." The constable had taken the man's measure and decided to take the upper hand. James Glover reminded the constable of a bully boy from his school days. He'd terrorized the other boys until Barnes had stood up to him.

Glover seemed to wilt before their very eyes. He slumped back in the chair, his mouth gaping for words that wouldn't come. Finally, he said, "Well, er, one does want to cooperate with the law."

"Yes, I expect one does." Barnes pointed at the empty chairs. "If it's all the same to you, we'll sit down and take care of this properly."

"Certainly, certainly." Glover nodded eagerly. "Of course, do make yourselves comfortable. Sorry. All this horrible business with poor Mr. Boyd has made me forget my manners."

They sat down, and Barnes whipped out his little brown notebook.

Witherspoon said, "Mr. Glover, what time did you leave the office yesterday?"

"What time did I leave?" Glover looked confused by the question. "You mean here?"

"That's correct."

He thought for a moment. "I'm not sure."

"Perhaps one of the clerks would remember," Barnes suggested as he started to rise to his feet. "Shall I . . ."

"No, no, that's all right, I believe it was about half past ten," he replied. "But it might have been closer to eleven. I'm not certain."

"You took some files to Mr. Boyd's residence, is that correct?" Witherspoon asked.

"That's right," Glover replied. "But I don't see what that has to do with Mr. Boyd's death. They were just files. He'd seen them dozens of times."

"Mr. Boyd was working from his home, is that correct?" Barnes looked up from his writing.

"Yes, he'd been working from home all week," Glover said. "He was a painter, you see. He'd have much rather been an artist than a banker, but his family owns a big portion of the bank and he was the only son, so he joined the firm. He had no choice, really. It was his duty."

"Who let you into the Boyd house yesterday?" Witherspoon watched Glover's face as he asked the question.

"No one," Glover replied easily. "I went around the back to the studio. I never even knocked on the door."

"You knew he'd be alone?" Barnes asked.

"No, I knew he was working in his studio. He'd instructed me to come directly there."

"You came around the side of the house directly to the studio," Witherspoon clarified. "Is that right?"

"That's right. There's a passageway between the kitchen and the house next door. It's a service yard that opens onto the street, but the gate is behind a hedge so you've got to know where to look to find it."

"Which files did you bring to Mr. Boyd?" Barnes asked.

Glover rubbed a fat finger against his cheek. "Let me see. He wanted the Simpson file, Bertram's, and oh, yes, the Heddington file. I do hope they aren't too badly damaged. Those are very important papers. When do you think we might have them back?"

"Are you in charge now that Mr. Boyd is dead?" Witherspoon asked.

Glover shrugged. "I'm the chief clerk, Inspector, so until the partners appoint another managing director, I'm the one who will be responsible for the office. Now, I ask you again, when can I get my files?" He'd regained some of his confidence.

"When we're through with them," Barnes replied. "Will you be a candidate for managing director?" he asked quickly.

"I expect so." Glover's chest expanded proudly. "None of the partners want the burden of the day-to-day running of the place, and none of the other clerks are up to the task. I'm the most experienced person here."

"So Mr. Boyd's death means you'll get a nice chance to have a promotion," Barnes said. "I imagine there's a substantial salary increase with such a change in position."

Glover gasped. "That's absurd."

"You mean there isn't an increase in pay?" Barnes asked innocently.

"That's not what I meant at all." Glover wiped at a bead of sweat that had suddenly rolled down his forehead. "It was your implication that I find offensive."

"Constable Barnes implied nothing," Witherspoon said calmly. "He merely asked some legitimate questions. But let's go back to the issue of you just walking into Mr.

Boyd's home unannounced."

"I've told you, he instructed me to come directly to the studio," Glover insisted. He pulled a white handkerchief out of his coat pocket and dabbed at his neck, mopping up the layer of sweat that had suddenly appeared. "If you don't believe me, you can ask Bingley. He was here with me when the note from Mr. Boyd arrived yesterday morning."

"Mr. Boyd sent you a note telling you to bring the files straight to the studio," the inspector clarified. "What time was this?"

"At nine, just after we opened."

"And Mr. Bingley saw the note?" Barnes pressed.

"Of course he did. I gave it to him so he could get the files Mr. Boyd had listed, the ones he wanted me to bring to him. Bingley can also verify I'd been invited to luncheon." Glover sat up straighter. "So I took the files over to Mr. Boyd's straightaway. I put them on the little table next to the door and went back to the house. It was quite warm and Mr. Boyd suggested I may want to tidy myself up before the luncheon. There were going to be some important guests and I wanted to look presentable."

Witherspoon nodded. "Did you speak to

Miss Clarke when you went back to the house?"

Glover hesitated. "No, I should have, but I didn't. Mr. Boyd had asked me to check her work, but frankly, I . . . uh . . . well, I'm not used to dealing with young women in business circumstances. Really, I found it quite absurd that Mr. Boyd had engaged her services in the first place."

"So you said nothing to her; you simply went into the drawing room and sat down?" Witherspoon pressed.

"That's correct."

"How is it she didn't hear you walking down the hall?" Barnes smiled slightly as he asked the question. "You obviously heard her quite clearly when she raised the alarm about the fire. How is it she didn't hear you?"

Glover looked down at the desk. "I walk very softly."

"Were you deliberately staying quiet?" Barnes pressed.

"Certainly not," Glover snapped. "That infernal machine makes such a racket a herd of goats could have been dancing in the hallway and she'd have not heard it."

Witherspoon shifted in the chair. "What time was this?"

"I've already told you that," Glover

dabbed at his neck again. "It was close to eleven o'clock."

"And the luncheon was scheduled for one o'clock," Barnes said softly. He leaned closer to Glover. "Tell me, Mr. Glover, were you going to sit quietly in Mr. Boyd's drawing room for two hours when your office is only a twenty-minute walk away. Why didn't you go back to work?"

"Of course not," Glover snapped. "After I tidied myself up, I fully intended to come back to the office." His pale face flushed red. "But I was tired and my feet hurt so I went into the drawing room to have a bit of a rest. The latest edition of the *Illustrated London News* was on the table, so I picked it up and sat down to have a quick glance at it. Reading always makes me sleepy, Inspector, and the room was exceptionally warm. I must have dozed off because all of a sudden, I was awakened by Miss Clarke. She'd shouted something, made some sort of call of distress. I leapt to my feet and saw her in the hallway running for the back door. She yelled that the studio was on fire." He paused and took a breath of air. "We both ran out to the back garden. We could see the flames through the front window of the studio, so I told Miss Clarke to fetch the fire brigade."

"And what did you do?" Barnes asked.

"I looked around for a bucket or something to use to try and put the flames out, but there was nothing that I could see that would be of any use." He sighed. "I finally grabbed the rug off the floor in the hall and tried using that to beat the flames out, but frankly, fire frightens me so I didn't want to get too close." His eyes filled with tears. "The truth is, I was so scared I didn't have the courage to even stick my head through the studio door. I kept calling Mr. Boyd's name, but he didn't reply. I think I must have known something awful had happened. I know it makes me sound a dreadful coward, but I'm terrified of fire."

"Fire frightens most people," Witherspoon said kindly. "What happened then?"

"A few minutes later, the fire brigade arrived and I got out of the way. It didn't take long to get the fire out." He broke off and laughed harshly. "It wasn't much of a fire in the first place. Yet I'd been too frightened to go through that wretched door. I'll never forgive myself; if I'd had the courage to go inside, Mr. Boyd might have been saved."

"I doubt that sir," Witherspoon said softly. "At what point did the servants come back?"

Glover tapped a finger against his lips. "I'm not sure. One moment I looked around and they were all standing near the back door looking frightened and shocked. But I've no idea how long they'd been there. Perhaps Miss Clarke will remember."

"Did you see or hear anything unusual after you gave Mr. Boyd the files?" Barnes asked.

"No, Constable." Glover shook his head. "As I said, I dozed off. I couldn't have heard anything in any case. The typewriter makes a very loud noise."

"Yet you dozed off?"

"It's noisy but very rhythmic," he explained. "A bit like riding on a train. One moment you're awake and the next, you're nodding off to the clackety clack of the wheels against the rails. I can't explain it, but that's what happened."

"Can you tell Mr. Horace Maitland that Luty Belle Crookshank is here to see him," Luty said to the young man in the reception office of Maitland, Warner, and Stutts, Merchant Bankers.

The clerk, who hadn't heard the door open, looked up. His eyes widened in surprise. An elderly woman wearing a bright emerald-green-striped day dress and an elegant hat and holding a frilly parasol, stood grinning at him. "Do you have an appointment, ma'am?' he asked.

"I don't think I'll need one," Luty replied easily. "You just skeedaddle on in there and tell him Luty Belle Crookshank is here to see him and it'll be fine. Go on now, git up off yer backside and git on in there." She waved her hand at him.

He leapt to his feet, frightened she might start waving her parasol next. "Uh, yes, ma'am, I'll just see if Mr. Maitland is available."

"Don't you fret, boy." Luty laughed. "He'll be available."

The young man disappeared into the office. A few moments later, Horace Maitland stepped into the reception room. The young man peered out from behind him. "Luty, this is a pleasure. Do come in. I'd heard you were ill."

Maitland was a clean-shaven man of medium height. He had brown hair and hazel eyes, and was dressed in a dark navy blue suit with a white shirt, blue waistcoat, and maroon tie. He took her arm. "See that we're not disturbed," he instructed the clerk as he led Luty into his office.

"I was, but I'm better now," Luty said. "I'm sorry to barge in on you like this, but I was hopin' you could help me with a problem I've got."

"Of course, of course, I'll do anything I can. Would you care for some tea?" He asked as he closed the door.

"No, thank you, Horace." Luty shook her head. "I'll not take up that much of your time. I know you're busy."

Maitland waved her into straight-backed leather chair opposite his desk. "Do sit down."

Luty sat and took a moment to gather her thoughts. It had been a good while since she'd been out "on the hunt" as Mrs. Jeffries would say, and she was raring to go. But she wanted to make sure she didn't frighten off her quarry. She was rich as sin and her American companies did plenty of business with Maitland's bank, but he was a banker and they tended to be more tight-lipped than lawyers. She knew she had to be careful.

"Now, what can I do for you?" Maitland leaned back in his chair and watched her curiously.

"I've got a little problem and I'm not sure what I can do about it." She smiled brightly. "You see, a good friend of mine has put a heap of money into a project that's goin' to be funded by Boyd, Stanford, and Sawyer, the merchant bank over on Blakely Street."

"I know who they are," he said.

112

"Well, I reckon you've heard what happened to the general manger, Lawrence Boyd . . ." She trailed off, hoping he'd jump into the conversation at this point, but he simply stared at her like a fish-eyed poker player, so she continued. "He went and got himself murdered. Now I'm stuck with my friend wonderin' whether or not he ought to pull his business from the bank."

Maitland stared at her for a long moment, and Luty was almost sure he didn't believe a word she was saying. Finally, he said, "Why didn't your friend come to us?"

"I told him to," she exclaimed. "But he's a stubborn cuss and he'd already started doin' business with Boyd's by the time he talked to me."

"So what you're asking is whether or not the bank is sound?" Maitland asked. "I should think that Mr. Boyd's death wouldn't have any bearing on the soundness of the enterprise."

"Don't take me for a fool," Luty said impatiently. "Of course the murder of a general partner is goin' to have a bearin' on the bank. My friend wants to know if the man's death means there's something bad goin' on. You know, hanky-panky with money, double dealin', that sort of thing. Have you heard anything?"

Maitland smiled. "Luty, tell your friend not to worry. There's nothing that suggests that Boyd's death has anything to do with any irregularities."

"But how can you be so sure?" Luty asked. This wasn't going as she had hoped. She'd forgotten how tight-lipped Maitland could be. She wasn't getting anywhere.

"You can't be certain, of course," he said. "But Lawrence Boyd had many enemies, and most of them had absolutely nothing to do with his business."

"Enemies," she repeated. "What do you mean?" Now they were getting somewhere.

Maitland glanced at the closed door of his office and then leaned closer. "Don't repeat this Luty, but the fellow wasn't very well liked."

Luty smiled eagerly and waited for more.

Maitland leaned back in his chair. "Are you sure you wouldn't like some tea?"

CHAPTER 4

"This is very nice but not very comfortable looking," Barnes murmured as he turned and surveyed the room. "I'd not fancy anyone could fall asleep on that settee. Thing looks as stiff as a plank board and so do those chairs. As a matter of fact, there's not a stick of furniture in here that looks like you could sit more than a few minutes without your backside going numb."

Witherspoon and Barnes were at the Boyd household. As they stood in the drawing room, waiting to speak to the housekeeper, the constable was studying the furnishings like a general surveying a battlefield. The inspector followed his lead and took a closer look at the furniture.

The room was done in the Empire style. The settee and the matching chairs had ornately carved backboards of heavy, dark wood and were upholstered with stiff green-and-white brocade fabric. The width of the seat on both the settee and the chairs was very shallow.

"I can't see Glover catching a catnap on anything in here," Barnes muttered. "He's too big and the seats on all the furniture too small."

Witherspoon continued his survey of the room. There was a green brocade loveseat in front of the fireplace, but it was upholstered in the same stiff brocade as the settee and had a very low back; certainly that didn't look inviting enough to sleep on. The other chairs in the room didn't look any better. "I can't imagine how Glover managed it. There's nothing in the room that looks at all comfortable, but perhaps he was really tired."

"Or perhaps he was lying," Barnes said.

"Did you sense that?" Witherspoon looked at the constable. He respected Barnes opinion as he wasn't given to rushing to judgment or assuming that everyone was guilty.

"I sensed he wasn't being completely candid," the constable replied. "But I can't put my finger on what's bothering me. Miss Clarke verified much of his story, and the clerk, Bingley, verified the note had arrived and that he'd been invited to luncheon."

The door opened and a tall, brown-haired

woman wearing a gray bombazine dress stepped into the room. "I'm Hannah Rothwell. I understand you wish to speak to me."

"I'm Inspector Gerald Witherspoon and this is Constable Barnes," he began. "I'm sorry we didn't get a chance to speak with you yesterday. There are some questions we'd like to ask you."

"I had to go to the shops and order provisions for the staff. The larders were empty. Even if there's been a death in the household, people need to eat." She stared at them for a moment. "Will this take long? I've a number of tasks to do this morning. Mr. Boyd's solicitor and the vicar will be here soon."

"Are they meeting Mr. Boyd's family here?" Witherspoon asked curiously. That was a bit of luck; he'd been planning on speaking to the victim's lawyer.

"They are coming to see me, Inspector. I'm Lawrence's cousin as well as his housekeeper. We've got to arrange the funeral." She walked to the settee, sat down, and gestured at the two chairs. "Please take a seat."

They seated themselves and Barnes took out his notebook. Witherspoon wasn't sure where to begin. It hadn't occurred to him that the housekeeper might be the victim's kin. "You're Mr. Boyd's cousin?"

"I just said I was," she replied.

"Did he have many relatives?" Barnes asked. Finding out how many heirs were left to squabble over the spoils was always a good place to start a murder investigation.

"He had some cousins in Scotland, but he hasn't seen or spoken to them in years," she replied. She smiled faintly at Barnes. "But I'm not the sole heir, believe me. If I know Lawrence, and I did, I suspect he's left his estate to some ridiculous charity or an art museum."

"Mr. Boyd was a generous man, I take it," the inspector commented.

"Gracious no." She laughed heartily. "Lawrence was a mean-spirited, nasty excuse for a human being. But he did love getting his name put about on everything. That's why he was always giving charities and societies money." She leaned slightly forward. "So far, he's got his name on a park bench, a plaque at Clapham Foundling Home, and at least three annual prizes at the Amateur Artists Guild. There's the Lawrence Boyd Prize for the best pastoral watercolour, the Lawrence Boyd Prize for the most outstanding cityscape done in oils, and . . . oh, bother, I can't remember what the third one was, but it was something equally silly. I think some of the groups he belonged to simply made up prizes so they could get a bit of cash out of him."

"I see." Witherspoon took a deep breath. Sometimes, he was glad he had so few relatives. At least no one of his own blood hated him. "Er, can you give us an account of the household's movements yesterday?"

"We went to a funeral, Inspector." She looked at him as though he were a half-wit. "I believe you were informed of that fact yesterday. Have you forgotten?"

"No, ma'am, I haven't forgotten. What I'm asking for is more detail," he explained patiently. "I'd like an accounting of everything that happened yesterday from the time the household awoke until you all returned from the funeral."

Her lips pursed disapprovingly, but she shrugged. "All right, well, let's see. I got up at half past five, which is an hour earlier than usual."

"Why was that?" Barnes asked.

"I knew we were going to the funeral, and as there was also a luncheon planned, we had to take extra time to get everything ready."

"Mr. Boyd didn't mind his staff leaving on the day he had a social engagement?" Witherspoon asked.

"He was furious." She smiled broadly. "But there wasn't anything he could do about it. Helen had worked here, and we were all very fond of the girl."

"Helen was the person who died?" Witherspoon interrupted. He wanted to keep everything straight in his own mind. These were the sort of details that might turn out to be important.

"Yes." She nodded. "Helen Cleminger. She was a housemaid here for four years. She was from a small village outside St. Albans, and when she took ill, she went home. Unfortunately, she didn't recover. She caught pneumonia this winter, and it kept getting worse and worse. It finally killed the poor girl. She was only twenty-two. But as I was saying, he could hardly object to the staff wanting to pay their last respects. Oh, he tried to bully us into not going. But these days, servants have more choices. No one has to work here. There are plenty of positions about." She laughed. "Cook flat out told him if she couldn't go to Helen's funeral, she'd be moving on, and so did the tweeny and the upstairs maid."

"So Mr. Boyd relented and gave you permission," Barnes pressed. "Was he angry about it?"

"He wasn't happy, but he had a difficult

time hanging onto servants in the first place so he'd not much choice. Cook came up with a menu for a cold luncheon that let him salvage his pride and act as if he were being generous in saying we could go, but I'm sure he planned on making everyone's life miserable for having the nerve to challenge his authority." She laughed again. "What he didn't know was that all of us were still planning on leaving."

"Including you?" Witherspoon watched her closely.

"Including me, Inspector," she admitted. "I'm going to Australia. I've got enough money saved to open a business and build a life for myself. Cook's going to retire, and the upstairs maid is getting married. The tweeny and the downstairs girl won't have any problem finding work as they're both fully trained."

"What time did you leave the house that morning?" Barnes asked.

"Early," she replied. "The food was all ready and in the wet larder. I'd made sure that Mary — she's the downstairs girl — had set the table properly, and I'd left Mr. Boyd's breakfast on a warming plate in the dining room. We left at half past seven; the funeral was set for ten o'clock, but it was in Helen's village church so we had to get to

Paddington Station in time for the 8:10 train."

"So you went to the funeral and then came back. Can you tell us what you saw when you arrived home?" Witherspoon shifted in his seat, his backside had gone quite numb. If the rest of the furniture was this uncomfortable, he knew Glover had to be lying. Napping on one of these chairs would be like trying to sleep on a bed of rocks.

"Mr. Boyd had insisted we return in time to serve luncheon, so we came back straightaway after the funeral." She sniffed disapprovingly. "You'd have thought he and his guests could serve themselves, but oh, no, we had to come back. We barely had time to pay our respects to Helen's family. But I digress. We arrived home to find the fire wagon outside and the fire brigade all over the place."

"Were Mr. Glover and Miss Clarke here?" Barnes asked.

"Yes, it was Mr. Glover who told us that Mr. Boyd was dead." She shrugged. "I know I sound heartless, but he wasn't a very nice person. I was one of the few relatives the man had, but do you think he'd let me live here as family? He did not. He put me to work as his housekeeper and insisted I call him Mr. Boyd."

"You said he had a problem keeping staff," Witherspoon said. "What exactly did you mean?"

"People wouldn't stay," she replied. "When one is in service, taking care of a single man rather than an entire family is supposed to be one of the easier situations. But he was as hard to please as a houseful of maiden aunts. Good gracious, if there was a speck of dust on the furniture he'd scream like a banshee. If cook was a minute late getting food on the table, he'd go into the kitchen himself and humiliate the woman, and he made the poor butler's life a living hell."

"Did Leeson plan on leaving as well?" Barnes looked up from his notebook.

"He was going to retire." Hannah Rothwell grinned broadly. "The poor man deserves some peace and quiet after what he's been through with my cousin."

"Why did he stay?" Witherspoon asked curiously.

"Lawrence paid well," she replied. "That's the only reason any of us stayed. But even decent wages don't make up for being treated badly. Not these days."

Witherspoon thought about asking if Boyd had enemies and then changed his mind as the question had already been answered. Instead, he said, "Had Mr. Boyd recently sacked anyone who might want to extract revenge against him?"

Mrs. Rothwell shook her head. "Lawrence didn't sack staff. They always left on their own. At least in the time I've been here, which is ten years. Before that, I couldn't say."

Barnes asked, "How many guests were expected for luncheon yesterday?"

"Four or five. The luncheon was buffet-style and people were supposed to help themselves, so I don't recall the exact number of people." She frowned thoughtfully. "Let me see, Mr. Gibbons was coming, Mr. and Mrs. Sapington, and I think one or two others. They were all quite stunned to find out he'd been killed, of course. Mind you, that didn't stop them from eating."

"Mr. Sapington stated you insisted the guests go ahead and eat," Witherspoon said. He had no idea why that had popped into his head, but it had.

"Nonsense," she snorted derisively. "I did no such thing. When I went into the dining room to supervise the clearing up, Maud Sapington was right on my heels. We were at school together, Inspector, and Maud delighted in sneering at how I'd come down in the world. But I digress again. Before I could so much as pull the trolley away from the butler's pantry, she grabbed a plate and began filling it with roast beef."

"Did she make any comment or did she just help herself?" Barnes asked curiously. Odd behavior by anyone at a murder scene was always worth noting.

"She looked at me and said, 'There's no reason to let all this food go to waste.' " Mrs. Rothwell snorted again. "Then she stuck her head out the door and called the others to come in and eat. I was amazed. I wasn't fond of Lawrence in the least, none of us were, but it was no longer a social occasion of any sort. But Maud was always like that, pushy and greedy."

Witherspoon nodded sympathetically. "It must have been a very awkward situation for you."

She actually laughed. "It was, but it was also funny. I'm sure the story of the whole lot of themselves eating themselves silly before their host's body was even carted off by the police is already making the rounds. The Sapingtons will hate that. Arnold Sapington is a stickler for the social niceties, which is a bit of an affectation if you ask me, considering he was nothing but a builder's son from Slough. Maud doesn't care what people think of her. She never did."

It was obvious Mrs. Rothwell had no love for Maud Sapington. "I take it you've known Mrs. Sapington for quite some time," Witherspoon said.

"As I said, since we were in school," Mrs. Rothwell replied. "She was a greedy thing back then, too. Which is odd, really; she grew up with everything. Oh, her family weren't aristocrats, but they were rich as Croesus."

"Are the Sapingtons and Mr. Boyd close friends?" the inspector pressed. He wanted to find out if all of yesterday's luncheon guests disliked their host.

"Oh, good lord, no." She laughed again. "Lawrence thought Maud a silly woman and considered her husband a social-climbing upstart. He only invited them for luncheon because Walter Gibbons was going to announce that it was Lawrence who'd won the chairmanship of the Bankers Benevolent Society and not Sapington." Her smile faded. "I told you, Inspector, my cousin had a cruel streak. He wanted to watch Arnold Sapington's face when he heard the news."

Witherspoon noticed that she now referred to the victim as "Lawrence" rather than "Mr. Boyd." But he didn't think that fact had anything to do with his murder. Furthermore, she might have disliked her cousin, but she did have an alibi. "Had Mr. Boyd been worried or unduly concerned about anyone or anything of late?"

"Not that I know about," she replied. "But he'd have hardly confided in me."

"Who would he have spoken with if he had concerns?" Barnes asked.

"No one. Lawrence kept his own counsel. He was a very secretive man, Inspector, in everything. He wouldn't even let anyone see one of his paintings until he was finished with it. He once sacked a gardner for sneaking a peek at an unfinished oil painting."

"So as far as you know, no one had been threatening him or doing anything of late to cause him alarm?" Witherspoon probed.

She shook her head and then glanced at an ornate carriage clock on a small table to her left. "Is this going to take much longer?"

"I think that will be all for now," Witherspoon said. "We appreciate your help in this matter."

Mrs. Rothwell got to her feet. "I don't know that anything I've said will help find who murdered him. If I were you, I'd stay a bit and have a chat with his lawyer. He should be here soon."

"Thank you for your time, Mrs. Rothwell. In the meantime, we're going to question the rest of the staff. I expect you'd like us to conduct our interviews below stairs. Do you have a space we might use, perhaps the butler's pantry . . ."

"You can talk to them here." She waved him back to his seat. "Who do you want me to send up first?"

Witherspoon smiled gratefully. "Could you ask Mr. Leeson to spare us a few minutes. We've a few more questions for him, and do let me know when Mr. Boyd's solicitor arrives. I'd like to insure he doesn't leave without speaking with us first."

Betsy stood on the pavement and shivered as a gust of wind slammed into her. The day had started out bright and sunny so she'd not bothered with her heavy jacket, just a light lavender shawl over her dress. But May weather was treacherous, and now dark clouds scuttled across the sky and the air had that raw heavy scent of impending rain. She debated going back to the house for her umbrella and jacket and then decided to risk the deluge. The worst that could happen was she'd get wet.

She pulled her shawl tighter, crossed the

road, and walked into the greengrocer's. The clerk, a young man with a prominent Adam's apple and wispy brown hair, was emptying cabbages into a bin. "I'll be with you in a moment, miss." He put the sack down on the floor, brushed off his hands, and came toward her.

After surveying all the shops in the area, Betsy had deliberately picked this one for her first stop. A lone male clerk was always best when it came to ferreting out information. "A pound of carrots, please." She gave him a wide smile.

The clerk shifted to one side and reached into the shallow bin holding carrots. "Would you like them topped?"

"Yes, please." She gave him another dazzling smile. "That's very kind of you."

He smiled self-consciously as he twisted the green leafy tops off the carrots, put them on the scale, and then reached back into the bin for another one to make up a pound.

"A friend of mine works in a household near here," she began. "But I'm not sure exactly where. I wonder how far away that is."

"I've lived in this area all my life. If you'll tell me the name of the street, I can probably help," the clerk offered.

"Oh, that's very kind of you. Let's see,

what did her last letter say? I've just moved up from the country and I'd like to call on her. We're from the same village, you see. It's Laurel Road; yes, that's the name of the street. I only found out this morning that it's so close by."

"Oh, that's just up the road a bit." He pointed to his left. "Not far at all. You can't miss it."

"Thanks ever so much. I'd like half a pound of those sprouts as well." She knew Mrs. Goodge would be glad of the extra vegetables. "I do hope my friend is still there. She'd written that she was thinking of looking for another position." Betsy stepped a bit closer and lowered her voice. "She didn't like the place very much."

"She'd not have a hard time findin' work," he replied as he dumped sprouts on the scale. "Not these days. Do you know the name of the family she works for?"

"It's not a family. It's a gentleman on his own. A Mr. Boyd."

"Lawrence Boyd, the banker?"

"I believe Emma did say her employer was a banker," Betsy replied. This was going even better than she had hoped.

"Your poor friend's not goin' to be havin' an easy time of it, then," he declared. "Lawrence Boyd was murdered yesterday.

130

It was in the morning papers."

"Murdered! Goodness, that's terrible." Betsy widened her eyes in pretended shock.

"Poor bloke was bashed on the head," the clerk said, repeating the information with obvious relish.

"The papers described how he was killed?" Betsy asked, her voice incredulous. The accounts she'd read this morning hadn't given any details at all.

"Oh, no." He leaned closed. "My mum got it from Mrs. Norton, who works next door to the Boyd house. She overheard the police talkin' about it when they was searching the grounds next to her house. She's got real good ears does Mrs. Norton, so I'm sure she didn't get it wrong."

"Why was the poor man killed?" Betsy asked.

"No one knows yet." He dumped the sprouts on the counter next to the carrots and pulled a sheet of brown paper off the roll. "Would you like anything else, miss?"

"No, that'll be all."

"Mind you, Mr. Boyd wasn't the nicest of people." The clerk slapped the paper down and then shoved the vegetables into the center. "My mum says that's why he never married again. No other woman would have him."

So Boyd was a widower, Betsy thought. That was certainly interesting news. "You mother didn't like Mr. Boyd?"

"Mum hated him. He used to buy from us, but he and Mum got into a dispute over a bill, so he took his business elsewhere." He folded the paper so that it made a nice package. "Mum had to threaten him with the law to get him to pay what he owed. But he finally did."

"He doesn't sound a nice person at all," Betsy agreed. "That's probably why Emma — that's my friend — wanted another position."

"We weren't the only merchant he squabbled with." He pulled a length of string off a roll and deftly twisted it around the packet of vegetables. "The chemists had stopped supplying him and so had the draper's shop over on Thornhill Lane. But I don't think any of the merchants were angry enough to bash the bloke's head in. That's not a particularly useful way of getting your bills paid, is it?"

"I suppose not," Betsy agreed. "Who do you think did kill him, then?"

"I've no idea." He shrugged, and then his gaze moved over Betsy's shoulder. He broke into a wide smile. "Good morning, Miss Devers. It's very nice to see you."

132

Betsy turned her head and saw a pretty, dark-haired young woman standing at the entrance. She wore clothes very much like Betsy's and had a shopping basket over her arm. "Hello, Mr. Clarkson." The girl smiled warmly at the clerk. "It's nice to see you as well. Have you any rutabagas today. Cook needs them for a stew."

"I've some lovely rutabagas," he replied. Without taking his gaze off the newcomer, he picked up Betsy's packet and handed it to her. "Thank you, miss," he said dismissively.

She handed him the money for the vegetables. Betsy was no fool. She wasn't going to get anything else out of this one, not when his lady love was right in front of him. "Thank you," she said politely as she turned to leave.

He didn't appear to hear her.

Smythe stood in front of the Dirty Duck Pub and hesitated for a moment before pushing the door open and stepping inside. He'd thought long and hard about the wisdom of asking Blimpey Groggins for help, but had decided that there was no point in not using a perfectly good source of information just to salvage his pride. He had plenty of money and he could afford

Blimpey's fees, and just because he chose to use him, it didn't mean he couldn't do his own investigating.

Even though it was only fifteen minutes past opening time, the pub was already crowded. Dockworkers, day laborers, tally clerks, and bargemen were two deep at the bar, and there wasn't a single empty seat on the side benches. The tables were full as well, but Blimpey was in his usual spot. A rough-looking man with wild black hair and a scar bisecting his right cheek sat next to him.

Blimpey glanced in Smythe's direction, then leaned over and said something to his companion as Smythe pushed his way through the crowd. As he drew close, the man got up.

"Sorry," Smythe apologized. "I didn't mean to interrupt, but I need to 'ave a quick word with Blimpey."

"After what your lot done for Tommy Odell, I'd gladly give up my seat to you," the man said. "It's rare that people like us get any justice in this old world."

Smythe was dumbstruck. Did the entire world know the inspector's household had kept a pickpocket from hanging for a murder he'd not committed? Blast a Spaniard, this was getting out of hand.

"This is Eddie Blanding. He's Tommy's uncle. He works on a merchant ship and he only got back a few days ago," Blimpey explained quickly.

"Pleased to meet you." Smythe extended his hand and the two men shook.

"If there's ever a favor I can do for you," Eddie said, "you've just to name it. I felt real bad that I wasn't here when Tommy and Edna — that's his mum and my sister — were goin' through their troubles. But I was at sea."

"You weren't to know then," Smythe said easily. "And I appreciate the offer of a favor. Maybe I'll take you up on it one day."

"I'm here for the next three months. Blimpey knows where to find me." Eddie nodded gravely, glanced at Blimpey, and then headed for the door.

Blimpey waved at the barmaid and mouthed "two pints" as Smythe took Eddie's chair.

"Now before you get all het up," Blimpey said, "I didn't say anything to Eddie. It was Tommy and his mum that let the cat out of the bag. But Eddie's a taciturn type; he'll not be speaking out of turn about what your lot is up to."

"That's good," Smythe said. "The fewer people that know what we're about, the better. But then, you know that better than anyone. It wouldn't do you much good if every mother's son was privy to your business."

"That's why I keep my 'ead down and my ears open," he replied. Blimpey was a ginger-haired man of late middle age with a ruddy complexion and a bit of a belly. He'd once been a petty thief. However, as he possessed a phenomenal memory and the ability to pick up bits and pieces of information from a variety of sources, he soon realized he could make far more money selling information than stealing. Blimpey had no stomach for violence or prison, so he changed careers and was now a successful businessman with a vast network of informants. Impoverished noblemen, court clerks, bailiffs, shopgirls, and barmaids fed him a steady stream of facts, gossip, and speculation that he turned into a useful commodity. He sold that commodity to whoever was willing to pay his price. Smythe had been using him for years, but on their last case, it had been Blimpey who had come to them seeking help.

"Not to worry, old sport. Those of us who know the truth can keep our mouths closed." Blimpey broke off as the barmaid brought their pints and put them on the

136

table. "Thanks, love." He waited till she'd moved off before he spoke. "I heard your inspector got that banker's murder."

"That's why I'm here," Smythe replied. He was certain that Blimpey knew as much about the victim as he did. "It's a bit of an odd one."

"Killer tried to make it look like an accident." Blimpey took a quick sip of his beer.

"That's what it looks like." Smythe lifted his pint and took a quick drink. It was a bit early for him, but he didn't wish to offend Blimpey. "Now I need you to find out what you can about Lawrence Boyd."

"Your victim?" Blimpey's eyesbrows shot up. "Is that all? I already know a bit about him. Don't you have any other names for me?"

"That's just it: we're not sure who we ought to be concentratin' on. There were only two people in the house when the murder was done, but Boyd was 'avin' a fancy luncheon that day and the guests turned up before they even carted off the body."

"Just give me the names you've got," Blimpey ordered.

"James Glover — he was Boyd's chief clerk — and there was a young woman, a Miss Eva Clarke. She's one of them typewriter girls. They were the two that were there when it happened."

"Who were the guests?"

"Arnold and Maud Sapington. He's another banker."

"I know who he is," Blimpey said. "Go on."

"And a man named Walter Gibbons. I don't know what he does for a living, but he was there to give Boyd some news about bein' the honorary chairman of the Bankers Benevolent Society."

Blimpey snorted. "There's no such thing as a benevolent banker, but this ought to do for now. Not to worry, I've already got my boys looking into the matter. Boyd had plenty of business rivals; that'll do for a start."

"You said you had some information for me already," Smythe reminded him. "What is it?" He hoped it was something really good. He'd like to show up at today's meeting with some interesting tidbits.

"Your Mr. Boyd wasn't very good at his job," Blimpey said. "He recently loaned a great deal of his bank's money to a mining enterprise called Bagley Hills out in Australia."

"I take it the venture isn't doing too well," Smythe said.

"It's a heap of red sand out in the middle of nowhere." Blimpey laughed. "You've been to the bush, Smythe. You know what it's like. Anyways, Boyd not only invested his bank's money in the thing, but he talked some of the bank's biggest clients into backing a loan for equipment and operating expenses. So not only are some of his clients furious at him, but his general partners aren't too happy."

"How come none of this has been made public?"

"Are you daft, man?" Blimpey laughed cynically. "This isn't the sort of news any bank wants bandied about. They bury this sort of information. I found out because . . . well, it's my job to know these kinds of things, and seein' as how I'm a bit beholdin' to you, I thought I'd pass this on. You might put a word in your inspector's ear to have a good look at the books."

"Thanks, Blimpey. I appreciate it."

Blimpey burped softly. "Oops, that slipped out. Sorry. Nell would have my guts for garters if she heard me belchin' this way."

"How is your good lady?" Smythe asked.

"She's fine. Mind you, a wife does change a man's habits. Time was I could break wind out of either end and not think anything of it, but not now. Nell's always going on about how to behave in public." Blimpey chuckled good naturedly. Then he sobered. "There is one thing I'd like to ask you about. It's more in the way of advice, if you know what I mean."

Smythe raised an eyebrow. "The last time I gave you advice, you ended up married."

"And it was the best bit of advice a man ever got," Blimpey declared. "That's why I'm glad you stopped by today. I need to ask you something else, and frankly, it's not the sort of thing I'd be comfortable askin' anyone else."

"What is it?"

Blimpey took a deep breath. "I told you before that the reason I wanted you and your lot to find Tommy's killer is because I thought Tommy was mine."

"I remember, and I've kept my promise. I've not told anyone. No one knows that Tommy is your son. Your secret is still safe." He took a quick sip of his beer.

"I know I can trust you. That's not what I'm worried about." He sighed heavily and looked down at the tabletop.

"Then what is it?"

"It's Nell. I feel bad about keepin' it from her. I think I should tell her."

Blimpey was still staring at the tabletop, and his voice was so low that Smythe had to lean forward to catch his words. He had no idea how to respond. This was very dangerous territory, so he took the coward's way out and said nothing.

After a long moment, Blimpey raised his head and stared at Smythe. "Well, what should I do? I don't like keepin' this kind of secret from Nell. She's been too good to me and it don't feel right."

"I'm no expert on women," Smythe muttered. "But if keepin' it to yourself makes you feel bad, then maybe you should tell her."

"You really think so?" Blimpey asked hopefully.

"She knows you weren't a saint all these years," he said.

"And she knows the kind of life I led. I never lied to her about how I made my living."

"So, she can hardly be surprised that you'd sowed a wild oat or two, can she?" Smythe pointed out.

"Of course she's got to understand," Blimpey agreed. "Once you get to be our age, you've got a past, and it's not always one you're real proud of, if you know what I mean."

"Blimpey, you're fifteen years older than me."

"I wasn't meanin' you." Blimpey shook his head impatiently. "I meant once you got to be mine and Nell's age. Mind you, you're no spring chicken. What are you, forty?"

"I'm thirty-eight," he said defensively. His age was a bit of a sore subject as Betsy was only twenty-four. It had once been an issue between them, but she'd put a stop to that nonsense.

"Now, now, don't get yourself all het up. I was only makin' a comment. So you think I ought to tell Nell?"

Smythe felt a great deal more confident now that the two of them had discussed it man to man. He also knew he'd not like to keep anything important from Betsy. "Nell's a good woman. I don't think she'd begrudge you spending a bit of time or lolly on your own flesh and blood."

"This will be a big load off my mind." Blimpey grinned broadly. "I like to share everything with my Nell."

"Glad I was able to help." Smythe drained his glass and rose to his feet. "I've got to be goin'. I'll come by in the next day or two. Thanks for the information about Boyd's business ventures. I'll put a flea in the inspector's ear to have a look in that direction."

■ ■ ■ ■

"Don't be nervous, miss." Inspector Witherspoon gave the red-haired young woman a reassuring smile. "I'm only going to ask you a few questions. What's your name?"

"Lydia White" she replied. "But I wasn't even here when the master was killed, so I don't see what I could tell you."

"Please sit down." The inspector pointed at the chair directly across from him. "I know you weren't here, but it's important we question everyone from the household."

She sat down. "All right, then, what do you want to know?"

"How long have you been employed here, Lydia?" Witherspoon hoped Barnes was having an easier time of it. So far, he'd not learned anything useful from Boyd's servants. Barnes, on the other hand, had gone to the house next door to see if they'd seen or heard anything out of the ordinary.

"A little more than a year, sir," she replied.

Witherspoon nodded. He'd expected that sort of answer. Except for the housekeeper and the butler, virtually the entire staff was relatively new. "Did you like working for Mr. Boyd?"

She hesitated for a second and then said,

"I know it's wrong to speak ill of the dead, but I didn't like it at all. Mr. Boyd wasn't very nice to us. Truth is, I was looking for a new position."

"How was he 'not nice'?"

"He never wanted to give us our full afternoon out," she said. "On your free day, you're supposed to be allowed off at noon, but he was always finding little jobs and things for you to do before you could go. It weren't just me; he did it to everyone. He kept a list of who had what afternoon off, and on those days, he'd make Mrs. Rothwell give us these stupid things to do that kept us here for half the afternoon. Last Friday he had poor Mary — she's the upstairs girl — cleaning out the attic before she could get off. She missed her train and didn't get to go home to see her parents."

He'd heard much the same from the others. Boyd wasn't very good to his servants, but from what the inspector had observed, half of London's gentry treated their staff badly. Strange, really, that people who had so much could begrudge those who had so little a few hours of leisure.

"And he wanted me to clean the paint off the floor in his studio on my day out last week," she continued. "The only reason I didn't have my afternoon ruined was because he suddenly decided he had to start workin' on a new painting. He never lets any of us in the studio when he's painting. Doesn't like people to see his work, not that any of us would want to anyway, but that's the only reason I got my day out."

"Did you see Mr. Boyd yesterday before you left for your friend's funeral?"

"No."

"When was the last time you saw him alive?"

"The day before he was murdered. I saw him come out of his study." Lydia grinned, exposing a mouthful of lovely white teeth. "He'd just had an awful row with Mrs. Rothwell and he looked fit to be tied."

"He had a row with Mrs. Rothwell?" Witherspoon repeated. "How do you know?"

"I heard it," Lydia replied. She looked over her shoulder at the door to the drawing room. "I don't suppose telling you about it will make any difference now. We're all goin' to be turfed out now that he's dead. Mind you, there's plenty of positions about, but I'm thinkin' about goin' back home and getting a job at the shoe factory. They've just opened up two of them in Nottingham and one's right close to my home. I don't really like London all that much . . ."

145

"That sounds perfectly splendid, miss," Witherspoon interrupted. "But could you tell me a bit more about Mrs. Rothwell's row with Mr. Boyd? Exactly when did this happen?"

"Like I said, the day before he was murdered. It was early of the morning and the two of them were in Mr. Boyd's study. I'd come down the back stairs to get my shoes out of the kitchen. They'd gotten wet in the rain, so I'd left them by the cooker to dry. The rest of the household was still upstairs; not even Leeson had come down yet. The house was real quiet, so I could hear everything." She paused and took a breath. "I'd started back up the stairs when I heard Mrs. Rothwell shouting loud enough to wake the dead. Then he'd shout right back at her and then she'd scream at him. It was awful but it was interesting, too."

"You were on the back stairs," he clarified.

"That's right. The back stairs are just on the other side of the study," she said.

"Could you hear what they were shouting at each other?"

"There's nothing wrong with my ears, sir; I heard them plain as I hear you. I sat down on the steps and had a good listen." She giggled. "I know it was wrong, but I couldn't help myself."

"Of course you'd be curious," he agreed. "Do go on."

"Mrs. Rothwell was shouting that she'd trusted him and now he'd let her down. Mr. Boyd was yelling that it wasn't his fault and that there were always risks involved. She called him a fool and an idiot. I thought he was going to sack her, but all he did was scream that it wasn't his fault and that he had enough worries without her adding to them."

"Then what happened?"

She frowned. "They seemed to realize how loud they were, so they dropped their voices and I couldn't hear. Then she left the room. I heard the study door open, so I got up and tiptoed up the stairs to landing." She smiled self-consciously. "I didn't want her to catch me sitting on the bottom stairs. It would have been obvious I'd been listening."

"Yes, that's very understandable," Witherspoon said softly.

"I was going to go back to my room, but I heard Mr. Boyd come out of the study and come down the hall. Honestly, he looked like he wanted to kill someone."

"You could see him from where you were standing?"

"Oh, yes, I just ducked back on the landing and stood in the shadows. He couldn't see me, but from where I stood I could see him as clear as day. His jaw was set and his face was redder than one of cook's strawberry tarts. He stomped down the hallway past the larders and out the side door. He slammed it as hard as he could, too. Didn't care a toss if he woke anyone else in the house. That's the kind of man he was, Inspector, selfish and mean to the core."

"Do you know where he was going?" Witherspoon asked. "You did say it was very early in the morning."

"Out to his studio," she replied. "When he was workin' on a painting, he liked to go out there for a time before he went into his office, and I know he was in a hurry to get this painting finished. I'd overheard him tell Leeson he needed it finished before the luncheon."

"You're sure you don't remember anything else?" the inspector asked. He'd found that people could often recall a tidbit or two if you pressed them just a bit.

"I might have," Lydia said slowly, her brow furrowed in concentration. "I think I heard her tell him something like, 'You'd better do something to make it right if you know what's good for you.' But they'd already lowered their voices by then so I can't be sure. But that's what it sounded like she was saying."

"You'd better do something to make it right," he repeated. He wondered what that meant.

CHAPTER 5

The rain began in earnest by the time they gathered at Upper Edmonton Gardens for their afternoon meeting. Mrs. Goodge had the table laid and the tea ready as the last one to arrive, Wiggins, walked in the back door.

"It's pourin' out there." He swept off his cap and shrugged out of his coat as he crossed the kitchen to the coat tree. "Cor blimey, I thought it was goin' to crack my head open, it's coming down that 'ard. Where's Fred?"

"He's upstairs under your bed, sound asleep," Mrs. Jeffries replied. More like he'd climbed up on the lad's bed, but she pretended she didn't know that. "There's a towel on the chair by the cooker. Dry yourself off and come have your tea."

"Can I go first?" Luty helped herself to a slice of Mrs. Goodge's warm brown bread. "I think it's only fair considerin' how I've been unable to help much in the last two cases we've had."

"Of course, Luty," Mrs. Jeffries replied. "I don't think anyone would object."

"Thank you." She reached for the butter pot and put a dab on her bread plate. "I didn't think I was goin' to have much luck today considerin' how it started." She frowned as she slathered butter on her bread. "I went to see one of my banker acquaintances, but he turned out to be as useless as teats on a bull . . ." She broke off as series of grunts and gasps erupted from the others. Betsy giggled, Wiggins was holding back a snicker and not doing a very good job of it as it escaped as a series of snorts, Mrs. Goodge had her hand over her mouth to smother a chuckle, and Smythe was laughing so hard his chair was shaking.

"Oh dear," Luty exclaimed. "What did I say . . . uh-oh, I guess you're not supposed to say 'teats on a bull.' "

"It's not generally a phrase one uses in polite company." Hatchet smiled broadly.

"But it is one that's quite useful," Mrs. Goodge declared. "I've known a number of people who fit that description."

"I'm sure it expressed precisely what you meant to say," Mrs. Jeffries agreed. "Do go on with your report."

151

The others quieted down and Luty continued. "As I was sayin', the banker was useless. The only thing I got out of him was that Lawrence Boyd wasn't well liked. Well Nell's bells, we already knew that. The fellow was murdered, so that means someone sure hated him. Anyways, I didn't let one little setback stop me; I went and paid a visit to my friend Fiona Arburton. Her husband's in banking, and Fiona loves gossip they way most of us love cream cakes. She had plenty to say. When I first got there, I thought I was in for another disappointment as she didn't know much about Boyd exceptin' that he was an artist as well as a banker. Then I happened to mention the names of the people who were due at the luncheon, and she had plenty to say about them."

"Who specifically?" Hatchet asked. He hoped that she'd not come across the same information he'd learned.

"For starters, she was surprised that Mrs. Sapington had agreed to set foot in the Boyd house." Luty paused dramatically. "Maud Sapington hated Lawrence Boyd. It seems Mr. Boyd had jilted Maud twenty years ago and eloped with her sister, Marianna. It was quite a scandal at the time. The wedding had already been announced and the banns read in the local church."

"That poor woman must have been terribly humiliated." Betsy shook her head. She was a bit disappointed that she wasn't the one to tell them that Boyd had once had a wife, but she didn't begrudge Luty her moment of triumph. "I can't say I'd blame her for wanting to kill the man who did that to her. But waiting twenty years is a bit odd, don't you think?"

"I thought Boyd didn't 'ave a wife," Wiggins exclaimed.

"He doesn't now," Luty explained. "Marianna died of scarlet fever a year after she married Boyd. According to what Fiona told me, Boyd didn't even let Maud and her parents know that Marianna was on her deathbed, so they never got to see her before she died."

"I take it there was a rift when Marianna eloped with Boyd?" Mrs. Jeffries said.

"Sure was. Maud and her parents were so furious, they refused to see or speak to the couple. When Marianna died so soon after marryin' him, it was a double blow." Luty shook her head. "Sad, isn't it."

"The family probably thought they had plenty of time to make it up with her," Mrs. Goodge commented. "I've seen situations like that before: families squabble and say terrible things to one another and for a few years no one speaks, then someone swallows their pride and before you know it, all is forgiven. But it seems like in this case they never got the chance."

"I agree with Betsy." Smythe frowned in puzzlement. "Why would Maud Sapington wait twenty years to take her vengeance?"

"We don't know she did, but I certainly think we should continue thinking of her as a suspect," Mrs. Jeffries commented. "That sort of public humiliation could be a powerful motive."

"Maybe it weren't just gettin' jilted," Wiggins suggested. "Maybe she was still mad about not gettin' to say a proper goodbye to her sister when she died."

"That's certainly possible," Mrs. Jeffries said. "It would be helpful if we knew her movements on the morning of the murder."

"I'll 'ave a go at that," Wiggins volunteered.

"That was really about all I learned." Luty grinned. "But I figured it was pretty good. Twenty years might have passed since Maud got left at the altar, but I've known people who could hold grudge for a lot longer than that. Maybe Maud Sapington was just bidin' her time, waiting for a chance to kill

154

him. Maybe yesterday, she got that chance."

"She might have hated Boyd," Mrs. Goodge said, "but I think she got over him well enough. She married Arnold Sapington, and before that, she was engaged to her cousin."

"Why didn't she marry him?" Betsy asked curiously. "Did she break her engagement?"

"No, he died."

"Maud Sapington didn't seem to 'ave much luck when it comes to 'angin' onto a fiancé," Wiggins said. "She let two of 'em get away."

Mrs. Goodge frowned at the footman and continued speaking. "His name was Nicholas Cutlip and he was a distant cousin. But he drowned in an accident, and a year later, Maud married her father's chief clerk, Arnold Sapington."

"So he married the boss's daughter," Smythe said softly. "That's one way to advance your career."

"But just because she was engaged to a fellow that died and married someone else doesn't mean she didn't hate Lawrence Boyd," Luty insisted. She wasn't about to give up her suspect without cause.

"That is very true." Mrs. Jeffries glanced around the table. "And we will most certainly keep her in the forefront of our

155

investigation. Hatchet, would you like to go next?"

"Thank you. I too found out something very interesting. According to my sources in the financial world, the general partners of Boyd's bank weren't very happy with the way Lawrence was managing the business."

"Did they want to sack him?" Wiggins asked eagerly.

Hatchet shook his head. "They couldn't even if they wanted to. Boyd controlled the majority of shares in the bank. But the board could make his life miserable enough that he'd resign and they'd be free to bring in a professional money man."

"What had he done?" Smythe asked.

"He made a substantial number of bad loans," Hatchet replied. "He recommended financing companies that went under and poured money into investments that went sour. One of my sources said the board was concerned that Boyd had gotten so involved in this charity work and his art that he'd completely lost interest in the bank's business."

"Were any of the board members angry enough to kill him?" Luty asked. "That's one way of gettin' shut of someone who's pouring your money down a rat hole — and the fastest, too."

"It's impossible to know precisely how angry any of the other board members might have been." Hatchet shrugged.

"How many people are on the board?" Smythe asked.

"Besides Boyd, there are three others: Evan Kettleworth, John Sawyer, and Harvey Holcomb. Next to Boyd, Sawyer and his family are the largest partners. James Stanford, one of the original partners, died years ago with no heirs."

"Do you think they warrant further investigation?" Mrs. Jeffries asked. "Should I mention their names to the inspector? Drop a few hints so he'll look in that direction?"

"For what it's worth," Smythe said quickly, "my sources told me much the same thing that Hatchet found out."

"Despite what madam says, murder is a rather drastic way of getting rid of an incompetent manager." Hatchet took a sip of tea.

"Not if the incompetent manager owns most of the bank," Luty interjected with a laugh. "But you're right, this isn't the Wild West."

Smythe wasn't so sure, but he'd wait his turn before he spoke.

"Let me have a day or two to see if I can ascertain where the board members were on the day of the murder," Hatchet suggested. He helped himself to a slice of seedcake. "That's the extent of my information, but I shall endeavor to learn more tomorrow."

"I've not found out a lot," Betsy said and then told them the few tidbits she'd gotten from the clerk at the greengrocer's, stretching it out and making more of the conversation than it had really been. She was covering up because she was a bit ashamed. Her attempts to get anything interesting out of the other shopkeepers had been a complete waste of time. All she'd heard was what the greengrocer's clerk had already told her. So she'd gone to the draper's shop he'd mentioned and gotten more interested in the curtains and the tablecloths than in asking useful questions. She'd given herself a stern talking to, tried her best to get something about their victim out of the shopkeeper — a stuck-up old stick of a woman who looked down her nose at Betsy — and gone to the shop next door. But it was a dressmaker's and it had been busy, so she'd sat down to look at the pattern book while she waited for the customers to clear out, and she'd gotten completely carried away. It was too much for any soon-to-be bride to resist. The outfits had been so beautiful — and the wedding dresses! There'd been over half a dozen patterns! "It's not much," she finished, "but I'll get back out there tomorrow and have another go at it."

"Why don't you see what you can learn about Maud Sapington," Mrs. Jeffries suggested. "Ask a few questions in her neighborhood. So far, she's the person who might have had the most personal reason to hate Boyd."

Betsy nodded enthusiastically. "That's a wonderful idea. The only thing the shopkeepers in Boyd's neighborhood want to talk about is what a tight-fisted miser he was."

"Do you remember where the Sapington's live?" Mrs. Jeffries suspected that the maid was having a difficult time concentrating on the case. She didn't really blame her; planning a wedding, even a simple one, was often a strain on a bride.

"It's Mayfair, isn't it?" Betsy frowned in annoyance. She'd forgotten the street address but didn't want to admit it.

"Number 34 Parrington Street," the housekeeper supplied.

"My turn," Smythe said. Without mentioning his source's name, he gave them a quick, concise report on the information Blimpey had given him. "So you see, my source is sayin' the same thing Hatchet heard, that Boyd is muckin' up his job. Only the way my source tells it, it isn't just the general partners that are furious, some of his clients are as well."

"Are there any particular clients that have lost enough to want to take their pound of flesh?" Mrs. Jeffries asked.

"My source is workin' on finding out that very thing," he continued. "Once I hear something, get any names of likely suspects, I'll take a look at what they mighta been doin' on the day Boyd was killed." He knew that Mrs. Jeffries would find a way to mention these new suspects to the inspector. She made certain that every idea, even the ones they'd decided were a bit far-fetched, was dropped into conversation with the inspector. "In the meantime, there's a number of pubs and a hansom stand not far from the Boyd house. I thought I'd have a chat with the drivers and see if any of them remembers takin' any fares to the Boyd house near the time of the murder. See if there was someone other than Glover and the luncheon guests that might have gone there that day."

"So you'd be lookin' for someone who went there between ten forty-five that morning and half past eleven?" Wiggins said.

Constable Barnes had told Mrs. Jeffries that based on the statements of Eva Clarke and James Glover, they were sure the murder must have happened during this time frame. "That's a busy neighborhood. You'll 'ave a difficult time sussin' out anything."

"I might get lucky, too." Smythe grinned. "That's happened to us more than once."

"Indeed it has," Mrs. Jeffries added. There were times when she was sure providence had deliberately sent them just the right information they needed to solve the case. But she always believed that God worked in mysterious ways, and deep in her heart, she knew he didn't like killers running about the streets.

"And you can always pick up a tidbit or two in a pub," Mrs. Goodge declared. "Nothing loosens tongues like gin or beer. Unfortunately, I didn't have many loose tongues in my kitchen today. The only bit I found out was that Lawrence Boyd was very pleased to have beaten out his rivals for the honorary chairmanship of that charity . . ." She broke off, frowning. "What's it called?"

"The Bankers Benevolent Society," Mrs. Jeffries supplied. "But not to worry, you weren't the only one who didn't learn anything useful. I went all the way over to St. Thomas's Hospital to find Dr. Bosworth only to be told he was in Edinburgh at a medical conference."

Dr. Bosworth was another one of their special friends. He'd been involved in one of their earlier cases and had helped them ever since. He'd spent part of his career in San Francisco, where he'd become an expert on gunshot wounds. His observations led him to the conclusion that a thorough examination of both the victim and even the scene of the crime would yield useful clues to the identity of the killer.

Bosworth tried his best to get all the surgeons working with the Metropolitan Police Force to take his methods seriously, but to date, he'd not had much luck. But the household of Upper Edmonton Gardens had great respect for him and his views. He was also very good at getting hold of post-mortem reports.

"So I guess that means we'll not find out anything about the postmortem," Smythe muttered. "Blast. That might have been useful in tracking down the kind of weapon that was used."

"When is the good doctor due back?" Hatchet helped himself to another slice of cake.

"Tomorrow," she replied. "And I intend to be sitting outside his office door when he gets to the hospital." She didn't tell the others, but she was sure she'd been followed today. This morning, just as she'd reached the corner and turned onto Holland Road, she'd seen a man step from the vestibule of St. John's Church. She'd thought nothing of it at the time; people frequently came in and out of St. John's. But she'd noticed the man had a long black scarf around his neck, and when she'd gotten off the omnibus at St. Thomas's, she was sure she saw the same fellow getting off as well. She'd recognized the scarf. She'd not seen him board the omnibus, but then she'd not been looking either. She'd told herself it was just a coincidence, that the man had business in that part of town. But when she'd spotted him again on her way home, she thought perhaps it wasn't just her imagination. But she couldn't be sure and she wasn't certain she ought to say anything to the others. They'd already been warned about keeping an eye out for Nivens and his minions, so they wouldn't do anything foolish. No, she'd wait and see if anything odd happened again. She didn't wish to cry wolf, upset the others, and then come to the conclusion that the entire incident was simply a coincidence. And coincidences did happen. She looked at Wiggins. "How did you do today?"

"Pretty poorly." Wiggins sighed. "I 'ad the worst run of luck. I got chased off Laurel Road by the woman I think is Boyd's housekeeper, and then I tried speaking to half a dozen other people in the neighborhood but no one knew anything. Honestly, it's shockin' 'ow little interest some people take in their neighbors. You'd think with a murder right under their noses, they'd be concerned. But no, most of the ones I spoke with didn't give a fig. People are selfish, aren't they. They're only interested in their own little world."

"You just had a run of bad luck," Mrs. Goodge said stoutly.

"I know." He smiled ruefully. "But it was odd, runnin' into so many people that just didn't seem to care a whit. But I'll get back out there tomorrow. I thought I'd try the housemaids at the Boyd house, and then I was thinkin' I might have a chat with someone who works at Miss Clarke's lodgin' house."

Mrs. Jeffries smiled broadly. "That's an excellent idea. You're absolutely correct. We mustn't ignore Miss Clarke. Considering all we've learned of Lawrence Boyd, she might have had reason to want him dead. But don't forget about Maude Sapington. You'll not have time to do everything."

Wiggins had forgotten he'd volunteered to try to trace her movements. "Maybe I ought to put off goin' to Miss Clarke's neighborhood until the day after tomorrow."

"Would you like someone else to try to trace Mrs. Sapington's movements?" the housekeeper suggested. "I could have a go at it."

"No, no," he said quickly. "I can do both. I can put off Miss Clarke's neighborhood until later."

"Good." The housekeeper nodded in approval. "Anything else you'd like to add?"

Wiggins hesitated for a moment. "No, that's all." He'd been tempted to tell them about the man he'd seen when he left the café today, but he decided they'd think he was being silly. It was just a fellow in a flat workman's cap and gray jacket, an ordinary working man. Yet Wiggins had spotted him through the window of the café when he'd been talking to the counter girl; the chap had stood right outside, staring in through the glass. He'd not thought much about the bloke. After all, working men were all over London. Yet he'd seen the man again an hour later, when he'd gone back to have another go at Laurel Road. For some reason, he'd glanced over his shoulder and there the fellow was, less than half a block back. The bloke had slowed then and began staring at the house numbers as he walked, trying to make it seem as though he was looking for an address. But Wiggins knew a trick when he saw one. He'd done that very same thing a number of times. There was something about the chap that put Wiggins on his guard. He didn't care if he was being silly; he'd keep a sharp eye out, and if he spotted this bloke again, he'd tell the others.

Mrs. Jeffries poured two glasses of sherry and handed one to the inspector. "Here you are, sir."

"Thank you, Mrs. Jeffries." He took a sip and sighed with pleasure. "One doesn't wish to become dependent on alcohol, but I must say, this does fill the bill nicely."

"I hardly think you're in danger of becoming dependent, sir." She sat down. "How did the investigation go today, sir?"

"As one would expect," he replied. "The house-to-house didn't yield any results and that was disappointing, though a maid at the house next door reported that she saw someone in a long coat climbing over the fence in their back garden shortly after the fire started."

"You don't think that's significant?" she asked.

"Not really." He smiled faintly. "I'm afraid it's a case of 'crying wolf.' According to the other servants, the girl has a habit of telling tales, so I'm not sure we ought to put much credence in the report."

"That's too bad, sir," Mrs. Jeffries said sympathetically. "You might have had a witness there. Did the girl get a look at his face? If she saw him again, could she recognize him?" She made a mental note to find out the maid's name and address. Maybe this time the girl wasn't crying wolf.

"I'm going to speak to her myself," he said. "But I'm not expecting very much in the way of useful information. But it's important to investigate all clues, even the ones that might be from unreliable people."

"Were you able to speak to Mr. Boyd's servants?" she pressed. "I know they weren't in the house when the murder happened, but they might have seen or noticed something out of the ordinary either before they left yesterday morning or after they returned."

"Actually, one of them told me that the housekeeper had had a dreadful row with Mr. Boyd the day before the murder," he said and then relayed the conversation he'd had with the maid.

"Oh dear, that certainly doesn't sound

very nice," she commented. "But of course, the housekeeper is the one person who couldn't have committed the murder. She was with the others at a funeral."

"But was she?" Witherspoon frowned thoughtfully.

"Do you have reason to believe she didn't go to the funeral?"

"No, but I didn't specifically ask any of the servants if they'd all been together the whole time."

"But surely someone would have told you if they hadn't," Mrs. Jeffries pointed out.

"Would they?" He looked doubtful. "Some people think the less they say to a policeman, the better."

"Yet the maid told you about the row," Mrs. Jeffries observed. "Surely she'd have mentioned it if Mrs. Rothwell hadn't gone to the funeral."

"Perhaps." He smiled cynically. "But I didn't specifically ask that question."

"I see."

"I concentrated on what time they'd all left that morning and what time they returned. I didn't ask anyone if Mrs. Rothwell had been absent for part of the time. I must make sure I do ask that very thing tomorrow. If I've learned one thing, Mrs. Jeffries, it's that one mustn't ever take anything for granted. Let's be honest here: there's a goodly number of working people who don't consider the police their friends. They don't ever volunteer information."

"That's true, sir," she replied, though she thought it highly unlikely that all the staff would protect the housekeeper. Besides, the maid hadn't been shy about telling Witherspoon about the housekeeper's row with Boyd, so she obviously wasn't trying to protect her. Yet she didn't wish to argue the point with Witherspoon. She didn't want him to have any reason to doubt his abilities or lose confidence in the investigation. "Were you able to get any useful information from Mr. Boyd's bank staff?"

"We spoke to James Glover again, but I suspect I'll have to go back. Merchant banking is quite complicated, and I'm not sure I understand how it works. I wasn't sure what questions I ought to be asking or even if I ought to be looking into his business affairs at all. But I can't ignore it, can I? Someone did murder the fellow."

"Of course you must look into his business," she declared. "As you always say, sir, one mustn't leave any stone unturned when dealing with murder."

"One must be thorough." Witherspoon relaxed a bit. Talking about his cases with

Mrs. Jeffries was so very helpful. It clarified his thoughts. "I had a brief word with Boyd's solicitor today, but he wasn't able to tell me anything about who benefits financially from Boyd's death because he says it's dreadfully complicated. I've an appointment to see him tomorrow morning." He yawned. "It's going to be a very busy day, I'm afraid."

"I'm sure you'll manage, sir," she said cheerfully. "You always do."

She continued chatting with him. She listened carefully and made sympathetic noises at the appropriate moment to bolster his spirits and raise his confidence. By the time he was ready to go in and eat his dinner, he'd gotten a great deal of frustration off his chest and she'd found out everything he'd heard and most of what he'd seen that day.

She also managed to slip in an idea or two of her own. Tomorrow, she was certain he'd have a closer look at Boyd's business partners. She rather agreed with Luty on that subject. People did get upset when you were pouring their money down a rat hole, and being murdered for incompetence might be unusual, but she'd bet her quarterly wages that it had happened before.

■ ■ ■ ■

The next morning, Mrs. Goodge got the others out of her kitchen only moments before her guest arrived. "Come in, Irma," she said as she ushered her in the back door and down the hall. "It's been ages since we've seen one another."

Irma Ballard was a former colleague of Mrs. Goodge. They'd worked together when Irma had been a lowly scullery maid and Mrs. Goodge the head cook at Lord Melbury's country estate near Reigate. Irma had risen substantially in the world since those days and now owned a small restaurant just off Sloane Street in Belgravia.

"Go right on in and have a seat and we'll have us a nice chat about old times." Mrs. Goodge pointed toward the kitchen table, which was set with a pot of tea and her nice china. A tray of freshly baked hot cross buns was sitting on the counter.

Irma stood in kitchen doorway and surveyed the room. "It's not as big as our old kitchen, is it?"

"No," Mrs. Goodge admitted as she picked up the plate of buns and put them on the table. "But then my employer is only a police inspector, not a peer of the realm."

She smiled at her guest.

Irma's hair was completely white, her eyes hazel, and her nose a sharp, hawkish shape. She was dressed in a gray-and-blue striped day dress with a high collar and long, puffy sleeves. Her hat was an elegant blue bonnet with a tiny veil and one small feather on the side. A long string of pearls was visible through the opening of her short blue cloak. She'd either dressed in her best or she'd been very successful in her life. "That's a bit of come down in the world for you, isn't it?" Irma sniffed and pulled a white lace-edged handkerchief from her sleeve.

"Yes, I suppose it is," Mrs. Goodge said cheerfully. "But I'm old and I was lucky to find the position. Not many people want to hire someone my age, and frankly, if I'd not found the inspector, I don't know what I'd have done."

Irma blinked in surprise and then her plain face split in a wide grin. "I expect you'd have done all right. Just the smell of those buns is making my mouth water. I'll warrant you can still hold your own when it comes to cookin' and bakin'."

Mrs. Goodge laughed. It was amazing how a bit of honesty could clear the air. "Then sit yourself down and let's have us a nice old natter. How's your husband?"

"He's even older and crankier than I am." She laughed. "But we're both in good health so we've no reason to complain. Sorry I was a bit stroppy when I first come in, but the truth is, I was ever so surprised to get your note yesterday. Well, I wasn't sure why you wanted me to come by."

Mrs. Goodge used her serving fork to put two buns on Irma's plate. "I imagine you were surprised. I wanted to see you. It's nice to chat with someone from the old days. So many of the ones we knew are gone now."

"I know just what you mean. Did you hear that Lizzie Drucker died this past winter? She was younger than both of us." Irma picked up a bun and took a bite.

"Oh no." Mrs. Goodge was genuinely distressed. "Lizzie was ever such a nice person."

"It was pneumonia that took her." Irma swallowed her food and reached for her tea. "She'd gone to live with her daughter in Bournemouth, poor thing."

They chatted about old friends and old times, which was precisely the way Mrs. Goodge had planned the conversation. "I understand that Minnie Pratt went to work for some banker. Now what was the name?" The cook trailed off and pretended to concentrate. "Oh, yes, now I remember, a

173

man named Lawrence Boyd. That's right, the man that was just murdered. That's what made me think of her. I do hope Minnie is all right. You remember what a timid little thing she was."

"That can't be right." Irma shook her head. "Minnie left service and went to Birmingham. She got a position as a matron at a girl's school. Which is odd, when you think of it — she could barely read or write. But I do know who you're talking about. That banker lived just around the corner from our restaurant. It's quite a posh area, if I do say so myself."

"My gracious, really? Did he ever eat at your restaurant?" This was going even better than she'd hoped.

"Only once that I know about. He came in with that awful Mr. Gibbons and they had a meal together."

"You knew him by sight?" Mrs. Goodge thought that a bit strange.

"Oh, no, Mr. Gibbons kept mentioning his name. This was only two weeks ago, so I quite recall the incident. They came in and had a meal together, but that awful Mr. Gibbons didn't seem to be enjoying himself at all."

"What's so awful about Mr. Gibbons?"

Irma snorted derisively. "He's one of our

regulars, and as such, he thinks he can walk all over people. Honestly, I wish he'd take his business elsewhere. He's just one of those people that have been soured on life, if you know what I mean."

"Maybe something happened to him when he was much younger," Mrs. Goodge suggested.

"Nonsense. He's not the first person to have had a fiancée go off and marry someone else," Irma said briskly. "That's supposedly why he's such a miserable old grouch. At least that's what Adelaide — she helps us do the washing up every night — says about him. Her aunt's been his housekeeper for years, so I expect Adelaide knows a bit about the man. But it seems to me that's just an excuse; some people simply enjoy being disagreeable. By the way, did you know that Harriet Day married a merchant sailor and went to live in one of them heathen countries in the Far East?"

"No, I hadn't heard that," Mrs. Goodge replied. Drat, she'd forgotten what a chatterbox Irma could be.

"Strange that I thought of her, isn't it?" Irma took a quick sip of tea. "But of course I would. We were talking about that cranky Mr. Gibbons, and Harriet was the maid to his fiancée. Now what was her name? Oh, yes, now I remember. She was Marianna Reese. Oh, my gracious, that's right! She married Lawrence Boyd." Irma's jaw dropped as she realized the connections. "Gracious, no wonder Gibbons looked like thunder that night. He was having dinner with the very man who'd stolen his fiancée."

"The Lawrence Boyd who was just murdered?" Mrs. Goodge asked softly. She reached for the teapot. "Do have some more tea."

"I don't want to overstay my welcome," Irma replied. "But honestly, it's lovely to see you and be able to talk about anything I like. When I'm at the restaurant, we've got to be so careful all the time. It does get so wearing, and John does tell me I do go on a bit."

"You don't go on at all." Mrs. Goodge refilled her cup. "It's wonderful to be able to chat with an old friend. Now, tell me more about your Mr. Gibbons and his dinner with Lawrence Boyd."

Inspector Witherspoon and Constable Barnes stepped into the office of Reese and Cutlip, Merchant Bankers. The clerks, all busily working at their desks, looked up one by one. Apparently, the sight of a uniformed policeman in their midst was a bit of a surprise for they all gaped at the two officers. The inspector stepped forward just as a door on the far side of the room opened and an older man appeared. "May I help you," the man asked as he came toward them.

"We would like to see Mr. Sapington," Witherspoon replied. They had been going to see Boyd's solicitor this morning, but as he'd been unexpectedly called out of town, Witherspoon had decided to speak to Boyd's luncheon guests again.

"Is Mr. Sapington expecting you?" The man regarded them over the top of his spectacles. "I'm Mr. Bateman, Mr. Sapington's chief clerk."

"Mr. Bateman, please ask Mr. Sapington if he can spare us a few moments," Barnes said.

"I can spare you as many moments as you need." Arnold Sapington stood in the open doorway just behind the elderly clerk. He stared at them. "Come in, please."

Witherspoon and Barnes followed him inside. Sapington went back to his desk and sat down. He regarded the policemen steadily. "Why are you here?"

"We'd like to ask you a few more questions," Witherspoon said. He noticed there were two empty chairs right in front of the man's desk.

"I don't see how I can help you." Sapington shrugged. "By the time my wife and I arrived for luncheon, Lawrence, Mr. Boyd, was already dead."

"That's true, sir." Witherspoon tried to think of why he wanted to speak to this person again, but for the life of him, he couldn't quite remember.

"Did you come to your office that day, sir?" Barnes asked. His knees were hurting him something fierce and he hated being kept standing like this.

Sapington's eyebrows rose in surprise. "I was here for a little while. Why? Am I considered a suspect?" He seemed amused by the prospect.

"We're only trying to establish the facts, sir," Barnes replied.

"What time did you leave for your luncheon?" Witherspoon asked. He too didn't like being kept standing. He was certain that Sapington was doing it deliberately.

Sapington thought for a moment. "It was probably eleven o'clock or thereabouts. No, no, wait, I left a bit earlier than that because I had to go to my tailor on Bond Street, then I went home and collected my wife. You know what women are like; it took ages

178

before she was ready, so it must have been half past twelve before we left our house."

"Let me make sure I understand this, sir." Barnes hadn't bothered to take out his notebook; writing while standing up was simply too difficult. He'd just make sure he remembered all the details of Sapington's statement. "You left here a few minutes before eleven, went to your tailors on Bond Street, then went home to collect your wife. By half past twelve you were on your way to Mr. Boyd's. Is that the correct sequence of events?"

Again, Sapington thought for a moment. "It was probably closer to half past ten or ten fifteen when I left here. Frankly, Constable, I wasn't really watching the time." He shrugged. "I had no reason to keep my eye on the clock, so I did what I came in to do and then went about my business."

"Perhaps one of your staff will recall exactly when you left?" Witherspoon suggested.

Sapington laughed. "I imagine they will, Inspector. I'm the boss, so I expect my comings and goings are of some importance to them. When the cats away, the mouse will play. By all means, go ahead and speak to the staff."

Witherspoon smiled faintly. "Thank you,

sir. That's very cooperative of you."

"I have nothing to hide," he replied.

"Then I'm sure you won't mind giving us the name of your tailor," Barnes added.

" 'E didn't give a toss about his bank," Jeremiah Fitch declared. "All he wanted to do was get 'is name in the papers and paint 'is ruddy pictures. It's a wonder they didn't toss 'im out on 'is ear."

Smythe had spoken to half a dozen people this morning, and this was the first time he'd found anyone who knew anything about the victim or any of their list of suspects. He measured his words carefully. Jeremiah Fitch was half drunk but not so far gone as to be useless. But if he had another pint of the fine ale here in the Gray Goose Pub, it might be a different story altogether. "You ought to know. You worked for Boyd long enough."

"Worked for 'im for ten years, I did." Fitch rubbed his nose. He was a balding man of late middle age with weatherworn skin, blue eyes, and a weak chin. He wore a gray coat two sizes too large for his skinny frame, a dirty gray shirt with a frayed collar, and black trousers held up with an old leather belt. "I used to watch him go into that buildin' 'e called a studio and do 'is pain-

180

tin'. I'm the one that tore the original windows out and put them big ones in for 'im."

"Why'd you stop workin' for 'im?" Smythe asked.

"I didn't." Fitch shrugged and took another quick sip. " 'E just stopped 'avin' work for me. I weren't a proper groundsman or gardner, you see, more like a jack of all trades. I'd do fer 'im whenever 'e needed a bit o' carpentry or somethin' like that done. I used to work in the buildin' trade, I did. Mr. Boyd would 'ave me in whenever 'e needed a stair replaced or windows done or a door to be hung. But the past year, 'e's not done much but paint in that ruddy studio. I don't see how 'e could stand all them hours out there. Cold as a whore's heart in the winter and stifling hot in the summer. It couldn'a been comfortable for him."

"Why not?"

"It were only half finished at best. The last job I did for him was them windows, and I was goin' to do the ceilin' next. But 'e told me not to bother. He said he liked it that way."

" 'E sounds a strange bird." Smythe took a quick sip of his beer. "The sort of fellow that had a lot of enemies."

Fitch laughed softly. "That's true. 'E weren't well liked. Odd though, he were right sociable. Always off to charity dos and vying to be the honorary chairman of this and that."

"Snob was he?" Smythe muttered. He really wasn't making any progress at all. This might be interesting general information, but it wasn't going to help them find the killer.

Fitch shook his head. "He were a toff, that's for sure. But it was more like he wanted people to take notice of 'im."

"When was the last time you saw 'im?"

"A day or so before the murder," Fitch replied. "I stopped in to see if he'd changed him mind about pullin' that old ceiling down, but he told me to quit worryin' about it, that it was fine the way it was. Boyd usually didn't talk much to me, but that day he was excited and I was the only one there, so he started chattin' with me like we was old mates. Told me he was goin' to get it this year, that they couldn't give it to someone else and that 'e'd be the one making the speech on the big night."

"What was he on about?"

Fitch's weather-beaten face creased in a frown as he tried to remember more details. Finally, he shook his head. "I don't know that 'e ever said the name of the charity. But he was excited to be beatin' the others out."

"Beating the others out?" Smythe repeated. "What does that mean?"

Fitch grinned broadly. "There was another bunch of bankers up for it as well, and what was really makin' him happy was that he was beatin' them out for the top spot. He didn't give a toss about the benevolent society. He was just happy the other blokes were losin'."

"Benevolent society? Is that the name of the charity?" Smythe asked.

"Yeah, somethin' like that," Fitch replied. He looked down at his now empty pint. "I don't suppose you'd stand me another, would ya?"

Smythe was fairly sure he'd gotten as much information as he was going to get out the fellow, so it didn't matter how drunk he got now. "Sure, you've been right good company." He nodded to the barman. "Another pint for me friend 'ere, please."

Wiggins stopped and stared in the shop window. But instead of actually looking at the beautiful bicycle displayed behind the glass, his eyes darted to the left and the right, trying to see if he really was being followed or if it was all in his mind. He saw nothing on either side except the rush of people going about their business on the busy High Street. Wiggins whirled around and spotted his prey disappearing into a doorway directly across the road from where he stood.

The man was quick but not fast enough, and Wiggins got a good look at him before he dived through the door of the chemist's shop. It was the same man who'd followed him the day before.

Wiggins had to warn the others, had to tell them to be careful. He turned and started back the way he'd just come, but he hadn't taken more than a few steps before he stopped. It was no use going back there now; the others would all be out. Besides, he had a much better idea. He looked over his shoulder. Sure enough, the man had just stepped out of the chemist's shop.

Wiggins made sure the man had spotted him, then he sprinted across the busy road, dodging between a hansom and a water cart. "Watch where you're goin', you silly git," the cart driver yelled as he pulled his horse up, but Wiggins ran on. He looked behind him and saw the fellow charging after him. He tore around the corner and then ducked into a small side street leading to a mews. Oh, yes, this was going to be lots of fun.

CHAPTER 6

Betsy stood in front of the dressmaker's shop and gazed at the traveling dress displayed in the window. The three-quarter-length coat was in a pale green check tweed wool and opened to reveal a matching waistcoat. A white blouse with a high neck and a simple bell skirt in a dark green completed the outfit. It was beautifully tailored, practical, and pretty. Betsy knew it would suit her perfectly. She'd never in her life even thought to own something so lovely, but now, thanks to her beloved fiancé, it was within reach.

Not that she loved Smythe because of his money, quite the contrary; she'd fallen in love with him when she thought him a simple coachman. His wealth had been quite a surprise to her, but one that she'd gotten accustomed to as time passed.

Betsy grasped the door handle and stepped inside the shop. It wouldn't hurt to see how much the outfit cost, she told herself. Besides, she was close to the Sapington house and there was a chance the dressmaker might know something about the household.

The shop was small but elegantly appointed. The walls were painted a soft pale rose, and opposite the door was an Empire-style chaise lounge in pink and white stripes. A maroon rug with a cream fleur-de-lys pattern covered the polished oak floor, and a dark red privacy screen was against the wall at the far end of the shop. A small table with three straight-backed chairs crowded around it stood next to the screen. The top of the table was piled high with pattern books.

A plump, red-haired woman wearing a plain gray dress with a high black collar stood behind the counter. She was winding a length of white lace around a spindle. Shelves filled with bolts of colorful cloth, laces, and ribbons were arranged on the wall behind her.

"May I help you, miss?" The woman put down the spindle and gave Betsy a wide, welcoming smile.

Betsy relaxed a bit. Shops like this one were just a bit daunting to her. When she was on the hunt and looking for clues, she could march into any shop on the face of the earth without so much as a by-your-leave. But when she was here just for herself, it was a little uncomfortable. She wasn't sure what to do or how to act. Growing up, her clothes had been hand-me-downs or bought from a street stall. But she really loved that traveling dress. It would be perfect for anything Smythe might have in mind. "I'm interested in that ladies traveling outfit in the window."

The woman stepped out from behind the counter. "That's a checked Harris tweed. It's a very popular pattern. The material for the jacket and the skirt comes in three different colours: burgundy, blue, or the green that's on the mannequin. With your coloring, I'd recommend the blue. It will look lovely with your eyes."

"But the green is so gorgeous." Betsy smiled in pleasure.

"The blue will be just as pretty, and with eyes like you've got, it will be absolutely perfect on you. I'm Geraldine Billingston, the proprietress. Have you visited us before?"

"No, this is my first time," Betsy replied. "How long would you need to get something like that made up for me?"

"Not long, a week or ten days at the most," she replied. "We'd need to take your measurements and do a fitting. Would that do you?"

"That would be fine." Betsy wondered if she dared ask the price. Perhaps this was the sort of place that simply handed you the bill when you came to collect the dress? Drat, she wished she knew what to do. "Do you do wedding dresses as well?" she blurted.

Geraldine Billingston's brows drew together. "Is it for you, miss?"

"I'm getting married next month."

"And you're just now getting the dress ordered?" She looked absolutely horrified.

"I didn't think it would take very long," Betsy mumbled. "I mean, I wasn't sure what I wanted and I've looked at a few patterns, but I couldn't seem to make up my mind. Don't worry, I've got plenty of money." She knew she was babbling but she couldn't seem to stop herself.

"Gracious, we've not a moment to lose. Step this way, please. We've some pattern books you can look at, but you'll need to pick quickly, and we'll also need to get your measurements taken today." She gave Betsy a gentle shove toward the table.

"I hadn't planned on a really fancy dress," Betsy admitted as she yanked out a chair and flopped down. "But I don't suppose it'll hurt to see what you've got."

The proprietress shoved a pattern book under Betsy's nose and opened it to the pages toward the back. "Here, start with this one. It's one of our most popular."

Betsy gasped in pleasure. The dress was every woman's fantasy: yards of white lace, an orange blossom headpiece with a sheer veil, and a train fit for a queen!

"This is a nice one, too." The proprietress flipped to the next page. "We can make any of these gowns up in Duchesse satin, silk, or even a patterned brocade. I've got the really nice bolts in the back room. I'll go get Emma. She can take your measurements while we're deciding on what you need, and we've plenty of tulle on hand for the veil, so you can get measured for that as well."

But Betsy wasn't listening; she was too busy drooling over the wedding dresses.

Wiggins trotted around the corner and crossed the road toward a tiny bookshop tucked between an ironmonger's and a chemist's. He knew his pursuer was still on his heels, and he was determined to throw him off the scent. The fact that he wasn't learning a ruddy thing about their case or the whereabouts of any of their suspects couldn't be helped. No, the fellow had to be convinced that following him would result in nothing more than a pair of very sore feet.

So far Wiggins had run for a good half mile, cutting through a mews and pretending to chase an omnibus. Then he'd sprinted to a boot shop a mile farther up the road and bought some boot blacker, trotted at a good pace for another half a mile and stopped for sweets at the newsagent's, and then doubled back and ended up here. He hoped the bloke trailing him had a painful stitch in his side and blisters on his feet. Wiggins was as tired as a pup and didn't know how much longer he could keep this up. He stopped long enough to catch his breath and then stepped into the shop.

"Can I help you?" asked an elderly man sitting on a chair behind the counter. He was reading a newspaper.

"Do you have the latest edition of *Whitaker's Almanac*?" Wiggins had been meaning to pick up this year's edition for ages now, but he'd not got around to it. He loved reading almanacs; they were filled with all sorts of useful information.

The clerk pointed to a shelf of books just inside the door. "Right there you are, young man."

"Ta, I didn't see it." Wiggins grabbed the

top one off the stack on the shelf, checked the date on the front page to make sure it was the latest edition, and then walked to the counter. He pulled some coins out of his pocket and paid the clerk.

"Will that be all, sir?" The clerk pulled a sheet of brown paper off a stack and began wrapping the book.

Wiggins glanced over his shoulder just as his follower ducked into a doorway across the street. "Do you have a back door out of here?"

"A back door?" The clerk raised his eyebrows. "Well, yes, I do . . ."

"I'll give you a shilling if you'll let me use it when I leave," Wiggins said. He had plenty of money and he had suddenly realized it was almost noon, his feet were killing him, and he was tired of playing chase the fox with this fellow. Apparently, this bloke didn't tire easily, and Wiggins didn't want to be the only one at their afternoon meeting with nothing to report.

The clerk handed him the neatly wrapped book. "Let's see the shilling."

Wiggins reached into his pocket again and pulled out the coin. He handed it over as he took his package.

"It's this way." The clerk waved him around the counter and through a small, narrow hallway into a dim back room. He led him through a maze of old bookcases, boxes of books, and broken chairs, finally stopping in front of a door. He threw the bolt and shoved it open. Wiggins stepped out into the bright sunshine and surveyed his surroundings. He was in a mews. He pulled another coin out of his pocket and handed it to the elderly clerk.

"What's this for?"

"A bit of silence." He grinned. "You know, just in case anyone comes into the shop and starts asking questions."

The old man laughed. "Don't worry, young man. There's been no one in my shop for the last half hour, if you know what I mean."

Wiggins nodded his thanks, turned, and hurried off. With any luck, he might be able to learn something useful before he had to head back to Upper Edmonton Gardens.

"What should we do about the note, sir?" Barnes asked the inspector as they climbed out of a hansom in front of the law offices of Oxley and Gardner. "It sounded a matter of some urgency." He turned away briefly to pay the driver.

"We'll go see the chap right after we finish interviewing the solicitor." Witherspoon pushed his spectacles up his nose, checked that his hat was on straight, and then crossed the pavement to the wide double doors of the office building.

"The bank closes at five, sir," Barnes reminded him as he hurried to catch up. "And I don't have the address of the clerk who sent us the note." He reached the wide, flat steps leading into the office block, surged ahead of the inspector, and grabbed the door handle. "Do you think we ought to send a message to the station and have a police constable go along and get the man's address?"

The inspector shook his head as they entered the building. "No, I don't want to draw too much attention to the clerk. After all, Glover is acting as the general manager for the moment. We don't want the chap put into an awkward position. We've no idea what he has to tell us."

They went down the long corridor toward a door at the far end, and a few minutes later, they were in John Oxley's office. The solicitor to the late Lawrence Boyd sat behind a massive mahogany desk and smiled benignly at the two policemen. "I'm so sorry I had to cancel our first appointment, but it was unavoidable. I do hope it didn't inconvenience you too much."

"We understand, sir." Witherspoon smiled faintly. The solicitor had actually put him off twice, but for the sake of cooperation, he wouldn't correct him. "These things happen. I know you're a very busy man, so we'll not take up any more of your time than necessary. I'm sure you know why we're here."

"You're interested in my late client, Lawrence Boyd." Oxley was a portly, brown-haired man with a full set of side whiskers and bright blue eyes.

"He had a will, I take it?" Witherspoon shifted slightly in his seat. He and Barnes were sitting in two straight-backed chairs and his wasn't very comfortable.

"Of course he had a will," Oxley replied. "He was a very prudent man."

"What can you tell us about the disbursement of his estate?" Witherspoon asked. He didn't like to come right out and ask who benefited from the poor man's death. That sounded so very crass and he'd observed that how one phrased a question often influenced the answer. He wanted facts here and nothing more.

"You mean who might have benefited from Boyd's murder." Oxley smiled slyly.

"Er, uh, yes."

"There's no one person in particular." Oxley's chair creaked as he leaned back. "Lawrence Boyd had no close family. His wife died many years ago and they'd had no children."

"What about his housekeeper?" Barnes asked. "Isn't she a relative?"

"She is, but she inherits very little," Oxley explained. "Hannah Rothwell along with two other of his cousins will each inherit a few hundred pounds. The rest of his estate is very complex. He made a number of bequests to various charities —"

"Was the Bankers Benevolent Society one of them?" Witherspoon interrupted. Solicitors could be just a tad longwinded and it was getting late. He wanted to get back to Boyd's bank and have a word with that clerk.

Oxley nodded. "So you know about that, do you? It was really bad form, but Lawrence would have his way."

"What was bad form, sir?" Barnes looked up from his notebook.

"The way Lawrence behaved." Oxley pursed his lips in disapproval. "I know he really wanted to be named this year's honorary chairman. It was very important to him, but honestly, telling the board of trustees that you're leaving them a rather large sum of money in your will is practically the same as buying the honor."

Barnes didn't see why Oxley was so offended. From his observations, money generally changed hands before honors were awarded. But usually it was done discreetly and diplomatically. "He told them he was leaving them a legacy?"

"Yes, at their meeting last month." Oxley shook his head. "What's more, they weren't the only ones. Lawrence told all of the charities he'd named in his will that he was leaving them money. The Amateur Artists Guild, the Society for Choral Singing, the Association for the Dramatic Sick Fund, the Royal Academy, the Doodlers Club. There are so many I can't even recall all their names."

Witherspoon's heart sank. He couldn't believe that any charitable institution would actually commit murder to gain a bequest, but considering his experiences as a policeman the past few years, he couldn't discount the notion either. "Wasn't that a bit unusual?"

"Of course it was," Oxley replied. "But Lawrence didn't care. He told me he wanted a monument to himself, something to leave on this earth so the world would know he'd been here."

"Which charity is getting the largest

bequest?" Barnes asked. "The Bankers Benevolent Society?"

"Oh no, but they're getting quite a bit, believe me. The charity benefiting the most is the Amateur Artists Guild. Mr. Boyd left them his house and his paintings. The place is to be turned into a permanent exhibition venue for the society providing Boyd's paintings are prominently displayed in the main gallery."

"Main gallery?" Witherspoon repeated.

"Actually, that's currently his drawing room," Oxley explained. "But he's left an enormous amount of money for the rooms to be redone as an art gallery. The upstairs rooms are to be turned into offices and work spaces for young artists. The whole place is to be renamed. It's to be called the 'Lawrence Boyd Memorial Gallery.' I don't know what the local council will say, and I'm quite sure the neighbors will have a fit. In that neighborhood I can't see the residents wanting the general public tromping up and down their street on a daily basis, I can tell you that. But Lawrence didn't care a toss about the difficulties in doing what he wanted. He simply instructed us to do as he directed. I imagine we'll be in court for years over this bequest."

"I should think that would benefit you,

sir," Barnes pointed out.

"I beg your pardon?" Oxley glared at the constable.

"You'll be able to charge his estate legal fees as long as the matter is under litigation."

"Are you implying I had anything to do with his death?" Oxley's face began to turn red. "I'll have you know, Constable, I tried to talk him out of doing such a foolish thing with his estate. But would he listen to me? No, he would not, and now he's left a fine mess for us to sort out."

"I'm sure the constable wasn't implying anything," Witherspoon interjected quickly. Ye Gods, if he didn't shut Barnes up they'd have a list of suspects longer than his right arm. Not only were half of the charities in London on the list, but now even the victim's lawyers had a good reason to want him dead. Why couldn't it just be a few greedy relatives? Why did his cases always get so complex? Sometimes he wished he was back in the records room at the Yard. Then he realized he mustn't think that way; for some reason, the good Lord had set this task before him and charged him with serving justice. But still, he wished the good Lord hadn't given him quite so many suspects.

"I should hope not." Oxley gave Barnes one last glare before turning his attention to the inspector. "Some cases are so complex they are simply not worth it, if you take my meaning. We'll earn every farthing of the fees we charge for handling this matter, I can tell you that."

"I'm sure you will, sir," Witherspoon said quickly. "Is there anyone else who is going to benefit under the terms of Mr. Boyd's will?"

Oxley frowned slightly. "There are some minor bequests to various individuals. As I said, he left his housekeeper and two other cousins a small amount of money. He also left the housekeeper one of his paintings. I believe there's a portrait of his late wife he's left to her sister, Maud Sapington. But other than that, everything goes to the various charities. I'll have my clerk give you a list."

"Thank you." Witherspoon smiled gratefully. "When was Mr. Boyd's will actually done?"

Oxley rolled his eyes. "It took ages to get it made up the way he wanted, but we finally got it signed and witnessed last month. I remember because Boyd kept insisting he had to have it completed by the time the trustees of the Benevolent Society had their monthly meeting. We had it ready for him with a day or two to spare."

"I see," Witherspoon replied. "You said that Boyd told all the various charities he was leaving them a bequest, is that correct?"

"That's right," Oxley snorted softly. "Oh, he wasn't crass enough to actually send them a letter or anything like that, but he made sure that when he was out socially and he'd run into a director or trustee from one of them, he'd be sure to mention the fact that he was remembering them in his will."

"He told you he'd done this?" Barnes said incredulously.

"Oh, no, he didn't actually tell me," Oxley replied. "I overheard it for myself. I happened to be standing right behind him at the opera, it was Mozart's *Magic Flute,* very good actually, top drawer if I do say so myself. I'm very fond of music, you know. But I mustn't digress. As I was saying, I happened to be standing right behind him when he ran into the president of the Amateur Artists Guild. I heard Boyd telling him every little detail of the legacy they were going to get when he died. Honestly, I couldn't credit my own ears, but he was speaking so loudly half the people in the lobby heard him. That wasn't the only time he bragged about it. My wife overheard him discussing the matter at the Art Institute dinner just last week. Lawrence Boyd wanted everyone to know which charities were getting his money, so he took every opportunity afforded him to discuss the matter at great length."

"Was it a lot of money?" the inspector asked softly.

Oxley leaned forward eagerly. "There was a great deal, Inspector. The value of the whole estate is over half a million pounds."

"Would you care for another drink?" Hatchet asked his companion, Reginald Manley. They were sitting in the small lounge of the Doodlers Club on a tiny street off Sheridan Square. Manley was a member. The fact that he was drinking with a butler, even though the butler had a net worth ten times Manley's, wouldn't be considered remarkable in any case. The Doodlers Club membership was composed of artists, cartoonists, fine craftsmen, glassblowers, and even a street portrait painter or two. Unlike most London clubs, this one actually required its members to be skilled at something difficult. Of course, the club was housed in an ancient two-story brick building that had a sagging roof, crumbling masonry, and several cracked windows. But the lounge was nicely furnished with comfortable chairs, a decent green wool carpet, and a meeting room that was large enough to use for member exhibits and the occasional lecture. A waiter, who also served as a barman, moved slowly around the room, taking orders or bringing drinks.

"I don't mind if I do." Reginald Manley caught the waiter's attention and then lifted his empty glass. He was a middle-aged man with a full head of black hair, sharp features, and deep-set gray eyes. "This is very kind of you, Hatchet. What is it you want?"

Hatchet took no offense. "You always did get right to the point, Reggie. I like that about you. You're right, of course; I do want something. Information. If you can help me with anything useful, I'll pay you. As I recall, you always did like money."

Manley laughed, revealing a set of perfect white teeth with exceptionally long incisors. "I'm not the only one who gets right to the point. I could use a few quid. My last few paintings haven't sold, and frankly, I'm getting too old to enchant the ladies much longer. I think I'm actually going to have to get married if I want to keep on eating and having a roof over my head."

Now it was Hatchet's turn to laugh. Manley made more money courting the ladies than he ever did selling his paintings. "Do you have someone in mind?"

"Of course, and despite what you probably think of me, once we're wed I'll be a very good husband. I may not be able to support the lady in question, but I will most certainly stay by her side for the rest of our lives. But that's enough about me. Do you still work for that odd American woman?"

"I do," he replied.

Manley smiled at the waiter as another glass of whiskey was placed on the table in front of him. "Thank you, Derrick. That'll be all. My companion is practically a teetotaler."

"Yes, sir." Derrick shuffled off.

"Do you know someone named Lawrence Boyd?" Hatchet asked.

"I did, but he was murdered a few days ago." Manley took a drink from his glass. "He was a banker who liked to play at being an artist."

"He was no good?"

Manley shrugged. "He painted things people liked to put on their walls, seascapes and pastoral scenes. He was competent but hardly inspired. He exhibited at the Royal Academy most years, which meant, of course that the rest of us were green with envy."

"Did you know him well?" Hatchet asked. He was fairly sure that even if Reggie hadn't known the fellow very well, he'd know the latest gossip about Boyd. Reginald Manley loved gossip more than he loved whiskey.

"We both studied under Trumwell, but that was years ago." Manley grinned. "Since then, we've hardly traveled in the same circles. But I do know that he was a rotten excuse for a human being. He eloped with Marianna Reese when he was already engaged to her sister and she was engaged to someone else."

Hatchet shifted in his chair. This was old news. He was hoping Manley might know something else about the victim. "Yes, I'd heard that."

"It was twenty years or so ago," Manley muttered. "Marianna Reese was a lovely woman. Boyd did a portrait of her. That's supposedly when they fell in love."

Hatchet glanced at the clock on the far wall. Time was getting on and he had to start for Upper Edmonton Gardens soon. "Yes, love does seem to make some people behave in odd ways."

"But that doesn't excuse his behavior. I might be a bit of a cad, but I don't go after engaged or married women and I limit my dalliances to ladies who know precisely what

205

I'm offering. Boyd betrayed his best friend and stole the man's fiancée, humiliated his own fiancée, and then had the gall to hold a grudge against the lot of them so that when Marianna Reese was dying, he didn't even let her family know until after the funeral."

"But isn't that all rather ancient history?" Hatchet sipped the last of his own drink.

"Not really." Manley grinned broadly. "Not when your former fiancée's husband is now in the running for the same charity post. From what I understand, Maud Reese Sapington was doing everything short of showing her petticoats to the trustees of the Bankers Benevolent Society in order to keep Lawrence from getting the position. You can't blame her for hating the man; he not only jilted her publicly but then he wouldn't let her near her own dying sister. After Marianna's death, Maud asked Boyd for the portrait of her sister. He wouldn't give it to her. She even offered to pay him to have a copy made, but he refused. He really was a dreadful man."

Wiggins was the last to arrive for their afternoon meeting. He slipped into his chair just as Mrs. Jeffries finished pouring the last of the steaming cups of tea. "I hope I didn't hold ya up," he apologized, "but I've had the devil's own time this afternoon."

"You're fine, lad," Smythe said. "We've only just sat down."

"Are you all right?" the cook asked. "You're face is as red as one of my good strawberry tarts."

"I've been runnin'. I 'ad to cut across the garden from the back gate down near Lady Cannonberry's," Wiggins explained. "I couldn't come down our road, you see. When I got to the corner, I spotted that fellow waitin' for me, but I managed to nip off and go the other way before he saw me."

There was dead silence for a moment, then they all began speaking at once.

"What man?" the cook demanded.

"What on earth are you talking about?" Mrs. Jeffries asked.

"You tell me if someone is threatenin' you," Luty commanded. "I can take care of that for ya."

"Oh, my goodness, Wiggins, are you all right? Did this man hurt you?" Betsy said anxiously.

"We can't have people following you with ill intent." Hatchet shoved away from the table. "Perhaps a quick word is in order."

"Is he still out there?" Smythe rose to his feet.

"Sit down." Mrs. Jeffries had to shout to

make herself heard. "Before we do anything, we'd best see what Wiggins has to say." She turned her attention to the footman. "The first order of business is to make sure you're all right."

"I thought I'd shaken 'im off my 'eels, but he must 'ave high tailed it back 'ere when I didn't come out of the bookshop. He was waitin' for me at the corner, but I'm fine. I never let him get close enough to lay hands on me."

"Good. Now, tell us what happened," Mrs. Jeffries instructed calmly. But inside, she was afraid her worst fears were being realized. Someone from their past, someone connected with a killer they'd helped apprehend was coming back to seek vengeance on them. She handed Wiggins a mug of steaming hot tea.

"Ta, Mrs. Jeffries." He helped himself to a spoonful of sugar. "Today wasn't the first time I've seen the bloke," he began. "But I didn't say anything because I thought it was probably just my imagination playin' tricks on me."

"When was the first time you saw him?" Smythe interjected.

"I think it was yesterday morning." Wiggins stirred his tea. "But I can't be sure. I know for certain that he was following me today." He told them the details of his morning and how he'd tried to tire his pursuer out by running all over London and then when that hadn't worked, by sneaking out the rear door of the bookshop. "But I guess I didn't fool the fellow. He was waitin' for me when I got to our street. It was just luck that I spotted him lurkin' about before he happened to see me. I think he works for Inspector Nivens."

"Inspector Nivens?" Mrs. Jeffries wasn't sure she liked that idea any better than her original one. "How do you know?"

Wiggins wasn't sure how to explain this part; he knew it wouldn't make sense, but he had to try. He knew he was right. "He's got a funny look about 'im. Even though he's wearin' a flat cap and an old coat, he looks like he's playin' a part, like it's not real."

"I'm not sure I know what ya mean," Luty muttered. "But you've got good instincts, so let's assume you're right and that the man is workin' for that no good polecat Nivens. What can we do about it?"

"I don't know." Mrs. Jeffries looked at Wiggins. "But it was very clever of you to throw him off the scent, so to speak."

"What are we going to do?" Betsy asked glumly. "We certainly don't need Nivens poking his nose into our business."

"We'll think of something," Mrs. Jeffries said briskly. "For right now, let's get on with our meeting."

"I do 'ave something else to report," Wiggins said eagerly. "I went around to the Sapington neighborhood and I wasn't 'avin' much luck, but then I spotted a street arab and we got to chattin'. He works that area regular like, and people are always usin' him to send messages to their friends or their husbands."

"Had Maud Sapington sent someone a message?" Mrs. Goodge demanded.

"Oh, no, but her next-door neighbor hired the lad to go to Throgmorton Street with a message for her husband, and the lad told me that as he was nippin' off, he spotted Mrs. Sapington slipping out of her house that morning. He noticed because she was the lady of the 'ouse and he claimed she slipped out the servants door like a thief makin' off with the family silver. He said she stopped and looked around, like she didn't want anyone seein' her leave."

"I don't suppose he happened to note the time he saw her," Betsy asked.

" 'E's not got a pocket watch." Wiggins grinned. "But he knew the time because Mrs. Barclay — she's the one that sent him with the message — said it was already half past ten and she needed her husband to have the message by eleven fifteen. But that's all I found out. I'll keep lookin', though, providin' we can think of a way to get rid of that bloke that's stickin' closer to me than my shadow."

"We'll think of something," Mrs. Jeffries said with more confidence than she felt.

"Of course we will," Hatchet said cheerfully. "If no one objects, I should like to go next. I believe you'll find my information rather interesting, especially in light of what young Wiggins just reported."

"We already know that Maud Sapington hated Lawrence Boyd. Besides, I thought you was goin' to try and find out about Boyd's partners and what they was doin' the day of the murder," Luty charged.

"Unfortunately, my source for that information was unavailable today, but I made an appointment to see him tomorrow." Hatchet smiled slyly. "And I must say there's a fact or two about Mrs. Sapington's relationship with the late Lawrence Boyd that you don't know."

Luty snorted faintly but said nothing.

"I had an interesting chat with a friend of mine, a painter. He has a vast amount of knowledge about the London art world."

Hatchet told them about his meeting with Reginald Manley. "You can see why I wanted to share this information as quickly as possible." He turned to Luty. "As you pointed out, we know that Maud hated Boyd, but we didn't know she wanted that portrait of her sister he'd painted and that even when she offered to pay to have a copy of it painted, he refused."

"But why would she wait years to kill him in order to get it?" Luty demanded. "And we don't know for sure she's going to get the danged painting. Maybe he's goin' to give it to someone else."

"Madam, madam." Hatchet gave her a pitying smile. "Not everyone has an intemperate nature. You have heard the saying, 'Revenge is a dish best served cold.' Perhaps Mrs. Sapington simply bided her time."

Wiggins nodded his head wisely. "And her waitin' to kill him now does make a bit of sense. He was gettin' all them big honors and such. That's why they was goin' to luncheon at his house, so that Gibbons fellow could announce to everyone that Boyd 'ad gotten to be the chairman of that bankers charity."

"That's a very interesting idea," Mrs. Jeffries interjected. "But let's not get ahead of ourselves. We're still in the early stages of the investigation and we mustn't jump to conclusions."

"That's right," Luty added eagerly. "Let's not jump to conclusions. Maybe the rest of us found out some interestin' bits as well."

"Why don't you go next, Luty," Mrs. Jeffries suggested.

"Why, thank you, I don't mind if I do. I didn't find out too much, but I did learn a little bit more about Hannah Rothwell." Luty paused. "She was supposed to have gone to that funeral, but she might not have actually been there. She met up with the others from Boyd's household when they got back to Paddington Station."

"You mean she doesn't have an alibi?" Mrs. Goodge asked.

"Oh, I wouldn't go so far as to say that," Luty replied. "Hannah Rothwell went with them all the way to the church, but it's one of them small country churches and it was crowded, so they all split up so they could find seats. My source said there was people standing in the aisles and crammed into every bit of space, so she could have actually been there, but the only way to prove it would be to find someone who saw her. There was a funeral reception at the girl's home and Boyd's servants all went to pay their respects to the family, but they weren't

213

together at that point. They'd not sat together, so I think everyone just paid their respects and went to station to get the next train back to London. Remember, they had to be back in time to serve that luncheon, so I think they each of them went to the station and got on the train. Then they met up at Paddington."

"But why would Hannah Rothwell want to kill Lawrence Boyd?" Betsy asked.

Luty shrugged. "She was his kin, but he made her work for her keep. That's got to rankle, and we know she and Boyd had that big ruckus the day before he was murdered. It had to have been about something important."

"We really must find out if she was at that funeral," Mrs. Jeffries remarked. "I'm afraid I might have made a terrible mistake. I should have been more encouraging when Inspector Witherspoon raised the issue."

"You mean our inspector wondered the same thing?" Wiggins said.

"Yes." Mrs. Jeffries nodded. "But it seemed such a strange scenario that I dismissed it out of hand. But I'll make sure to bring it up this evening."

"That's all I found out." Luty settled back in her chair with a smug smile on her lips.

Mrs. Jeffries looked at the Betsy. "Were

you able to find out anything about Maud Sapington?" she asked.

"Not really," Betsy admitted. "But I heard a few bits about her husband. It's not much, but he was hoping to get the chairmanship of the Bankers Benevolent Society as well. He's considered a real social climber. His father was actually a builder and wanted him to go into the business with him, but he had other ideas and became an articled clerk when he left grammar school."

"What's wrong with bein' a builder?" Wiggins asked.

"Absolutely nothing," Hatchet explained. "But generally, people from the 'trades' don't end up climbing very high in social status."

"Sapington seems to have managed it," Betsy continued. She'd only found out about Arnold Sapington because she'd brought up Maud's name when she was at the dressmaker's. The seamstress hadn't known anything about Maud, but the little apprentice had come from Slough, the same town as Arnold. "Mind you, my source says the man worked hard for what he's got. He went to grammar school on a scholarship and then came to London and worked his way up at Reese and Cutlip."

"Marryin' the boss's daughter probably

helped a bit," Smythe reminded her.

"True and he is the lucky sort," Betsy agreed. "He only got the scholarship because another lad had it but he died, so Arnold got to take his place."

"Looks like he's lucky again," Wiggins laughed. "Now that Boyd's dead, maybe he'll get to be the honorary chairman."

"So I take it none of us were actually able to ascertain all of Maud Sapington's movements on the morning of the murder?" Mrs. Jeffries probed.

"We know she snuck out of her 'ouse," Wiggins said. "But that's all I was able to learn."

"I'll be out again tomorrow," the maid declared.

"Me, too," Wiggins added.

"I 'ad a bit of luck myself," Smythe said. He told them about the drink he'd shared with Jeremiah Fitch. "From what he told me, Boyd's greatest pleasure in his charitable work was beatin' someone else out of an honor, especially on this Bankers Benevolent Society. Boyd was an odd bird, wasn't he? From what we've 'eard about him, he didn't have any genuine love for people yet he was bound and determined to do charity work and be recognized for it. It doesn't make a lot of sense, does it?"

"It does if he had an ulterior motive," Mrs. Jeffries replied. "He might have been hoping to eventually get a knighthood or something along those lines. We'll simply have to keep on digging to find out what happened that day."

"Did you see Dr. Bosworth?" Betsy asked eagerly. "Was he able to get his hands on the postmortem report?"

Mrs. Jeffries shook her head. "I spent hours waiting for him, but there was some sort of industrial accident and Dr. Bosworth was in surgery all day. I'll have another go tomorrow."

The time spent wandering the environs of St. Thomas's Hospital hadn't been entirely wasted; she'd had many hours to think about the case. She'd walked up and down the path by the river while she waited to see Dr. Bosworth after surgery; however, even the stiff breeze off the water and the sharp scents of the air hadn't helped her thinking. So far her recalcitrant brain had produced nothing useful about this case. None of the facts they'd learned thus far had formed into any sort of reasonable theory. She was still as much in the dark as she'd been two days ago.

On the other hand, she was quite certain she'd not been followed today. She glanced at Wiggins and felt a tug of panic. What on earth were they to do? They couldn't continue if their every step was going to be dogged by one of Niven's toadies.

"Mrs. Jeffries, were you through?" Betsy asked. "You've got a worried look on your face. Is everything all right?"

"Oh, sorry, I just got a bit distracted. I'm fine and that was all I had to report." She forced a bright smile. "Does anyone else have anything to report?"

"I've got just a bit to say." Mrs. Goodge had been patiently waiting her turn. "An old colleague of mine came around today for morning tea. Her name is Irma Ballard and she's done quite well in the years since I've seen her. She and her husband now own a restaurant just around the corner from one of our suspects."

"That's right handy," Wiggins commented. "Who is it?"

"Walter Gibbons," the cook replied. "He's one of their regular customers. Irma says he's as miserable and mean a soul as she's ever seen."

"Worse than Lawrence Boyd?" Betsy asked. She found that hard to believe.

"It'd be a close race, but so far Gibbons has avoided being murdered." Mrs. Goodge took a deep breath. "Walter Gibbons was

Marianna Reese's fiancé before she ran off with Lawrence Boyd."

"Gibbons was engaged to Marianna Reese?" Betsy exclaimed. "And we're just now finding this out?"

"Better late than never," the cook replied. "It all happened years ago, and we were so concerned about Maud Sapington having been jilted by Boyd that none of us thought to ask too many questions about Marianna."

"That's true," the housekeeper said, "but it's often difficult to determine what is important and what isn't, especially when the incident was so long ago." She wondered what else they may have overlooked. She was annoyed with herself because the inspector had specifically mentioned that Gibbons seemed to actively dislike Boyd. She hadn't pursued the matter as carefully as she should have.

"We do the best we can, Mrs. Jeffries. Sometimes we get lucky and we come across a tidbit that's interesting or useful." Mrs. Goodge beamed proudly. She had more to say. "This might have happened years ago, but Irma doesn't think the passage of time has made Gibbons any more forgiving. She says he's as bitter a man as she's ever seen."

"And Gibbons was the one that had to

decide who got to be the honorary chairman?" Luty exclaimed. "And he gave it to Boyd? Why? Why would he do that?"

"I don't know," Mrs. Goodge admitted. "But I'm sure there must be a reason."

"Perhaps he wasn't the one who made the decision," Mrs. Jeffries said. "Most charities are run by an administrative board or a set of trustees. Perhaps he had no choice; perhaps he had to give the honor to Boyd. But this at least explains Gibbons attitude about Boyd. Remember, the inspector mentioned that Gibbons made a point of saying it wasn't a social call and he'd not have been there except for the charity business."

"And he wasn't the only one there that day that hated Boyd," Wiggins added. "No wonder the man ended up dead. Seems like everyone who ever crossed his path became his enemy. What a miserable way to live your life."

CHAPTER 7

Witherspoon and Barnes arrived at the bank offices just as the clerks were putting away their ink pots and closing the ledgers. Bingley, a middle-aged man with thinning hair and spectacles, leapt out of his seat and rushed toward them. He gave a nervous glance over his shoulder toward Glover's office. "If you'd like to wait out in the hall, I'll be right with you," he whispered.

Taken aback, Witherspoon gaped at the man, but Barnes grabbed the inspector's elbow and yanked him back through the door. As soon as they were safely out of the bank, Barnes said, "Glover must still be here and Bingley obviously doesn't want to speak in front of him."

Just then the door opened and Bingley slipped out into the hall. He shoved a battered looking brown bowler on his head, looked at the two policeman, and then charged toward the street door. "Come along, gentlemen, we must hurry. There's a café around the corner where we can speak privately. Hurry, hurry. Mr. Glover is right behind me and I don't want to end up losing my position over this." He looked over his shoulder to see if they were following and then increased his pace to a fast trot when he saw they were right on his heels. "Hollinger is going to try to delay him, but I do believe he's already suspicious about me, so please, do come along. You mustn't let him see you."

With Bingley in the lead, they dashed out of the building, around the corner, and up a tiny side road, and then took a quick right that brought them, finally, to a café. Bingley sighed in relief as he sank into a chair facing the window. He took off his hat and placed it on the table in front of him. "Could I have some tea, please?" he asked breathlessly.

"I'll get us all a cup," Barnes offered.

"Do relax a bit and steady yourself," Witherspoon said as he took the chair next to Bingley. "We've plenty of time to hear what you've got to say."

"I hope Mr. Glover didn't see me with you." Bingley wiped the perspiration off his forehead. "He'd sack me for certain."

Witherspoon gave him a few moments to

222

compose himself. "Does he have the authority to dismiss you?" he asked.

Bingley took a deep breath and nodded. "He's temporarily in charge, but you can see from the way he struts about the place that he's fairly sure the position will become permanent."

"Here's your tea, sir." Barnes put a cup of tea in front of the clerk, handed another cup to Witherspoon, and then went back to the counter to get his own. A moment later he slipped into the empty seat facing the inspector.

"Thank you, Constable Barnes," the inspector said. He looked at Bingley. "Why did you want to see us?"

Bingley took a quick sip from his cup. "I saw something today that I thought you ought to know about. One of my duties at the bank is sorting the mail. Usually it's a very simple task. I simply pass out the envelopes that are addressed to individuals directly to them, but the letters that are just addressed to the bank, I open those and pass them along." He paused and took another deep breath. "Today we got a letter that wasn't addressed to anyone, so I opened it. It was from the Metropolitan Police. At first I couldn't understand what it was, then I realized it was some sort of receipt for the files that Mr. Glover took to Mr. Boyd's the day he was killed."

"That would be an evidence receipt, sir," Witherspoon said. "We took the files into evidence and we always issue a receipt to the legal owner. The bank will get them back as soon as I've had a chance to go through them." He knew he ought to have already read the files, but he simply hadn't had time.

"That's not important, Inspector," Bingley replied. "What was important is that one of the files was missing."

"Missing?" Barnes exclaimed. "That's absurd. The Metropolitan Police does not lose evidence."

"I didn't accuse you of losing evidence," Bingley snapped. "That's why I wanted to speak with you. I'm fairly certain the missing file was stolen before your lot even got there. Mr. Glover took it."

"Oh, sorry," Barnes smiled sheepishly. "Go on Mr. Bingley."

"Thank you," Bingley said waspishly. "The reason I suspect he took it was because I'm fairly certain he's been playing about with the books."

"What, precisely, do you mean by that?" Witherspoon asked.

"It means I think he was stealing from the

bank," Bingley said. "You see, the day before Mr. Boyd was murdered I'd sent him a note saying he really ought to take a look at the Pressley file, especially the income and expenditure statements. That's one of Mr. Glover's accounts, and frankly, I've been suspicious for several months now that he's been taking money out of the expenditure account and putting it in his own pocket. But I had no proof until the day before Mr. Boyd's murder." Bingley smiled triumphantly. "I got the receipts you see, and when I went to match them up to the expenditures, I realized the receipts were far less than the ledger amounts. So I sent Mr. Boyd the receipts with a note and told him to take a good look at the file. The next day, Glover gave me a list of files he said Mr. Boyd wished to see and the Pressley file was on the list."

"You're certain that Mr. Glover actually took him that particular file?" Barnes asked.

"Absolutely. I handed it to him myself along with all the others," Bingley answered. "Glover wouldn't have dared show up without it. Mr. Boyd would have sacked him on the spot. He was a very hard man."

"And now it's missing?" Witherspoon clarified.

"Yes, it wasn't on the list I received from

your lot," Bingley replied. "And as Glover was bragging to the general partners about how he'd tried to put the fire out before the fire brigade arrived, it all made sense. He didn't fight any fire. He grabbed the file and hid it on his person so that no one would ever see it."

"He did say he was just outside the studio door, sir." Barnes looked at Witherspoon.

"But he said he never went inside," the inspector murmured. "He was frightened of fire."

"Believe me, he's more frightened of going to jail," Bingley said. "And what's more, now he can blame the Metropolitan Police for the missing file. It's worked out rather well for Mr. Glover."

Before the meeting broke up, Wiggins once again asked what he should do about the man who'd been following him.

"Don't worry, lad," Smythe said. "I'll take care of it."

"Smythe, you mustn't put yourself at risk," Mrs. Jeffries cautioned. "Nivens wouldn't hesitate to arrest you or anyone else that gets in his way."

The coachman grinned. "No one's goin' to be arrested," he promised. Under the table, he grabbed Betsy's hand and gave it a reassuring squeeze. "I know what I'm about." He looked back at Wiggins. "Go out tomorrow as usual, lad. I'll take care of the matter."

"What are you goin' to do?" the footman asked eagerly.

"Call in a few favors," he replied cryptically.

Mrs. Jeffries decided that she had to trust that Smythe knew what he was doing. He'd never let her down in the past and she didn't think he was going to start now. "Excellent, then, that's settled. Luty, can you and Hatchet come by early tomorrow morning?"

"Certainly," Hatchet replied. "Is there any special reason?"

"Only that I've a feeling the inspector may have learned quite a bit today," she explained, "and I want to make sure the both of you have the same information as the rest of us."

"We'll be here," Hatchet responded. "Come along, madam. Let's get you home. You've got a dinner engagement with Count Romanov." He ushered Luty toward the back door.

"Let's hope the inspector has plenty to say tonight," Luty called over her shoulder. "We need all the help we kin get."

"Speak for yourself, madam," Hatchet was heard to say just before the door closed. They always left by the back door because Luty insisted on keeping her carriage around the corner. She didn't want the neighbors or the inspector knowing just how often she and Hatchet were visitors to the house.

It was getting dark by the time the inspector got home. "I'm sorry I'm so late," he said as he handed Mrs. Jeffries his bowler. "But it's been an extraordinarily busy day. Er, was there anything interesting in the mail?"

"You received a letter from Lady Cannonberry, sir," Mrs. Jeffries replied. "I put it on your desk." She prayed he wouldn't want to read it yet. She wanted to hear about his day.

"I'll read it after dinner." He smiled happily. "Let's have a glass of sherry."

They went into the drawing room and she poured both of them a glass of Harvey's. "I take it the case is making progress," she said as she took her seat.

"We're learning quite a bit, but I'm not certain I'm making any progress." He took a quick sip. "Honestly, Mrs. Jeffries, I do believe everyone who crossed Lawrence

Boyd's path had a reason to want him dead. Everyday my list of suspects gets longer."

"How very inconvenvient, sir," she prompted. She listened carefully as he spoke, occasionally asking a question. By the time he'd finished his sherry, he seemed far more relaxed than when he'd arrived home. He put his glass down, got to his feet, and started for the dining room. "I had better eat my dinner. I don't want to keep the whole household hanging about the kitchen all night."

"That's most considerate of you, sir." She followed him out into the hall. "I'll just go bring it up, sir. It's all ready."

Witherspoon paused by the open dining room door. "Gracious, Mrs. Jeffries, it does so help me to clarify things when I talk them over with you."

"That's very kind of you, sir. I enjoy hearing about your cases."

He went on into the dining room and she went down to the kitchen. She noticed that the coachman was nowhere to be seen. "Has Smythe gone out?"

"Yes, he said he'd be back in an hour or two." Betsy picked up the inspector's dinner tray from the counter and handed it to the housekeeper. "He told me not to worry, but that's not possible. I don't like him being

229

out in the dark."

"Smythe knows how to take care of himself," Mrs. Jeffries said firmly. "So do as he says and stop fretting. He'll be home soon."

Mrs. Jeffries was the last one to go up that night. She made sure the front door was latched properly, picked up her lantern, and made her way up the darkened staircase. She hadn't wanted the others to know, but she was very discouraged about this case. She reached the first floor landing and stopped for a moment to catch her breath. On nights like this, she felt her age. She glanced at the inspector's closed door and went on up the next flight of stairs to her rooms. Opening the door, she slipped inside, put the lantern on the table, and then got ready for bed. But she knew that she wasn't going to be able to sleep, so after she'd changed into her nightclothes, she blew out the flame in the lantern and went to the rocking chair by the window.

Mrs. Jeffries stared out into the night, fixing her gaze at the streetlight across the road. Sometimes, if she simply let her mind go blank, if she deliberately thought of nothing, some sort of pattern about the case would emerge.

Keeping her gaze on the faint glow of the

light, she took a deep breath and relaxed her body. Who wanted Lawrence Boyd dead enough to take the risk to murder him? It had to be someone who knew he was going to be alone that morning — but no, she caught herself, that wasn't true. Boyd wasn't alone that day; the typewriter girl, Miss Clarke, was in his study. But maybe the killer didn't know that? She thought back to everything the inspector had mentioned and tried to ascertain who actually knew Miss Clarke was going to be at the house that day. She frowned thoughtfully; she didn't think any of the suspects knew the typewriter girl was going to be there. The servants had all left early that morning, and the guests that were due to come for luncheon wouldn't know anything about Boyd's business arrangements.

Perhaps everyone thought he was alone. But he wasn't and that appeared to be why the killer's plan went so awry. She shifted in her chair and pulled her shawl tighter against her shoulders. But had the murderer actually had a plan, or had the killing been done on the spur of the moment? In her view, the murder itself had been badly bungled, especially if the killer had been counting on the fire getting rid of all the evidence.

And exactly who hated Boyd enough to want him dead? Maud Sapington had reason to hate him, but he'd scandalized her family years ago. Why wait till now to do something about it? If Boyd's clerk was stealing money from one of the accounts, he might risk murder rather than face a prison sentence. The inspector hadn't come right out and said it, but she could tell he didn't believe Glover's story about falling asleep in the drawing room. And what about Boyd leaving all his estate to those charities? It was a peculiar idea, but perhaps there was someone on the board of the Amateur Artists Guild or the Benevolent Bankers Society that thought they might hasten Boyd to his grave and help their cause as well.

She spent another half hour letting the bits and pieces of the case drift in and out of her mind. Finally, she realized she wasn't going to come to any conclusions just yet. She got up and slipped into her bed. But it was hours before her eyes closed in sleep.

The next morning, as the inspector was leaving out the front door, Luty and Hatchet were coming in the back one. They had a quick meeting, and Mrs. Jeffries shared what she'd learned from the inspector. As they broke up to go their separate ways, Mrs. Goodge reminded them to be back by half past four.

"Don't you worry, we'll be here," Luty called over her shoulder as she and Hatchet raced toward the back door.

Wiggins and Mrs. Jeffries had already gone, leaving Betsy and Smythe alone in the hallway. Betsy grabbed Smythe's hand as soon as the door closed behind Hatchet and Mrs. Goodge had disappeared back into the kitchen. "I didn't want to say anything in front of the others, but I picked out a wedding dress yesterday."

"It's about time, lass. I was beginnin' to think you were goin' to walk down the aisle in yer apron and cap," Smythe replied. "And I don't want any sass from you about the cost, either. You just give me the name of the dressmaker's and I'll take care of everythin'. I hope you got some other dresses as well."

Betsy giggled. "I wonder how long you'll be saying things like that after we're married. But yes, I did buy a traveling costume as well. But I felt ever so guilty spending that much money on two dresses!"

Smythe stopped in front of the back door and took her by the shoulders. "We've been over this before, love. I've got more money

233

than either of us can spend and you're to 'ave anything you want. A couple of your dresses won't put me in the poor house."

"I know," she said softly. "But I'm not used to spending like that."

"Well, you'd best get used to it," he said. "I'm goin' to be takin' care of you for the rest of our lives."

"You like taking care of things, don't you." Her smile faded. "Oh, dear, I should have let you go off with Wiggins. I know he's nervous about that man following him."

"I took care of that last night," Smythe replied. He'd made a quick trip to the Dirty Duck Pub and had a word with Blimpey Groggins. "Don't worry about the lad. He'll be fine."

"Should I keep my eyes open, then?" she asked. She was tempted to ask him what he'd done, but she had a feeling she might not like his answer. Mrs. Jeffries was right; she had to learn to stop worrying about him. He could take care of both of them.

"Always keep your eyes open, love," he said, his expression suddenly dead serious. "I couldn't live if something happened to you."

Betsy didn't like the somber mood that had overtaken them both. She forced herself to laugh. "Nothing's going to happen to either of us, and in a few weeks, we're going to be man and wife. I've got to be off. If I don't find out something useful today, I'll never forgive myself."

"You've got time to give us a quick kiss," he insisted. "And then we can leave together. I'll walk you to the omnibus stand." He leaned down and kissed her on the lips.

Betsy moved closer to him and at that very moment, there was a loud knock on the door. She leapt back, stumbling slightly in her haste. Smythe caught her by the shoulders and made sure her stumble didn't turn into a fall. "Are you alright, love?"

"Just startled a bit, that's all." She reached for the door knob as she spoke.

"Hello, Miss Betsy," the butcher's boy gave her a wide smile. He was pulling a huge wicker cart behind him. "I've got your meat order here."

"Mrs. Goodge," Smythe called over his shoulder. "Your lad is here."

"We won't keep you long, Miss Johnston," Witherspoon said to the young maid. "But I do need to ask you a few questions." He and Barnes were at the house next door to the late Lawrence Boyd. The young woman sitting across from them at a rickety table in the butler's pantry was Miss Lorraine

235

Johnston, scullery maid.

"The other copper asked me questions yesterday. I told him what I saw, but then I overheard Letty Wilson tellin' the bloke I told tales." Lorraine's brown eyes narrowed and she cast a withering glance at the closed door of the pantry. She was a thin young woman with pale skin, brown hair, hazel eyes, and slightly protruding front teeth.

"But you're not telling tales, are you?" the inspector said kindly. He noticed her front tooth was chipped.

"I'm tellin' the truth. I know what I saw," she said indignantly. "I don't know why Letty's always makin' up nonsense about me, but I don't tell lies."

"Why don't you tell us what it was that you did see," Barnes suggested. There was a hint of impatience in his tone.

"I saw a fellow climbing over the fence that separates the Boyd property from the mews," she replied. "You can see it as clear as day from the top of the back steps."

"Is that were you were standing?" Witherspoon asked.

Lorraine nodded. "I'd gone outside to get some air. It was so hot in the kitchen I almost couldn't breathe, so I nipped out for a bit of fresh air. I was standing on the top step when a bit of movement caught my eye.

When I took a closer look, I saw it was a man climbing over Mr. Boyd's fence."

"What time was this?" Barnes glanced at the inspector. If by chance the girl had seen something, this might give them the time the murder had been committed.

"I don't rightly know." Lorraine shrugged.

"Come now, surely you've some idea," Witherspoon coaxed. He knew he oughtn't to lead the witness, but this might be very important. "Was it just after breakfast?"

"No," she frowned. "I'd done the breakfast dishes much earlier so it was well past that. It was fairly close to lunch. I know that because that's why the kitchen was so boiling hot. The mistress was having a luncheon and cook had both ovens on. I think it was around half past eleven." She nodded to herself. "Yes, that's right. I remember now. I'd looked at the clock just a few minutes before I went out."

Witherspoon wished he'd not pressed the girl. He couldn't tell whether she was telling the truth. "You're certain about this?"

"I said I was, didn't I?" She looked irritated. "Honestly, I don't know why everyone believes Letty and not me. When I saw the man, I ran back to the kitchen to tell the others. Go and ask Annie if you don't believe me. I drug her outside to have a look as well, but by the time we got back out here, the fellow was gone."

"Who is Annie?" Barnes asked.

"She's the tweeny. She'll tell you I'm not makin' it up."

"Can you tell us what the man looked like?" Witherspoon asked.

"Not really. There's a lot of greenery by Mr. Boyd's fence. I just barely saw the top of the fellow's head and shoulders as he nipped over. He had on a flat black cap and what looked like a long black coat."

"You didn't get a good look at the man, but you could tell he was wearing a long coat?" Barnes voice was skeptical.

"That's what I said, isn't it?" Lorraine snapped. "I didn't get a look at his face as the top of the ruddy pine tree kept blocking my view. But I noticed the coat because it blew open as he reached the top of the fence." She got up off the rickety chair she'd been sitting on. "I've got to get back to the kitchen. Cook will have my guts for garters if I don't get them carrots peeled. I've told you what I saw, and you can ask Annie if I didn't come running in to get her when it happened. I tried to tell cook about it, but she's a silly old stick and wouldn't listen to me. I'll admit that sometimes I do tell a bit of a story, but I'm not tellin' one now." She stared defiantly at the two policemen.

"Thank you, Miss Johnston. Your information has been very helpful." Witherspoon smiled kindly at her. "We appreciate your cooperation. Now, could you please send Annie into us?"

She nodded, dropped a quick curtsey, and then hurried out.

"Do you think she's telling the truth?" Barnes glanced at the inspector.

"That's just what I was going to ask you," Witherspoon replied. From behind the closed door, he could hear voices.

"I do," Barnes said softly as the pantry door opened again and another young woman stepped into the room.

"I'm Annie Barker," the girl said. She was tall and slender with light red hair, blue eyes, and a wide mouth. "Lorraine said you wanted to speak to me."

"We do. Please have a seat." Witherspoon gestured at the chair Lorraine had just vacated. "We'll not take much of your time."

Annie sat down in the empty chair and stared expectantly at the two police officers on the other side of the table.

"Do you remember the day Mr. Boyd died?" Witherspoon began.

"It was only a couple of days ago." Annie laughed. "Of course I remember it."

"Did Lorraine come and fetch you that morning and ask you to step outside to see something?" He was careful to avoid saying too much. He wanted only her recollection of the event.

"She come running into the kitchen saying there was a man climbing over Mr. Boyd's fence. So I went outside to have a look with her, but I didn't see anyone," Annie replied.

"Why didn't anyone mention this event to the police constable when he was here?" Barnes asked.

Annie shrugged. "Because no one paid any attention to Lorraine when she come running in; the kitchen was noisy, so she couldn't get anyone to listen to her."

"You listened," Witherspoon pointed out.

"I was in the hallway getting more polish out of the cupboard. Besides, I felt sorry for her. Lorraine likes to natter on a bit too much, so some of the others aren't very nice to her. Frankly, I wasn't sure that she wasn't making something up, but I went outside so her feelings wouldn't be hurt."

"So you've no idea if there actually was a man or not?" the inspector pressed.

"No."

"And Lorraine does sometimes make up stories?"

240

Annie sighed. "Everyone ignores her. Sometimes she makes things up just to get a bit of attention, if you know what I mean."

"Do you think she's making this up?"

Annie shook her head. "I don't think so. She saw someone climbing over that fence and came running into the kitchen to tell someone about it hours before we knew Mr. Boyd had been murdered."

Betsy spied the young maid coming out the servant's entrance to the Sapington house and instantly changed her plans. The neighborhood shopkeepers could wait. Here was someone who actually lived in the house, and even better, she was dressed for a day out, not for running an errand for the mistress of the house.

The girl started down the street and Betsy hurried after her. She followed her for several blocks, not allowing herself to get too close until the girl halted at the omnibus stop. Betsy walked up and stood next to her. She could see the girl was quite pretty with black hair, blue eyes, and very fair skin.

"Excuse me," Betsy said, "but do you know when the next omnibus is due?"

"The one for the train station is due any minute," the girl replied. "The one for

Baker Street isn't due for another half hour."

Betsy wasn't sure how to respond. She wanted to make sure she got on the same one as this girl. But before she had to comment, the girl continued. "I'm goin' to ride the station. It's my day out and I'm going to visit my gran."

"That's what I'm doing as well." Betsy smiled shyly. "I mean I'm having my day out. Where are you going? That is, if you don't mind my asking."

"I'm going to Reading," she announced. "I'm actually going to get to spend the night with my family. I've some exciting news to tell them and I wanted to do it in person, not by post. Oh look, here comes the omnibus. Where did you say you were going? My name is Margaret Blakley, but everyone calls me Meg. What's yours?"

"I'm Lizzie. Lizzie Thompson." Betsy lied. She mentally calculated how long the train journey would take from London to Reading and back. She was taking a big risk here; she might waste hours and find out nothing. On the other hand, she'd seen the girl coming out of the Sapington house. She had to know something. "Gracious, isn't this a coincidence? I'm going to Reading as well."

"It'll be lovely to have someone to ride

with," Meg said eagerly. "I hate taking train journeys on my own." The omnibus pulled up and they clambered on board. "There's two in the back." Meg pointed to the only empty seats in the conveyance.

Betsy pushed her way down the narrow aisle and eased into the seat nearest the window. Meg slid in next to her. "We ought to make the 10:33. My family will be ever so pleased to see me. I've not been home in almost a month."

"Your mistress doesn't allow you an afternoon out every week?" Betsy grabbed the handhold as the omnibus lurched forward.

"She does," Meg replied. "She's a hard enough time keeping staff, what with that stingy husband of hers, so we get our day out. It's just that I've been spending mine in London." She laughed merrily. "That's why I'm going home. I want to tell them I'm engaged. They'll be ever so pleased for me, especially my sister Clara. She used to be in service too until she married Bert and they moved back to Reading to open a shop."

Betsy fought the temptation to mention her own engagement. "Is your fiancé in service with you?"

"Oh, no." Meg shook her head. "Billy works down at the Edgington Arms —

that's a pub just up the road from me. His father owns the place, so when we marry, I expect I'll be working there as well. Mind you, it'll be a lot easier than what I'm doin' now."

"What position do you have now?" Betsy was beginning to think this was a mistake. Maybe when they reached the station she could come up with some excuse not to board the train. Yes, that's what she'd do; she'd claim she'd forgotten her mother's medicine or something like that.

"I'm the tweeny." Meg made a face. "It's a miserable job. The mistress is all right, but the master is as tight as two ticks on a fat dog's tail. I've never seen such a miser, and you'd think that him comin' from ordinary people, he'd be a bit more generous. But he's the kind that's only good to himself, not the rest of us."

"That's too bad." Betsy's spirits were sinking by the minute. "Maybe he doesn't have much money to spare."

"Don't be daft. He's a ruddy banker," Meg snorted. "And he's got the first shilling he ever made. He's always goin' on about how he got where he is by hard work and good planning." She snorted again. "But he actually got where he is by marrying a rich man's daughter. Honestly, he's an arrogant pig. He comes down and checks the larders to make sure we're not sneaking food. He's so miserly with the heat in the winter in our part of the house, that one of the maids walked about with bronchitis for two months. Mind you, he had it nice and toasty in his study and the mistress's bedroom. But that's the way he is, tight with us and really extravagant when it comes to him or her. The silly fool tosses out anything that isn't perfect, and his wife is almost as bad. But picking up after their leavings isn't reason enough to stay. Last month Mr. Sapington threw out two good shirts just because the collar was frayed. The footman got his hands on those before I could grab them for my Billy. The month before he tossed out two good pair of trousers, and of course, that little weasel of a footman, George, got to them before anyone else could. I did manage to get hold of one of Mr. Sapington's kerchiefs for me dad. All it had was little stain on the corner. One little stain on his bloomin' handkerchief and Mrs. Sapington tosses it in the bin and orders me to go clear across town to buy him a new batch. And they couldn't be any old kerchiefs, could they? Oh, no, I had to go all the way over to Bond Street to buy those fancy ones that cost the earth. I'll be glad to get out of there, believe me."

"Sapington? Now where have I heard that name before? Was it in the papers recently?" Betsy dangled the bait and hoped Meg would mention the Boyd murder.

Meg didn't appear to have heard her. She continued talking like Betsy wasn't even there. "I told Evelyn — she's the one that had bronchitis — to keep an eye on Mr. Sapington, and the next time he tossed out a perfectly good piece of clothing, I told her to grab it before George could get his hands on it. It's not like he needed the things, either. He sells whatever he gets his hands on at the Saturday market." The omnibus rolled to a stop and half the passengers got off. Moments later, another bunch took their place.

"Oh dear, that isn't very nice," Betsy murmured.

Meg laughed. "That's all right. She beat George to Mr. Sapington's boots and gave them to her brother. George was furious that he'd lost them but he didn't have the nerve to complain. When Evelyn started bragging about how there wasn't anything wrong with them exceptin' for a few stains on the back heel, George got up and stomped out of the butler's pantry. We all had a good laugh."

"The Sapingtons don't sound very nice at all." Betsy craned her neck to look out the passenger window. How much longer before they were at the station?

"They're mean and nasty. He can't be bothered to heat the house properly, but he spends plenty of money trying to impress important people. He and Mrs. Sapington are always entertaining, and it's not because they're sociable or nice. It's so Mr. Sapington can move up in the world. He's always plannin' this or that or something else. That's his favorite activity, making plans. She's a bit nicer, but not by much. Mind you, at least she doesn't watch every bite we eat like he does. The man drives us all mad."

Betsy thought she was going to go mad as well.

Witherspoon and Barnes stood in the drawing room of the Boyd house and waited for Leeson. "Exactly why are we back here, sir?" Barnes asked. "I thought we were going to have a word with Mr. Glover this morning."

"We'll see him soon enough," Witherspoon replied. "But as we were in the neighborhood, I thought it might be a good idea to double-check a few details. I want to make sure that everyone who went to that funeral on the day of the murder can actually verify they were in the church."

The door opened and the butler entered. "You wanted to see me?" He tried to smile but couldn't quite manage it.

"Yes, we've a few more questions to ask you," Witherspoon said.

"I'm glad you're here." Leeson moved toward them. "Mr. Boyd's lawyer, Mr. Oxley, has been badgering me about Mr. Boyd's painting. He says it's got to come back to be inventoried. I told him I wasn't sure who took it in the first place."

"It's been taken into evidence" Barnes said smoothly.

Leeson sighed. "Mr. Oxley has been asking me endless questions about the picture, wanting to know what it was, where it was, or who had it. I don't know how he could have expected me to know anything. Mr. Boyd never let anyone see what he was working on. He kept all his paintings locked in a cupboard or covered with a cloth when he wasn't there."

"Tell Mr. Oxley to contact us," Witherspoon said quickly. "May we sit down, Leeson?"

"Certainly, sir," he gestured toward the chairs and settee. "I'm dreadfully sorry. I'm forgetting my manners."

Witherspoon sat down on a chair while

Barnes lowered himself onto the settee, wincing as his backside made contact with the stiff, uncomfortable brocade seat. The constable pulled out his notebook and then looked expectantly at the inspector.

Witherspoon cleared his throat; there was no polite way to ask this question. "Leeson, when you and the other staff members went to Helen Cleminger's funeral, were you all together the entire time?"

Leeson's brows drew together in a puzzled frown. "We couldn't sit together on the train. It was crowded, so we moved about until everyone found a seat. But we all got off at the other end and met up on the station platform."

"Was the funeral close to the station?" Barnes looked up from his notebook.

"No, it was in Helen's village church, which was a mile or so from the station," Leeson replied cautiously. "It was a bit of a walk, but we managed."

"Did you sit together in the church?" Witherspoon continued.

"We couldn't. It's a small church, so everyone just made do with what they could find. The church was very crowded. There were people standing in the aisles and even in the entryway at the back."

The inspector nodded in encouragement.

"But you all met up with one another after the service, is that correct?"

Leeson hesitated a fraction too long before he answered the question. "More or less."

"What does that mean?"

"It means most of us were present and accounted for." Leeson looked over his shoulder at the closed door. "Oh dear, I hadn't wanted to say anything, but well, you're going to find out anyway if you question the others." He sighed heavily. "Mrs. Rothwell didn't come to the funeral. When we got to the station, she told me she had some pressing business to take care of and that she had to do it that morning. She told us she'd meet us at the church, but she never came. I know because I was watching for her. She never showed up at poor little Helen's funeral at all. The next time I saw her was on the platform of Paddington Station here in London. And she pretended like she'd come to the funeral and been standing at the back the whole time, but she wasn't. I know because I was standing back there and she never arrived at all."

"But the other servants think she did?" Witherspoon clarified. "Is that what you're telling us?"

"I think several of them have guessed the truth, but no one wants to say anything because we all like Mrs. Rothwell and . . . well, what with Mr. Boyd being murdered, we didn't want you to think she'd done it."

"Why would you think she wanted her cousin dead?" Witherspoon asked.

"Because she had that great row with him," Leeson cried. "The whole house heard her screaming at the man. But she isn't a murderess. Despite her anger, she's a decent, good woman who put up with one humiliation after another from that awful man." He clamped his mouth shut as though he'd said too much.

The inspector said nothing for a long moment and the room was silent save the ticking of the clock. Then he said, "Thank you, Leeson. I know this must have been very difficult for you. Can you please ask Mrs. Rothwell to step inside?"

Leeson stared at him. "I know one shouldn't speak ill of the dead, but Mr. Boyd was not a very nice person. He was an absolutely dreadful human being and none of the staff liked him. But none of us, including Mrs. Rothwell, wished him dead." He turned on his heel and stalked into the hall, closing the door softly behind him.

Barnes glanced at the inspector. "You'd have thought one of them might have shared that information with us a bit earlier," he grumbled.

"They obviously didn't want to get Mrs. Rothwell in trouble," Witherspoon replied. "I'm wondering why she didn't tell us herself. Surely she must have realized that eventually we'd find out she didn't go to the funeral."

"I'll check on train times from St. Albans to Paddington," Barnes muttered. "We'll have to see if she'd have had time to get back here, murder Boyd, hide the weapon, and then get to the platform at Paddington in time to meet the others."

"She would have had time." Witherspoon shook his head. "Mark my words."

There was a soft knock on the door and a second later, Hannah Rothwell stepped inside. "I understand you wish to speak to me again."

"Indeed we do," Witherspoon replied. "Why don't you sit down, Mrs. Rothwell."

"There's no need for me to start acting like a guest, Inspector," she said bluntly. "Leeson told me he's already told you that I didn't go to poor Helen's funeral that day."

"Where did you go?" Witherspoon resisted the urge to stand up. He felt awkward sitting in the presence of a woman.

"I came back to London, but I expect you already know that."

"Mrs. Rothwell, please do sit down. My knee is bothering me terribly and if you insist on standing, I'll have to stand as well."

For a moment, he thought she was going to refuse, but then she walked over and sat down on the chair opposite him. "You're obviously very much a gentleman, Inspector. Is this better?"

"Much, thank you. Now, can you please tell us why you came back to London on the morning that Mr. Boyd was murdered?"

"That's simple. I went to see a solicitor," she replied. "There's one very near the station. I had it all planned. When we got off the train in St. Albans, I told the others to go ahead and I'd meet them at the church. Of course, I had no intention of meeting them. Instead, I took the next train back to London, saw my lawyer, and then got to the station in time to meet them when they came back."

"What's the name of your solicitor?" Barnes glanced up from his notebook.

"Jonathan Lampton. He's a partner at Lampton and Beekins. Their offices are at number 12 Holston Road."

"You told no one where you were going, is that correct?" Witherspoon regarded her quizzically. He wasn't sure what to ask next.

"That's correct."

The inspector blurted out the next question that came to mind. "Why did you want to see a solicitor?"

"I wanted to file a lawsuit, Inspector," she replied. "One generally needs a solicitor to do that."

Barnes asked the next question. "Who were you going to sue?"

"Let's stop dancing about this matter, shall we?" She smiled coolly. "I was going to sue my cousin Lawrence, and the reason I was so secretive about my movements is because I didn't want one of the others inadvertently letting Lawrence know what I was up to. I wanted it to be a surprise."

"A surprise," Witherspoon repeated.

"Oh, yes, Inspector, I wanted to be standing right next to him when he got served with the legal papers. I wanted to see that horrid smug smile wiped off his face when he knew that someone was finally going to take him to task for his negligence and his incompetence. I wanted to be a witness to the anguish it would cause his social-climbing soul to know that he was going to have his name and his professional reputation dragged through the courts. In short, I wanted to watch him suffer the way he'd made so many others suffer."

"I take it you didn't like your cousin very

254

much," the inspector muttered.

"I hated him. He ruined what little life I have left. Wouldn't you hate someone who'd taken away everything you've ever wanted," she replied.

"What time was your appointment?" Barnes shifted slightly in an attempt to keep his backside from going completely numb.

"Ten o'clock."

"What time did you leave Mr. Lampton's office?" Witherspoon asked. He had recovered his equilibrium enough to think straight.

"Half past ten." She laughed. "And yes, I would have had time to get here, kill him, and then make it back to the train station to meet the others. We've very good cab service in this neighborhood. There's a stand just up the road."

"Why were you suing your cousin?" Witherspoon leaned forward slightly.

"I thought you'd have guessed, Inspector. Lawrence was an incompetent fool. He lost all my money," she said. "Money that I'd spent the last ten years saving. It was sitting in a post office account and it was nice and safe. Then Lawrence insisted he could make it earn more for me, that I'd do well if I gave it to him to invest. He harangued me about the matter so often that I finally gave in and let him have it."

"You hadn't wanted him to invest your money?" Barnes asked curiously.

"Oh, no, you see, I'm the real fool here. I should never have given him my money in the first place. I knew he didn't care a fig about financial matters. But I assumed that he had people working for him that did know what they were doing and that my money would be safe. That was a foolish mistake on my part. One that I'll regret until my dying day."

"If you felt it was your mistake in trusting him with your money in the first place, why did you want to sue him?" Witherspoon was almost sure that wasn't the reason. "Were you trying to recover your losses?"

"I've already told you why, Inspector." she smiled again. "I wanted to watch him suffer. That's why I filed suit. Furthermore, I'm going ahead with the lawsuit. I'm going to tie his estate up in court for years."

"But aren't you inheriting something from him?" Barnes asked. He wanted to know if she knew about her legacy.

"Humph. He's left me a few hundred pounds. But that's nothing compared to what I lost. Oh, yes, I know precisely how much he was leaving me. He told me what I'd get when he died. But that's not important to me."

"But Mrs. Rothwell," Witherspoon said softly, "you'll be out of a position soon, so surely even a few hundred pounds would be welcome."

"I don't care, Inspector." Her eyes narrowed and her expression grew fierce. "I want the estate tied up in court. It'll be a cold day in the pits of hell before this place is turned into a memorial to that odious man!"

CHAPTER 8

Dr. Bosworth's office fascinated Mrs. Jeffries even though she'd been there several times. The office was small and rather cramped. Most of the available floor space was taken up by the doctor's desk. Books, papers, and medical instruments were strewn willy-nilly across its top, and in the corner there was a jar of clear liquid with a green, oblong object floating in it. Dim light seeped into the room through the tall window of frosted glass just behind his chair. A glass-fronted bookcase filled with medical volumes stood next to the door, and the only other seat in the room was stacked high with papers and magazines.

Dr. Bosworth, a tall man with red hair and a pale, bony face, lifted the clutter off the chair. "Do sit down, Mrs. Jeffries," he said. He put the papers he was holding on top of the bookcase. "Forgive the mess. I meant to tidy up before you arrived, but the time simply got away from me. Sister said you'd come by yesterday, so I was expecting you."

"I hope I'm not catching you at an inconvenient time." She sat down. "But I am so hoping you can help us."

"It's not an inconvenient time in the least. I'm sorry I wasn't able to break away and see you yesterday." He smiled apologetically as he sat down behind his desk. "The sister said you'd waited most of the day."

"That's quite all right," she replied. "I know you were busy. Industrial accidents are terrible, aren't they? The papers said five people were killed and dozens injured."

"I thought they'd never stop bringing them in." He shook his head. "And the awful part was, the accident was preventable. A pressure gauge on the main boiler wasn't working properly. Can you believe it? The owners couldn't be bothered to make sure their equipment was in decent working order and as a result five people died. Dozens more were mangled by the explosion, and half of them probably won't be able to work again. I wonder when this country will start forcing factory owners to spend some of their precious profits on a few, simple safety precautions." He stopped, smiling ruefully. "You mustn't get me started on that topic, Mrs. Jeffries, otherwise we'll both be here for hours."

"I understand how you feel," she replied. "It does seem utterly senseless. How was your trip to Edinburgh?"

"It was most interesting. There were some fascinating papers presented. But you're not here to hear about the latest surgical techniques for removing the gall bladder." He opened his top drawer, reached inside, and pulled out a flat brown file. "This is the postmortem report on Lawrence Boyd."

Her eyes widened in surprise. "How on earth did you know what I needed? I didn't mention it to anyone when I was here yesterday."

"You didn't need to." He laughed. "When I heard you'd dropped by to see me, I knew it was because your inspector must have gotten a murder case. After that, it was easy to track down the identity of the victim."

"You'd make quite a good detective yourself," she said.

"I'll keep that in mind in case I should ever tire of medicine." He smiled. "The postmortem was done at University College Hospital on Gower Street. Getting a copy of the report wasn't difficult, but I warn you, I haven't had time to go over it as thoroughly as I'd like."

"Do you have time to take another look at

it now?" she asked. "They've no idea what the murder weapon might have been."

"Whatever it was, it's probably at the bottom of the Thames by now." Bosworth flipped open the file and began to read.

Mrs. Jeffries sat quietly, giving him a chance to absorb the information in the report. While he read, she thought about the case and about what an odd person the victim had been. He was a rich banker who really didn't care a toss about business and an artist who was more concerned with building monuments to himself than with creating brilliant paintings. The only relationships that interested him were those that reinforced his own sense of importance.

Why he was thoroughly disliked was easy for her to understand. What was difficult to comprehend was why anyone would care enough about the man to murder him. That was what was bothering her about this case. Boyd had been the sort of man people would go out of their way to avoid, not someone who could inspire the kind of personal hatred it took to commit murder. Twenty years ago he jilted his fiancée and stole another man's intended. Mrs. Jeffries imagined that a good number of people had been enraged with him then, but people rarely held onto rage for such a long period of time. Strong emotions tended to dim with the passage of the years. But then again, perhaps she wasn't seeing the entire picture. Perhaps the murder had nothing to do with hatred, but was committed for an entirely different reason. It was quite possible that the chief clerk had committed the murder in the hopes of hiding his thievery. Or maybe the housekeeper had done it; she had been furious at Boyd as well. It was all very confusing. Mrs. Jeffries had the feeling that there was something right in front of her that she simply wasn't seeing.

She was jerked out of her reverie by Dr. Bosworth's voice. "Mrs. Jeffries, are you all right?"

"I'm fine. I'm sorry. I was thinking about the case."

"You were obviously deep in thought. I called your name twice." He smiled widely and closed the file. "I'm afraid the postmortem isn't going to be of much help to you. The attending physician didn't do anything except give a very general description of the wounds. He didn't take any measurements nor did he give a detailed description of the shape."

She was disappointed. She had so hoped he'd see something in the report that could help. "Oh, that is most unfortunate. Finding the murder weapon might be very important. This case isn't going well at all."

"I'm sorry." He shrugged apologetically. "I'd have a look at the body myself, but it's already been released to the undertakers."

"You've no idea what kind of weapon might have been used?" she pressed.

"Mrs. Jeffries, without actually seeing the wounds or reading a good description of the precise size or shape, it's impossible to say. The killer could have used anything: a hammer or a rock, a candlestick, or even a police truncheon. Without knowing the size and shape, I simply can't speculate."

Mrs. Jeffries mentally cursed the incompetence of most police surgeons. "I do wish other police surgeons would avail themselves of your methods. It would make our task so much easier."

"Perhaps one day they will," he replied. "Look, I can't tell you what the weapon was, but I can tell you this much: Boyd died from massive head injuries, and the surgeon wrote that he thought no more than two blows were struck. There's no mention that the skull was particularly thin, so I have to conclude that the blow was struck with a great deal of force."

"Which leads you to what conclusion?" she queried.

"The killer was either very strong or the murder weapon was very heavy." He gave her another apologetic smile. "I wish I could narrow it down further, but that's really the best I can do."

"You've been very helpful." She rose to her feet. "Thank you, Doctor. I appreciate your assistance. I know you're busy, so I won't take up any more of your time."

"It was a pleasure seeing you. Give my best regards to the others in the household." He got up, came out from behind the desk, and went to the door. "I wish I could tell you more, but with the scarcity of detail in the report and not having seen the body, I really mustn't speculate further. But do let me know how it all comes out."

"Let's just hope it all comes out with the right person being arrested for the crime," she said somberly.

Wiggins quickened his steps and dodged around a family huddled together in front of the entrance to Hyde Park. Following people was a lot harder than it looked, but he was determined not to lose his quarry. He glanced over his shoulder again, needing to make sure there was no one hot on his heels. But he saw no sign of the man in a flat workingman's cap nor of anyone else for that matter. He knew he was being overly cautious, but he couldn't help himself. Just the idea that one of Niven's lads had been pursuing him made him half sick to his stomach. But whatever Smythe had done last evening must have worked; he'd not seen hide nor hair of anyone since leaving Upper Edmonton Gardens.

He moved closer to the young woman he'd been trailing for the past ten minutes. She was a tall girl with dark blonde hair tucked into a topknot under a red bonnet that had seen better days. She wore a short gray jacket over a simple green day dress and sturdy black shoes. Under her arm, she'd tucked her umbrella and a small purse. Wiggins had seen her come out of the servant's entrance at the Boyd house this morning, so he was fairly sure she was a housemaid. He knew he should have tried to find out a bit more about Maud Sapington's movements on the morning of the murder, but as he knew Betsy was going over that way, he thought he might have another go at the Boyd servants. No one had really had any contact with them.

She rounded the corner and then slowed her pace. She stopped abruptly, looked around and then pulled open a door and stepped inside. Wiggins couldn't see what kind of establishment she'd gone into, but he hoped it was a café.

He ran up to where he'd seen her disappear. "Oh blast," he muttered aloud. She'd gone into a pub. A ruddy pub! Young girls in service weren't supposed to hang about in pubs on their own. But maybe she wasn't on her own, he thought. Maybe she was meeting her fella. He hoped not. He couldn't have much of a chat with the girl if her bloke was standing there watching them.

Wiggins yanked open the door and went inside. As it was just past opening time, the room wasn't very crowded. All three of the small tables were empty, and there was only one old man on the bench along the side wall. His quarry stood alone on this side of the bar. She was engaged in an intense conversation with the barmaid.

Moving nonchalantly, he ambled up to the bar and stopped a few feet away from where she stood. From behind him, he heard the door open, so he glanced over his shoulder, just to be sure it wasn't the man in the flat cap. But it was just an old woman carrying a shopping basket. She trudged up to the bar and eased in between him and the girl.

"Hello, Mum." The barmaid smiled brightly at the old woman. "Janie and I have been 'avin' a nice old natter. We expected you five minutes ago. Where've you been?"

"It's all right, Mum. Lallie's just pullin' your leg. I only just arrived myself."

Blast, Wiggins thought. It was a ruddy family reunion. He'd never get close enough to the girl to find out anything now. He wondered if he ought to leave.

"Don't you worry about me." The old woman put her basket on the bar. "You just worry about findin' another position. Get somethin' decent like your sister's got. But while you're standin' there, make yourself useful and pour me one."

"Oh, Mum." The barmaid rolled her eyes and then seemed to realize she had a customer. She smiled at Wiggins. "What can I get for you?"

Before he could stop himself, he said, "Please serve the lady first," he bowed at the older woman, "and then the young lady. If you wouldn't think me forward, it would be my pleasure to buy the both of you a libation."

"What's a libation?" the old woman asked.

"He means a drink, Mum." The barmaid stared at him suspiciously.

Wiggins pulled a half crown out of his coat pocket and handed it to the barmaid. "I'd like a pint as well."

She hesitated and then reached for the

money. "That's right nice of you. Are you buyin' me one, too?"

"Of course," he replied. He was suddenly very glad the pub wasn't full. The elderly gent propped up on the bench in the corner was watching him avidly. Wiggins had a sudden, horrible thought that perhaps the old fellow worked for Nivens. Then he realized he was being stupid. The man had been sitting there when he'd come in. "It would my pleasure. The three of you remind me of my mum and sisters." He searched their faces carefully, trying to tell by their expressions whether he was being too bold. It wouldn't do him any good if they accepted the drinks and then ignored him.

"I'll have a gin if you don't mind." The barmaid grinned broadly. "My name's Lallie. That's short for Eulalie. And this here's my sister Janie and me mum."

"The name is Mrs. Mull." The old woman grinned. "And if you're buyin', I'll 'ave a gin as well."

"A half pint will do me," Janie replied.

"And what would you like?" Lallie grabbed a half-pint glass from underneath the bar and filled it from the pump.

"A half pint will be fine for me as well." Wiggins wasn't sure what to do next, but his offer hadn't ended in disaster, so he figured he might as well try to see what he could find out. "I don't suppose any of you fine ladies might know of an establishment in need of a fully trained footman, do you?"

"You're lookin' for a position, then?" Mrs. Mull stared at him suspiciously.

"I'm not in desperate need of one just yet," he lied. He didn't like the way the old woman's expression had hardened. He didn't want them thinking he was down and out. "The household I'm currently in is gettin' set to go out to India and they want me to go with 'em. But me mum, she lives over in Stepney, and she wants me to stay. I'd quite like to see one of them strange foreign countries, but I promised Mum I'd have a look around and see about gettin' another position here."

Mrs. Mull relaxed a bit. "No mother wants her children so far away."

"There's nothin' goin' where I work," Janie added. "Our master just died, so we're all goin' to be lookin' for positions ourselves."

Wiggins gaze at her sympathetically. "That's a bit of bad news for ya, isn't it? Won't the mistress of the house keep you on?"

"He weren't married." Janie grinned. "But it weren't really bad news, not for me anyways. I was lookin' for a new position anyways. It wasn't a very nice place to work."

"It was perfectly decent." Mrs. Mull frowned at her daughter. "Your Mr. Boyd was a bit of an old maid, but there's worse employers about. You should hear some of the troubles your father and I have had over the years tryin' to make ends meet. At least your Mr. Boyd fed you decently and you had a roof over your head."

"That's about all we had," Janie muttered.

"It's not nice to speak ill of the dead," Lallie said softly.

"Rubbish," Janie snapped. "Just because he died doesn't make him a better person than he was in life."

Wiggins thought they'd forgotten he was standing here.

"It's still not nice to speak ill of him," Lallie shot back. "He's not here to defend himself."

"That's true, I suppose. He might have been a bit of a tartar, but at least he's not as bad as some."

"Has either of you heard anything about the Sapington household?" Wiggins blurted. He knew this was a dangerous tactic. He didn't want to say too much and give the game away. "I've heard they have a position open."

Janie's jaw dropped in surprise. "I know about them. I'd not go there if I was you. That's about the only household in London worse than Mr. Boyd's."

"What's so awful about it?" Wiggins asked.

"On the day that Mr. Boyd were murdered, our household was set to go to a funeral. But Mr. Boyd had a luncheon planned for one of his silly charities. Do you know that the Sapingtons sent a lad over to find out what was bein' served that day? Bloomin' cheeky."

"Your Mr. Boyd was murdered?" Wiggins pretended to be shocked. "That's terrible."

"I suppose so." Janie took a sip of her drink.

"Why did the Sapingtons want to know what was bein' served?" he asked. "I mean, you're right, that's a bit of cheek. No one's ever come around and asked my mistress what was on the menu when they were 'avin' a do."

Janie stared at him blankly for a few moments, then she shrugged. "The lad said Mr. Sapington had sent him over to make sure shrimp wasn't bein' served. Seems he's got an allergy to shellfish and it'll make 'im deathly ill. But Mrs. Rothwell told the boy it was just going to be a cold luncheon of ham and roast beef because we were all to be gone that morning and nothing was bein' cooked."

"How does that make him the meanest master in London?" Wiggins asked.

"Because when Helen — that's the girl who died, the one whose funeral we all went to on the day Mr. Boyd was done in — when she first got ill and went round to the doctor's, she run into another girl there who had the same thing. They both had bronchitis. She and this girl got to talking and it turns out the girl worked for the Sapingtons and that she'd been ill for over a month. She'd asked Mr. Sapington for an advance on her quarterly wages so she could pay the doctor, and he wouldn't give it to her. The bastard had made her wait till the end of the month. All I can say is even Lawrence Boyd wasn't that mean. When Helen got sick, he gave her an advance right away so she could get seen to!"

"And you remembered Mr. Sapington's name all this time?" Wiggins thought that odd. He rarely recalled the names of people who he'd heard mentioned in casual conversation.

"Only because Helen come back and was tellin' us all about it and Mr. Boyd happened to overhear her. Mr. Boyd never said a word to the likes of us unless it was to scream or scold, but he flopped his big arse down right there in the kitchen and made Helen tell him all the details."

"That's peculiar," Wiggins said.

"Not for Mr. Boyd. A few days later, after Helen had gone home to recover, I heard Mrs. Rothwell tellin' Mr. Leeson that Mr. Boyd was spreadin' the story about Mr. Sapington all over town. It was like he wanted everyone to know that Mr. Sapington was a terrible person."

Smythe pushed through the door of the Dirty Duck and headed for Blimpey's table. He was sitting in his usual spot, but he was hunched over and staring at the tabletop like it was a racing sheet. He glanced up and frowned. "Humph, it's you. I might have known the day wasn't going to get any better."

"What 'ave I done?" Smythe sank down on the stool.

"What have you done?" Blimpey repeated. "What have you done? Let me tell you what you've done: you've given me the worst advice I ever had. Nell's so angry she's not said a kind word to me since I took your bloomin' advice and told her the truth about Tommy and his mum."

Smythe was dumbstruck. He didn't know

what to say. "But everything was fine last evening," he blurted. "I saw you less than twelve hours ago and you never said a word."

"Twelve hours ago I hadn't told Nell the truth," Blimpey shot back. "But after you left, I decided it was the right time. Nell was in nice mood and we was havin' a nice natter about the upstairs curtains. So I told her the truth. Well, guess what, Smythe? She wasn't in the least happy about the wild oats I'd sowed in my past."

Smythe grimaced. "Oh Blimpey, I'm sorry. I thought she'd be reasonable."

"And what's more," Blimpey continued, "Tommy's mum is furious at me as well. Seems she liked things the way they were and didn't appreciate the fact that now there's a few people about who know Tommy's my lad and not her dead husband's. Though I can't see that she really thought she was foolin' anyone. Tommy were born eleven months after Angus died."

"But you kept her son from bein' hanged," Smythe protested. He was willing to take the blame for Nell being angry, but he drew the line at Tommy's mum. They'd done her a great favor. "I mean, you come to us . . ."

Blimpey waved him off impatiently. "I know what you meant."

"I'm sorry, Blimpey," Smythe said. "I never meant for this to happen." He would never, ever give anyone advice about women as long as he lived.

"Oh, what's the use?" Blimpey sighed heavily. "I know it's not really your fault. I was goin' to tell Nell the truth all along."

"Then why'd you ask my advice?" Smythe demanded.

"Because if things went wrong, which they did, I'd have you to blame." He grinned broadly.

"I didn't mean for my advice to cause you grief. But remember, you did ask me and all I did was tell you what I thought."

"I know, I know. Like I said, it's not your fault. Besides, Nell will get over it and so will Tommy's good mother." He sighed again. "Edna's just a bit embarrassed, but once she gets past that, she'll be fine. Now, let's get down to business." He caught the barmaid's attention. "Two pints, please."

"What have you got for me?" Smythe was relieved to be moving off this sticky subject.

"Quite a bit, actually." Blimpey leaned forward. "Half of London disliked your Mr. Boyd. Turns out that Maud Sapington loathed him so much, she used her influence to try and get him turfed out of the Amateur Artists Guild, but he fought back by givin' 'em a huge donation, so she wasn't able to do much except sully his reputation."

Smythe nodded. "Yeah, that's what we've found out."

"As for the guests that were comin' to luncheon that day, the one you might want to keep your eye on is Walter Gibbons." He smiled at the barmaid as she brought them their beer. "Thanks, love."

Smythe waited until the barmaid had moved out of earshot before speaking. "What about Gibbons? What did you find out?"

"He hated Boyd," Blimpey replied.

"We know that." Smythe struggled to keep the impatience out of his voice.

"But did you know that he was seen walking down Queens Road in Bayswater around the time of the murder?" Blimpey grinned triumphantly.

"How do you know that?" Smythe asked.

Blimpey shrugged. "It's my business to find out such things. Not only that, but Gibbons recommended to the board of the Bankers Benevolent Society that the honorary chairmanship be given to Arnold Sapington and not Lawrence Boyd."

"But it was Boyd who got it," Smythe pointed out. "How did that happen?"

"Gibbons was overruled." Blimpey took a quick sip of beer. "There was quite a dustup at that board meeting. Gibbons told the other members that if they gave it to Boyd, he'd resign from the board. They still overruled him and he resigned."

"But he went to Boyd's house that day to tell him the news."

"Did he?" Blimpey shrugged. "Or did he just show up after the fire to make sure the job was done properly?"

Smythe shook his head. "I don't understand any of this. Are you sayin' you think Gibbons did the murder?"

"All I'm sayin' is that he was spotted in Boyd's neighborhood at the time of the killin'."

"He was on his way to luncheon at the Boyd house," Smythe protested.

"You don't show up for a luncheon an hour and a half early. As I just said, Gibbons had resigned from the board, so one of the other board members was goin' to take his place at the luncheon," Blimpey explained. "But then Gibbons relented and said he'd do it. The other board members weren't keen on him doing it, considerin' as he'd just resigned over the matter, but they couldn't stop him as he'd made his resignation effective for the following day. Seems to me he was planning on more than just givin' Lawrence Boyd some good news. Seems to me he was plannin' on a lot more than that."

Luty stood on the pavement and stared through the window of Brougham's Fine Art. The elegant establishment catered to the rich and the powerful. She grabbed the doorknob, gave it a twist, and stepped inside. She paused just inside the doorway and surveyed the room. Tables covered with colorful brocade runners or fringed silk shawls were strategically placed to best display the shops offerings of antique Chinese vases, ornate woodcarvings, crystal glassware, porcelain statues, and other fine home furnishings.

Opposite the door, a young man with slicked-back hair and dressed in formal coattails was standing in front of a glass display case. He was speaking with a well-dressed matron. He glanced at Luty and then immediately turned back to the matron.

The door at the back of the shop opened and a tall, dignified man with iron-gray hair and wearing a pin-striped suit stepped inside. His eyes widened in surprise when he saw Luty by the front door. "Oh, gracious, Mrs. Crookshank, how long have you been here? Gaspar, why haven't you offered Mrs. Crookshank a chair?" He flew down the length of the shop.

"That's all right, Harry." Luty chuckled as the hapless clerk's expression changed from haughty indifference to one of dismay. "Your clerk was helpin' this other lady. I kin wait my turn."

"Nonsense. I'll be pleased to take care of you myself." Harry Brougham took Luty's elbow, shot the hapless Gaspar a dirty look, and then led her to a seat at a small round table near the window. "Gracious, Luty, it's been ages since I've seen you. What can I do for you? Would you care for tea?"

As Luty planned to be back at Upper Edmonton Gardens in an hour, she thought it best to decline. "No thank you, Harry. What I'm really after is a bit of information. I'm hopin' you kin help me."

"But of course." Harry smiled brightly. Mrs. Crookshank was a bit eccentric, but then again, she was an American and they were all a somewhat odd. Still, he'd known her for years and she was an excellent customer.

"I'm tryin' to find out about that banker that was killed. I expect you've heard of him. His name was Lawrence Boyd."

Harry's smile faltered. "I saw something about it in the newspapers. But I don't know that I could be of any help."

"But he was an artist and a banker," Luty said doggedly. "Are you tellin' me you never met the man?"

"Perhaps I might have met him a time or two, but certainly I didn't know him well enough to make any sort of comment about his circumstances." Harry picked a piece of nonexistent lint off the arm of his pin-striped jacket.

"Oh, don't be such an old stick, Harry." Luty poked him in the ribs. "You and I go way back. I remember when you were running a stall out of the East End and pushing stuff you'd bought cheap off widows and orphans."

Harry looked around quickly. "Shh . . . Really, Luty, keep your voice down. That was a long time ago."

"I know. I'm just remindin' you to git off that high horse of yours. This is me you're talking to. Now, can you help me or not?"

Harry Brougham had been a friend of Luty's late husband before he'd gone to America to seek his fortune. They'd renewed their acquaintance when the Crookshanks returned some years later. By then, all of them had been successful. Luty had used

Harry's services in redecorating her house in Knightsbridge, and over the years since, she'd also steered thousands of pounds worth of business his way.

Harry glanced over his shoulder and gave Gaspar, who was staring openly at them, a good glare. "Continue helping Mrs. Morgan," he ordered. He turned back to Luty. "Alright, I did know him. But he was a dreadful man and certainly not someone I'm going to remember with any great fondness."

"Now we're gettin' somewhere." Luty grinned. "I knew you had to know the fellow. I ain't looking for a testimonial to the man's character. I just need some information."

Harry's eyes narrowed suspiciously. "Why? Did he lose your money?"

Luty nodded, relieved she didn't have to make up some tale about why she was interested in Lawrence Boyd. "Yep, and I aim to git it back. A friend of mine recommended his bank for a commercial transaction, so instead of goin' to my usual bankers, I went to him. Then I found out the fellow got himself murdered and that don't sit well with me."

"Come now, Luty, pull the other one. This is me, remember? Unless you've completely lost your mind, you wouldn't have given Boyd a farthing. You're far too good a businesswoman to do something that foolish." Harry grinned and leaned closer. "Tell me the real reason you're asking questions and I'll tell you what I know about him."

"You always did drive a hard bargain." Luty laughed. She'd forgotten that under that fake upper-class exterior Harry adopted, there was still the sharp, hungry boy from the mean streets of the East End. He wasn't easily fooled. "All right, I'm trying to find out who might have wanted to murder him."

"Half of London," Harry shot back. "And why do you care? I know he wasn't a friend of yours. Boyd didn't have any friends."

"No, but a friend of mine might be in a lot of trouble soon if the police don't catch the real killer," Luty replied. Her explanation was close enough to have a ring of truth. It wasn't a lie. The inspector might get into difficulties if this case went unsolved and Luty considered him a friend. "So tell me what you know."

Harry shrugged. "I don't know any more than most people who have some connections with both art and commerce in this city. Boyd was an exceptional artist, a miserable businessman, and a dreadful person.

He's spent virtually the last ten years pushing himself forward to be head of one committee or another. Honestly, the man positively delighted in building monuments to his name. I heard a rumor that he promised the board of the Amateur Artists Guild his house when he died if they'd elect him to their board. Can you believe such gall?"

Luty nodded. Harry wasn't telling her anything she didn't already know about Boyd. "How about the Sapingtons? Do you know them?"

"You mean Arnold and Maud Sapington?" Harry shook his head. "I've heard of them, of course. But I don't know them. They shop at Coventry's on Regent Street." He sniffed disapprovingly at the mention of his rival's name. "People like to say that Arnold Sapington got where he is by marriage to Maud Reese. He was the chief clerk at Reese and Cutlip when they got married."

"Wasn't she the boss's daughter?"

"She was but I don't think she married Arnold Sapington because she couldn't find anyone else," he replied. "And that's frequently what people say when they hear about a marriage such as hers. I think she married him out of gratitude."

"Gratitude?" Luty repeated. "Why would she be grateful to her father's chief clerk?"

Harry laced his fingers together on the tabletop and stared at her. "Because she'd lost the true love of her life, her cousin Nicholas Cutlip. He drowned in a boating accident just a few weeks before they were to marry. Some say Maud only married Arnold because he'd tried so hard to save the young man."

"Sapington was with him when the accident happened?"

"Yes, they were out rowing. The boat tipped over. According to witnesses, Sapington tried his best to pull the young man to shore, but he couldn't manage it. Nicholas kept going under. It was sad. Sapington is a bit of a social climber but he's no fool, and he's not brought Reese and Cutlip to the edge of bankruptcy."

"Was Boyd's bank at the edge?"

Harry shrugged again. "I've heard the other partners have had to put in some infusions of cash and that there was a movement afoot to oust him from his position. But as Boyd held the most shares, it was going to be difficult to get rid of the fellow."

Luty was getting desperate. She hated the thought of being the only one at their afternoon meeting who hadn't found out anything useful and so far, she'd learned nothing they didn't already know. "What about Walter Gibbons? You heard of him?"

Harry thought for a moment. "The name sound's familiar, but I can't say that I've heard anything about him."

"Did Boyd have any other enemies . . . Oh, of course he did. You've already told me half of London hated him." Luty sighed deeply. "But who hated him enough to want him dead? That's the question."

James Glover stared at the two policemen. "I don't know what you're talking about, Inspector," he finally blustered. "The police have all the files that I took to Mr. Boyd that morning."

"They don't have the Pressley file," the inspector said. He wasn't in the best of humor and he wasn't inclined to beat about the bush with Mr. Glover. After he finished here, he was going to have to go back to the Boyd household, and as he'd already been there once today, he felt a tad foolish. But it was his own fault as he'd forgotten to question Boyd's servants about an interesting idea he and Mrs. Jeffries had discussed over breakfast this morning. Drat, he hated being so forgetful.

"You were the last one to have that file," Barnes added.

Glover glared at the constable and shoved

his chair away from the desk. "That's ridiculous. I put those files on the table in Mr. Boyd's studio and that's the last I saw of them."

"Are you sure about that, sir?" Witherspoon pressed. He edged closer to the door, wanting to be at the ready in case Glover should try to bolt. His experiences of the past few years had taught him to be very cautious when he was pressing a suspect, so he'd stationed two constables at the street door. They were under instructions to stop anyone who came running out of the building. Witherspoon sincerely hoped there wasn't a fire. "Are you sure you didn't take it when the fire started?"

Glover's eyes narrowed angrily as a dull red flush crept up his face. "Who told you I'd taken that file?" he demanded. "They're lying."

Barnes pulled a piece of paper out of his pocket. "This is the list that Mr. Boyd sent over by messenger on the morning he died. The file is on the list."

"Where did you get that?" he snapped.

"Mr. Bingley had put it in his desk," Witherspoon replied. "He gave it to me when I was last here. I compared this list to the files we took into evidence. The ones from Mr. Boyd's studio. The Pressley file is missing. Can you explain that?"

Glover took a deep breath. "The only explanation is that the police must have lost it."

"We didn't lose it," Barnes said softly. "But you'd have reason to want it to be lost, wouldn't you?"

"I've no idea what you're talking about." Glover swallowed nervously.

Witherspoon sighed deeply. He hated it when people behaved as if the police were fools. "Mr. Glover, you're not doing yourself any good at all."

"I don't know what you mean." Glover's eyes bulged and he leapt to his feet. "I think you'd better leave. We're very busy and I've a number of important matters to see to this afternoon."

"Sit back down, man," Barnes said wearily. "We're not going anywhere and neither are you. If you like, you can accompany us to the station to help with our inquiries, or we can take care of the matter here. Which is it to be?"

Glover's gaze cut to the door and then back to the two policemen.

Barnes slapped his notebook shut and tucked it back in his pocket. Witherspoon shifted so that his weight was on his good knee. Both men knew that Glover was weighing the odds of running for it.

Suddenly, Glover flopped back into his chair, buried his face in his hands, and started to wail. His pudgy shoulders shook and he started rocking back and forth. "Oh . . . no . . . no . . . no . . ." he cried.

Alarmed, the inspector started toward him, thinking that if he kept chugging back and forth like a demented freight train, he'd topple over and hurt himself. But Barnes was quicker. He darted toward Glover and grabbed his arm. "Mr. Glover, for goodness sake, get hold of yourself."

"I didn't do it," Glover wailed. He raised his eyes to the constable. Tears streaked down his cheeks, his skin was dead white, and the hair around his temples was standing straight up. "I tell you, I didn't do it."

"No one has accused you of anything," Witherspoon said softly.

"But you're going to. I know you are. I've always had rotten luck, and now you're going to think I did it because of that stupid file, but I didn't kill him. I swear, I didn't kill him."

"Why don't you tell us exactly what you did do?" Witherspoon suggested kindly. He sat down and motioned for Barnes to take the chair next to him. He was fairly certain the danger was past and that Glover wouldn't charge for the door.

Barnes relaxed his stance, sat down, and pulled out his notebook. He looked at Glover expectantly.

"I'm not sure where to start." Glover pulled out a handkerchief, blew his nose, wiped his face, and took a deep breath.

"Start from the time you received the note from Mr. Boyd," Witherspoon replied.

"That's as good a place as any, I suppose," Glover said wearily. "As you know, I was here at the office when a street lad popped in with a note from Mr. Boyd. The note instructed me to bring some files to his studio and that I was to stay to luncheon. It told me to come straightaway and that's what I did. When I arrived, he told me to put the files on the table and go tidy myself up. He said there was a bathroom in the hallway I could use."

"According to your original statement, you went into the drawing room and fell asleep," Barnes said, reading from his notebook. "Would you like to amend that statement."

"No, that's what I actually did."

"But Mr. Glover, the furniture in there is horribly uncomfortable," the inspector protested. "I can't imagine anyone falling asleep on the settee or any of the chairs."

"But I did, Inspector. I was exhausted you see. I've not slept much for the past few weeks so I really did nod off. I agree, though; the furniture is dreadful." He smiled weakly. "I was awakened by Miss Clarke's cry of alarm. She'd cried out in some fashion and it startled me. I went out into the hall and saw her running toward the back door. She saw me and yelled that there was a fire in the studio. I told her that I'd go to the studio and for her to go get the fire brigade, that there was a station just around corner. She ran off and I continued on to the studio. There was smoke everywhere, and I could see flames through the window."

"But you went in, didn't you?" Barnes said softly. "You knew this was your one chance, so even though you were frightened of fire, you opened the studio door. Right?"

He nodded. "That's right. The fire wasn't as bad as I'd first thought, and when I went inside, I called out for Mr. Boyd. Then I saw him on the settee. It was obvious he was already dead, so I grabbed the Pressley file, stuck it under my shirt, and stepped back out into the garden."

"How did you know he was dead?" The inspector watched him carefully. He didn't know whether he believed him.

"I just knew," Glover replied. "He was so still. It was dreadful of me, I know, but I didn't care in the least that he was dead. I simply wanted to get that awful file and hide it away so no one could ever, ever see it. But that's silly, isn't it? Whether the file is there or not, the money is still missing."

"Did you know that Mr. Boyd had hired a typewriter girl that morning?" Barnes asked.

Glover shook his head. "Not until I arrived. Mr. Boyd told me to stick my head into the study and make sure she was working. He said it never hurt to keep an eye on people." He laughed bitterly. "He was certainly keeping an eye on me."

"What do you mean by that, sir?" Witherspoon asked.

"He knew what I was doing, Inspector." Glover laughed bitterly. "That's why he asked for the Pressley file."

"What did he know?" Witherspoon pressed.

Glover looked him straight in the eye. "He knew I was embezzling money, Inspector. But that makes me a thief, not a murderer."

Chapter 9

It was quite late by the time the inspector and Barnes went back to the Boyd residence. "Barnes, you really ought to go on home," Witherspoon said as they waited for someone to answer the front door. "It's already past five and I'm sure your wife will have your supper on the table soon."

"You said this wouldn't take long, sir, and the missus is used to warmin' up my food." Barnes thought they might be on a fool's errand, but the inspector had been adamant about coming back and speaking to the servants again.

Leeson opened the door and stared at them expressionlessly. "Good afternoon, gentlemen."

"Good afternoon, Leeson. We'd like to have a quick word with the staff. If you'll just tell Mrs. Rothwell we're here —"

"Mrs. Rothwell is at the undertaker's," Leeson interrupted wearily. "She took them

Mr. Boyd's clothes so they can prepare him for the funeral tomorrow. After she leaves there, she said she was going to visit a friend. I don't expect her back until later this evening." He pulled the door open wide and stepped back. "But you may as well come inside. Go into the drawing room and I'll send them up."

"Thank you. Can you send up the cook first?" Witherspoon asked. He and Barnes crossed the threshold and stepped into the foyer.

"Yes, Inspector," Leeson replied.

They made their way down the hall and went into the drawing room. Barnes sank down on one of the chairs, wincing as he tried to make himself comfortable. "Why do people buy rubbish like this? The seat is as hard as a blooming rock."

"Some people are more interested in appearance than comfort." Witherspoon remained standing. He wandered over to the wall and gazed up at a painting of a seascape. "Boyd was an artist. Apparently beauty was more important to him than comfort."

"Humph," Barnes snorted and pulled out his notebook. "I'll bet he's got a nice old soft chair tucked away somewhere. I can't see anyone sitting for more than a few minutes on this lot."

The cook appeared in the open doorway. "Leeson says you want to speak to me again," she said. She didn't look pleased by the prospect of another chat with the police.

"We would indeed." Witherspoon smiled at the woman. She stared stonily back at him. "It will only take a few minutes. Why don't you sit down?"

"I'd just as soon stand, sir," she said bluntly. "I've a cake in the oven and I need to get back downstairs. Those girls are useless when it comes to baking and they'll let it burn. Now, what do you want to know?"

Witherspoon hesitated. He wanted to ask this question properly, but he didn't want to lead the witness, so to speak. At breakfast this morning, Mrs. Jeffries had handed him his coffee cup and made a comment about the murder weapon and the fact that the Boyd household was in such a busy, crowded neighborhood. That casual remark got him thinking that the killer must have been taking an awful risk walking about with a bloody weapon hidden on his or her person. Then it had occurred to him that perhaps the weapon hadn't been carried off at all. Instead, after the murder, it might have been cleaned off and put back in its proper place here in the house with no one the wiser.

"Inspector, are you going to speak up or just stand there all day?" the cook said impatiently.

"Sorry." Witherspoon took a deep breath. "When you arrived back from the funeral that day, did you notice anything amiss in your kitchen?"

"Did I notice something amiss?" The cook frowned in confusion. "No. Not really. None of the guests had been down there if that's what you're asking. No, now wait a minute, I tell a lie. Janie complained that someone had moved the sugar hammer. It wasn't in the right drawer."

The inspector glanced at Barnes and then back at the cook. "May we see this hammer, please?"

"You want to see my sugar hammer?" The cook looked at him, her expression incredulous. "Right now?"

"That's right," Witherspoon replied. He walked out to the hall. "I'm sorry to put you to so much trouble, but it is important."

"Well, I never," the cook grumbled, but she followed along after him. Barnes fell in step behind her.

A few minutes later, they were standing in the dimly lit kitchen. The cook pulled open a drawer from the center work table and reached inside. She brought out a huge hammer-like thing with an incredibly large head on it. "It's a big one," she said. "Fourteen inches in length and it's got a nice two-inch metal and wood head. We do a lot of baking and I got tired of using that poxy little thing Mr. Boyd had here, so I insisted that he buy this one. It's made by a firm in Germany. They like sweets in Germany. Now if it's all the same to you, I'll get back to my cake." She handed it to the inspector.

"Thank you." He examined it for a moment and then handed it to Barnes.

The constable looked at it closely, then waited until the cook was fussing about at the stove before he spoke. "This could do it, sir. One blow from something this heavy would kill anyone."

"And the killer could have gotten in and out of the kitchen." The inspector pointed to a door leading to the side yard. "The kitchen was empty and the side door probably unlocked. He or she could easily have crossed down the edge of the garden to the studio without being seen by Miss Clarke. The desk in the study faces the hall door."

"Too bad we don't have any way of knowing for certain," Barnes murmured.

"Perhaps we do." Witherspoon glanced at the cook. She was bending over the open oven door holding a straw. The inspector waited till she'd pulled the cake out, poked the center with the straw, and then examined the tip. He and Barnes watched as she picked up the cake and put it on a stone slab lying on the counter. "Excuse me, Mrs. . . ." He spoke loudly hoping she'd turn and look at him. He'd forgotten her name.

"Yes, what is it?" She frowned irritably.

"After Mr. Boyd's murder, did you use this hammer?"

"I'm not sure I understand what you mean?" The cook's frown deepened.

"Did you use this the day you came back from Helen Cleminger's funeral?" Witherspoon hoped that was clear enough.

"That's a funny thing to inquire about. Why would you want to know something like that?"

"We just do," Barnes interjected, "and we'd be obliged if you'd just answer the question."

"I used it that very afternoon," she snapped. "The others were upset, so I made a nice bread pudding to calm everyone's nerves. Mr. Boyd's guests had made real pigs of themselves, so there wasn't much left for us to eat. Honestly, you'd think a murder right under their very noses might have affected their appetites, but not that lot. There wasn't so much as a crumb of Battenberg cake left."

"I'm sure the pudding was delicious," Witherspoon soothed. "When you pulled the sugar hammer out of the drawer, was it as it always was?" He wasn't certain he'd phrased the question so she would understand what he was asking, but he really didn't want to put words in her mouth.

"I don't understand. What would have been different about it? It's a piece of kitchen equipment. It's not going to grow mold or be any different from one moment to the next."

"You're right, of course." That answered his question. "Thank you. You've been very helpful."

"It was different though," a voice said from behind them.

The two policemen turned around. A young scullery maid was standing in the doorway. She was holding a flat wicker basket filled with carrots and tomatoes. "Don't you remember, Mrs. Milford? I got the hammer out for you and it was in the wrong drawer."

"I already told them that," the cook said.

"But I told you that it was wet as well."

"You'd probably not dried it properly."

The cook brushed aside her explanation. "In this damp weather, things don't dry out very quickly."

"But I 'ad dried it properly," the girl insisted. "I always dry everything properly ever since Mr. Boyd raised such a fuss about that Wedgwood platter last month. Remember? He threatened to sack me."

"That's right, he did, didn't he? Now that you mention it, I do recall you sayin' the hammer was wet."

"Had you used the hammer that day before leaving for the funeral?" Barnes asked.

"Oh, yes, I used it that morning."

"And I washed it right afterwards." The maid walked over to the worktable and put down the basket of vegetables. "Everything was washed, dried, and properly put away before we left for the funeral. That hammer was dry as a bone when I put it in the drawer, and what's more, I put it in the right drawer, not the one it was in when we come back that day."

"Thank you, ladies," Witherspoon said. "If anyone needs us, we'll be out in Mr. Boyd's studio. We'd like to have another look around."

They left by the side door, Barnes walking slightly behind the inspector. As soon as they were far enough away not to be over-heard, he said, "Do you think it's the weapon, sir?"

"Yes, as a matter of fact I do," the inspector replied. "But even with the statements from the cook and the maid, we can't be absolutely sure." He stepped off the path onto the lawn. "Mind you, if that hammer was used to kill Boyd, it solved a number of problems for the killer."

"All he or she had to do was give it a good wash under the pump and toss it back in a drawer."

They reached the studio. Witherspoon pulled open the door. "I think the killer knew the house was going to be empty. Helen Cleminger's funeral had to have been planned for several days, and I think the murderer knew that the servants would be gone."

Barnes followed Witherspoon into the studio. "That's possible, sir," he said. "But it seems to me the killer couldn't be certain there wasn't going to be someone left home. Boyd wasn't known in the area as a particularly kind or generous master, and there was a good chance he'd have made someone stay that morning. The murderer was taking an awfully big chance."

"Most killers are prepared to take quite

large risks to get what they want," Wither-spoon replied. "That's one of the reasons we're able to catch them. No matter how much planning a murderer does, something unexpected often happens."

"I hope you lot have found out something useful today." Mrs. Goodge put a plate of sliced maderia cake down next to the teapot. "My sources have been positively useless. The only thing I heard was some old gos-sip."

"Not to worry, Mrs. Goodge." Wiggins dropped into his seat and reached for a slice of cake. "There's always tomorrow."

"Let's get started then." Mrs. Jeffries slipped into her place at the head of the table and glanced at the empty chair next to Smythe. "I'm sure Betsy will be here any moment. It's only just gone half past four."

"I'm here, I'm here," Betsy called out as she hurried down the hallway. "I'd have been back on time but that ruddy train was late."

"Train?" Smythe repeated. "Where'd you go that you had to take a train?"

"It's a long story." She took off her hat and jacket, hung them up, and then sat down at the table. "Don't worry, you'll hear all about it, and I'm not even sure what little information I got was worth the trip."

Wiggins grinned broadly. "Sounds like you 'ad an adventure. I did, too. I was in a pub and I ended up buyin' drinks for three ladies. I've never done that before."

"I'm sure we've all quite a bit to report," Mrs. Jeffries interjected. Today was going to be one of those times when she had to keep a firm grip on the meeting if they were to get through everyone's report. "Who would like to go first?"

"If it's all the same to everyone, I've found out an interesting fact or two," Hatchet volunteered. "It's not going to be of much help in finding out who murdered Boyd, but it will eliminate some of our suspects."

"Git on with it," Luty said impatiently. "I don't know why you always have to draw everything out."

"I'm not drawing it out, madam," Hatchet said sarcastically. "I'm merely reciting pertinent facts in a forthright and intelligent manner. Now, if you'll let me continue with my narrative, I'll, as you so succinctly put it, get on with it. As I mentioned at our last meeting, I had an appointment to find out some information about Boyd's partners. As we discussed, they weren't happy with the way he conducted bank business, but I don't think any of them could have killed him." He pulled a slip of paper out of his jacket pocket and began to read. "Evan Kettleworth left for the Continent two weeks ago, Harvey Holcomb is in bed with a case of gout and has been incapacitated since three days before the murder, and John Sawyer was in Leeds negotiating a merger. So, unless they hired the murder done, none of them could have committed the crime."

"It wasn't a hired killing," Smythe said softly. "A professional wouldn't have bothered to try to burn the place down."

"I agree." Mrs. Jeffries looked at Hatchet. "Did your contact have any idea what happens to Boyd's share of the bank?"

Hatchet grinned broadly. "Indeed he did. As Boyd didn't have any direct heirs, the terms and conditions of the charter are such that his shares can only be bought by the other partners."

"You mean it's not part of 'is estate?" Wiggins asked.

"It is, but Boyd didn't have the legal right to will the shares to whoever he wanted. The partnership agreement was originally drawn up to keep the bank private. If a partner dies with no direct heirs, then the other partners must buy those shares at the current market value."

"So Boyd's estate gets paid the value of his shares, but the bank stays in the hands of the partners," Smythe murmured. "Only now there are three partners, not four."

"That's a handy motive for wanting him dead," Betsy said.

"True, but my source also told me that Boyd's partners are going to have to take out loans in order to buy the shares, so it's not likely they were eager to see him dead. It's going to cost them all an arm and a leg. Kettleworth is going to have to mortgage his country estate, and Sawyer is putting up his interest in Stratford's Shipping as collateral for a loan to pay his third of the cost. Harvey Holcomb's got a rich wife, but from what I hear, she doesn't care overly much for his company, so getting the cash for his third out of her isn't going to be very pleasant. No, much as Boyd's partners thought him incompetent, his death is causing them no end of problems."

"Then I suppose we'd best concentrate on our other suspects," Mrs. Jeffries said slowly. But she wasn't going to discount the partners completely. She'd keep an open mind about the situation. "Who would like to go next?"

"I found out a bit about Walter Gibbons," Smythe said. He gave them the information he'd learned from Blimpey without, of course, mentioning Blimpey's name. When he'd finished, he reached for a slice of cake and waited for the others to comment.

"So Boyd caused Gibbons to resign," Hatchet said, his expression thoughtful. "That could bring back a lot of old anger and resentments. Perhaps we ought to have a closer look at Mr. Gibbons."

"And he was seen in the neighborhood before the murder," Mrs. Jeffries said, repeating the coachman's words. "Do we know exactly when he was seen?"

"My source says it was close to the time of the murder, and that means he was in the neighborhood a good hour and a half before the luncheon."

"That doesn't mean anything," Betsy pointed out. "Perhaps he had an errand to run."

"Or perhaps he was murderin' Lawrence Boyd," Luty suggested. "Besides, rich people like him don't do their own errands."

"We'll definitely have a closer look at Mr. Gibbons," Mrs. Jeffries said quickly. "Did any of you find out anything about Maud Sapington's movements?"

"I did," Betsy said.

"I didn't," Wiggins admitted. "But I managed to pick up a few bits and pieces from me own sources. Go on, Betsy. Tell us what you 'eard."

"Thank you." She laughed. "Mrs. Sapington was the reason I had a train journey." She told them about how she'd spotted the maid slipping out of the Sapington household and had followed her. Betsy had developed several tricks to help her recall conversations almost word for word. She paused in the middle of her recitation and brought Meg's face into focus in her own mind. Then she continued. "We already know that Maud Sapington slipped out the house that day by the servant's entrance, but what I found out is that she told her husband she was going to spend the whole morning with the cook, going over menus."

"Wonder why she did that?" Luty frowned. "Surely the woman must have realized that the staff wouldn't hold their tongues for long."

"The staff likes her better than they do him," Betsy continued. "He is a miserable person." She told them about the other details that Meg had shared with her, including how Arnold Sapington's boots had ended up with a hansom driver. "So you see, Maud Sapington could be almost sure that her secret was safe. The servants avoid him like the plague."

"But that still doesn't tell us where she went that morning," Mrs. Jeffries murmured.

"Meg didn't know," Betsy said. "But she felt sorry for Mrs. Sapington. He's a monster. He wouldn't even give that poor maid an advance on her wages so she could go to the doctor."

"I 'eard that story, too," Wiggins said. "Oh, sorry, I didn't mean to interrupt."

"I was through," Betsy said. "Go on."

"Ta, as I was sayin', I 'eard the same story you did, only I 'eard it from one of Lawrence Boyd's servants," Wiggins continued. He told them how he'd followed the girl to a pub and ended up buying drinks for her whole family. He took his time in the telling, taking care to give them all the details. When he'd finished, he reached for his tea. "Seems to me it's a close race, but Sapington is a hair meaner than Boyd was, at least Boyd let poor Helen go to the doctor when she 'ad the bronchitis."

"It didn't do her much good, though," Betsy interjected. "The poor girl still died."

"They both ought to be ashamed of themselves." Luty shook her head in disgust. She was rich, but she treated her servants and anyone else that worked for her decently.

"What did you learn today, madam?"

Hatchet inquired innocently.

"Quite a bit, but I was waitin' my turn." She sniffed. "Some of us know our manners."

"That's all right," Wiggins told her. "I was finished."

"Alrighty, then." Luty took a deep breath and told them everything she'd learned from Harry Brougham. "So now we know why Maud married Sapington. He tried to save Nicholas Cutlip and she was real grateful."

"Do women marry out of gratitude?" Smythe asked, his expression skeptical.

Luty shrugged. "My source told me she was very grateful and that Sapington was very persistent."

"She lost one fiancé by being jilted and another one to an untimely death," Betsy added. "I don't imagine she had any romantic notions left. She probably just wanted a good husband."

"But he isn't good. He's a mean piece of work," Wiggins protested. "Why would she want to marry someone like that?"

"By the standards of her class, Sapington is no worse than most," Hatchet said. "Remember what Mrs. Goodge's source said about Gibbons: he's no better. Most wealthy households in this city treat their servants dreadfully, so I don't think either Boyd or Sapington should be singled out as monsters."

"Seems to me the whole system is miserable," Mrs. Goodge muttered. "But that's a discussion for another time." She glanced at Luty. "If you're finished, I'll tell my bit."

"I'm done. It weren't much, but you never know what's goin' to end up bein' important," Luty declared.

"Yours is a sight better than what I found out." The cook sighed. "All I got was some old gossip about Cutlip and Reese. Seems a few years back one of their clerks was arrested for embezzlement."

"That might be important." Wiggins reached for slice of cake.

"Don't be daft, lad." Mrs. Goodge smiled to take the sting out of the words. "It's got nothing to do with Boyd's murder, but I appreciate your tryin' to spare my feelings. I've more sources coming in tomorrow."

Mrs. Jeffries looked at the clock and noted it was well past the hour. "Right then, it's my turn. I finally managed to see Dr. Bosworth and I'm afraid the news isn't very good." She told them what the good doctor had shared with her.

"He couldn't tell you anything?" Luty exclaimed. She'd been counting on Dr. Bosworth for some additional clues.

"He did say that from his reading of the police surgeon's report, the killer must have used a very heavy object to strike the blows or been very strong. Only two blows were actually struck. It's not much, I'm afraid, but he said the report wasn't very extensive. The police surgeon merely ascertained the cause of death and left it at that."

Wiggins shook his head in disgust. "You'd think these ruddy doctors would take care to add a few important details."

"Wiggins, the only police surgeon who does do that is Dr. Bosworth and only because he's made a study of bullet wounds. Most of them simply verify the cause of death," Mrs. Jeffries explained. "We've all gotten a bit spoiled by Dr. Bosworth's willingness to look beyond the obvious."

"Seems to me his methods ought to be used by all police surgeons," the coachman argued. He was a great admirer of Dr. Bosworth.

"I agree and perhaps one day they will." She gazed around the table. "Does anyone have anything else to add?" She waited a moment and then asked her next question. "Were any of you followed?"

"Not me." Wiggins smiled gratefully at the coachman. "Whatever you did, it worked. I didn't see 'ide nor 'air of the bloke in the flat cap, and I was lookin'."

Witherspoon was exhausted when he came in that evening. There were dark circles forming under his eyes, and his spectacles had slid so far down his nose it was a wonder they'd not fallen to the floor. "You look very tired, sir," Mrs. Jeffries said as she hung up his hat. "Would you like to go straight in and have your dinner?"

"Dinner sounds lovely. I am very tired." He gave her a weary smile. "But I insist you pour yourself a glass of sherry and keep me company while I eat. It's been an extraordinary day and I want to tell you about it. That comment you made at breakfast got me to thinking, and well, I don't like to boast, but I think I've deduced what the killer used as a weapon."

"That's most kind of you, sir. You know how I enjoy listening to you talk about your methods. Go on into the dining room and I'll be right up with your tray." She told her conscience to be quiet when it protested that he did look dead on his feet and that she should insist he go up to rest. She hurried down to the kitchen and got his tray.

When she walked into the dining room,

he'd poured her a glass of sherry. "Why, thank you, sir," she said nodding at the glass sitting in front of the empty chair next to him. "But I could have done that." She put his tray on the table and began to serve.

"And I can serve myself, Mrs. Jeffries. Do go sit down. I'm sure you're as tired as I am."

She did as she was told. "What happened today, sir?"

Witherspoon spread his serviette on his lap. "Quite a bit, if I do say so myself. As I mentioned a few moments ago, our discussion this morning got me to thinking about the weapon." He told her about he and Barnes stopping in at the Boyd house on their way home and what they'd found out from the cook and the maid. "I'm fairly certain the sugar hammer was the weapon," he finished.

"But would it have been big enough to kill someone?" she asked, thinking of the one downstairs in their own kitchen.

"This was a commercial one from Germany. It's much larger than the kind one usually finds in a household."

"The killer was taking a great risk," she remarked. She wasn't sure what this information might mean. "He or she couldn't be certain the house would be empty that morning." As she spoke, an idea flashed through her mind and then was just as quickly gone.

Witherspoon picked up his fork. "Oh, but I think they were certain," he explained. "After all, Helen Cleminger's death was known in the neighborhood, and I think the killer knew the servants would all go to the service. Boyd lived alone, so there was no one else to worry about, and what's more, Boyd was working at home and had been for several days. From the murderer's point of view, it was a perfect time to commit the crime."

"And the killer couldn't have known about Glover bringing the files or Miss Clarke being in the house," she mused. "Those events all transpired that morning."

"That's absolutely correct." He beamed proudly. "But that's not all that I found out today. As I said, it was most extraordinary." Between bites of shepherd's pie and wilted lettuce salad, the inspector told her about Hannah Rothwell and James Glover.

She listened carefully, occasionally nodding her head in encouragement or making a comment. Finally, when it appeared he was finished, she asked, "Are you going to arrest Glover for embezzlement?" Again, there was another nudge at the corner of her mind, but it was gone before she could grab it.

He shook his head. "Not yet. If he's the killer, I'd rather arrest him on that charge." He took a quick drink of water. "He's free for the moment, but I've got some men watching his flat."

"What about Mrs. Rothwell?" Mrs. Jeffries asked. "Do you have someone watching her?"

"I don't think that's necessary. I put the lads on Glover because he's actually admitted to a crime." He frowned. "He insists he's innocent of murder, but I don't know if I believe him."

"Do you think he admitted to the lesser crime to avoid being arrested for murder?" she asked. It didn't seem to her to be a very clever strategy. Most policemen would already have the man arrested and behind bars. Witherspoon wasn't like other detectives, but she didn't think Glover could possibly have known that fact.

"No, I think he admitted what he'd done because he knew we were on to him." He leaned back in his chair, covered his mouth with his hand, and yawned.

"You're exhausted, sir." Mrs. Jeffries put down her glass and rose to her feet. "I'll ask Wiggins to take Fred for his walk."

Witherspoon smiled gratefully and stood up. "Thank you. I am tired. Good night, Mrs. Jeffries."

"Good night, sir." She stacked the dishes on the tray and went down to the kitchen.

Mrs. Goodge was sitting alone at the table. "Wiggins took Fred out for walkies, Smythe and Betsy went out to the garden, and I'm going to my room. Did you find out a lot from our inspector."

"Yes. We've much to discuss at the morning meeting." She took the tray over to the sink and put it on the counter.

"Leave those. Betsy said she'd clear up when they came back," the cook said.

"No, that's all right. I'll do them. Sometimes doing mundane tasks helps me think. Are you off to bed?" Mrs. Jeffries rolled up her sleeves.

"Yes, good night, then." The cook yawned. "See you in the morning."

Mrs. Jeffries put the dirty crockery in the pan of warm soapy water. She let her mind wander as she began to work. She went over every detail of the case she'd learned thus far, hoping that the little nudges she'd felt when she was speaking with the inspector would come back. But they didn't. By the time she'd put the last dish in the drying rack and was hanging up the tea towels, the others had returned.

Wiggins and Fred went right up to bed, and Smythe went to double-check that all the doors and windows were locked. Betsy frowned at the empty sink. "I was going to finish that," she protested.

"I know, dear." Mrs. Jeffries smiled kindly. "But you've had a very tiring day and I needed something to do to keep my mind occupied. Now go on up to bed. We've a very busy day tomorrow and you're going to need your rest."

"So are you," Betsy smiled gratefully. "But thank you. It was nice for Smythe and me to have a few moments to ourselves. I can't believe we're going to be married in a few weeks." She started for the back stairs. "Tell him I said good night."

"I will." Mrs. Jeffries waited till she heard Betsy's footsteps hit the top landing, and then she went to the cupboard and pulled out two mugs.

She was sitting at the table with two steaming mugs of tea when Smythe came back to the kitchen. He raised his eyebrows. "I take it we're going to have us a natter."

"I thought it would be a good idea," she replied. "Betsy said to tell you good night. She's gone up."

He slipped into the empty chair across

from her and she handed him his tea. "I think I know what this is about. You're wantin' to know how I called off Nivens' dogs, right?"

"That's correct." Mrs. Jeffries had thought long and hard about asking him what he'd done to alleviate that problem. "I don't want you to think I'm not grateful for your actions. I am, as is everyone else in the household. But Nigel Nivens is a dangerous enemy, and I don't think it fair that you should have had to deal with the problem on your own."

"I'm not scared of that little popinjay."

"Don't underestimate him," she warned. "You've helped solve enough cases to know full well that a rat will bite when it's cornered. I don't want you harmed by that odious man."

"Don't worry, Mrs. J." Smythe shrugged. "I know what I'm about. All I did was call in a few favors."

"It was more than that, Smythe." She looked him directly in the eye.

He sighed. "I also flashed a bit of cash about."

"What do you mean?" Alarmed, she gaped at him. "Did you bribe someone?"

" 'Course not." He grinned. "Blimpey Groggins has got some connections in the

Home Office. I 'ad him put some pressure on one of them to get Nivens off our patch, that's all. Blimpey owed us a favor or two."

Relieved, she eyed him speculatively. "That must have cost you a pretty penny."

He grinned. "It was money well spent. Blimpey might 'ave felt beholdin' to us, but gettin' him to put pressure on a Home Office bureaucrat cost."

"You mean you paid him because now he can't use that resource for other tasks." She wanted to make sure she understood.

"That's right. Blimpey said he knew someone that owed him a big favor," he fibbed. Blimpey had actually said he knew someone "he had the goods on," but Smythe didn't want to share that with Mrs. Jeffries. "But he could only get the fellow to pull strings once," he explained. "I was a little annoyed, seein' as how we helped Blimpey with Tommy, but lookin' at it from his point of view, it was costin' him quite a bit. I also had Eddie Blandings come along this morning and watch the back garden gate, just in case Blimpey's sources didn't come through in time."

"Eddie Blanding — that's Tommy Odell's uncle, right?" She thought the name sounded familiar.

"That's right. He was 'appy to do it for

318

us." Smythe took a quick sip of tea. "He said he didn't see anyone larkin' about. Tell me what's got ya so worried?"

Mrs. Jeffries shrugged. "I wouldn't say I was worried, but I am concerned."

"Alright, what are you concerned about?"

"Nivens has his own sources in the Home Office. If he was reprimanded, he'll be furious. He'll also assume it was our inspector who is the cause of his problems."

Smythe shrugged. "He already thinks that. I couldn't just let us be followed about while we were on the hunt, Mrs. Jeffries. I 'ad to do something."

"I'm not being critical, Smythe," she said quickly. "Your actions were absolutely correct. I'm sorry you had to spend your own money, though. That's hardly fair."

"I've got plenty to spare." He waved a hand dismissively. "So don't fret over it. But you're not tellin' me everything."

"We've got to catch this killer," she replied, "and I'm so muddled about the whole matter, I'm afraid we're going to fail."

He looked at her for a long moment and then burst out laughing. "You always feel like that when we're on the hunt."

"I'm glad you find it so funny," she said indignantly. "But I'm quite concerned about the matter."

"Don't be. You'll figure it out; you always do."

"But this time it's imperative the case is solved," she persisted. "If our inspector doesn't bring in the killer soon, Nivens will destroy his career. I can feel it in my bones. The only thing keeping Witherspoon really safe is that he can solve crimes no one else can deal with and the Home Office knows it."

"And as long as he's got us, our inspector will keep on solvin' them," Smythe said bluntly. He got up, picked up his mug, and grinned down at her. "Stop frettin'. You'll come up with the answer."

"I'm glad you've so much faith in me," she muttered. "Go on up to bed. I'll see to the lamps."

"Are you sure?" He didn't want to leave her sitting in the kitchen and feeling bad about herself. "Honestly, Mrs. Jeffries, you get like this on all our cases and it's always just before you come up with the answer."

She laughed. "Oh, get on with you. I'm fine."

"Good night, Mrs. J," he called as he headed for the back stairs.

Mrs. Jeffries sat in the quiet kitchen and finished her tea. She hoped that Smythe was correct and that she would be able to figure out who murdered Lawrence Boyd. She'd meant what she'd told the coachman: Nivens would ruin their inspector if he was given half a chance. She vowed he wasn't going to get that opportunity. They would solve this case. Someone killed Boyd; someone walked into his studio that morning as big as you please, whacked him on the head, and then tried to burn the place down to hide it was murder. But who?

She got up and took her mug to the sink. Who had a compelling reason to want him dead and also had the means to do the deed? Maud Sapington certainly had no love for Boyd. She'd hated him for years. She didn't have an alibi, either. But why pick that day to finally extract vengeance?

Mrs. Jeffries looked out the window over the sink. She fixed her gaze on the street lamp across the road and let her mind wander. Who else could have wanted Boyd dead? Hannah Rothwell had the most reason to hate him. He'd lost her entire savings. But she claimed she was going to punish him by dragging him into court. What about Walter Gibbons? He was seen on the Queens Road close to the time of the murder. What was he doing there? Could he have been on his way to kill Boyd?

But she couldn't think of the answer to

any of these questions. Tomorrow morning, when she told the others the information she'd learned from the inspector, perhaps one of them would see something she'd missed and point her in the right direction. She yawned and picked up the little lamp. As she reached the kitchen door, she paused to give the room a quick look, making sure that all was as it should be and nothing had been left burning. She turned and started for the back stairs. Just as she reached the stairwell, she felt another tug at the back of her mind. But before she could grab hold of the thought and make any sense of the feeling, it was gone.

The next morning, Witherspoon and Barnes once again waited in the parlor of Eva Clarke's lodging house while the maid went to fetch the young woman. "I thought it a good idea to have a follow-up interview with the lady," the inspector said to Barnes. "After all, she was in the house that morning, and now that she's had a few days to get over the shock of murder, perhaps she'll recall something she might have seen or heard."

"I don't see how she could hear much of anything with the noise one of those type-writing machines makes," Barnes muttered.

"I also want to ask her why she wanted Glover to stay that day," Witherspoon said. "Perhaps I'm grasping at straws, but I do believe it's important to understand all these little details, don't you?"

"Indeed I do, sir. Speaking of details, when we leave here, sir, are we going to see Hannah Rothwell's solicitor?" Barnes asked. "It's not far and we still need to confirm her story."

"That's a good idea," Witherspoon replied. "After that, I thought perhaps we might have another word with Walter Gibbons —" He broke off as Eva Clarke came into the room.

"Inspector, Constable." She nodded politely at the two men. "You wanted to speak to me?"

"Yes, it won't take long," Witherspoon replied. He noted that she wore a simple white blouse and black skirt. "I do hope we're not going to make you late for an appointment."

"I've no work today, Inspector." She smiled ruefully. "Do make yourselves comfortable." She sank down on the chair as the policemen settled upon the sofa. "Now, what can I do for you?"

"Miss Clarke, we were told that on the day of the murder, Mr. Glover made a statement that he was going to leave the Boyd house and it was you who prevailed upon him to stay. Is that correct?" the inspector asked.

"That's right," she admitted. "He said he wanted to go back to the office and tell the staff about Mr. Boyd's death. But I asked him to please stay."

"Why?" Witherspoon hoped she'd tell him something that would help him solve this case. The elation of perhaps finding the murder weapon had passed and he was beginning to feel a bit desperate.

She blushed and looked down at the floor. "I'm ashamed to admit the truth." She raised her head. "But I suppose the truth must come out."

Witherspoon's spirits soared. She knew something and she was going to tell him. "The truth generally does. Do go on."

She took a deep breath. "I wanted him to stay so that I could speak to him privately. Oh, this is most embarrassing, but you've got to understand, I need every farthing I can earn and the agency doesn't pay me until the client pays them."

The inspector stared at her blankly. "I'm sorry, I don't understand."

"Mr. Boyd was dead," she explained. "I wanted Mr. Glover to stay so I could speak to him about making sure the secretarial agency was paid promptly. Otherwise it might take ages for me to get my wages. But the situation seemed to get more and more awkward as the hours passed, and frankly, Mr. Glover wasn't very approachable, so I thought better of saying anything to him. The poor man was in a dreadful state."

Barnes' eyes narrowed. "Can you be a bit more specific?"

"It's difficult to describe," she said. "But he seemed to be in a fog. His eyes were unfocused, and if you said something to him, he took a long time to respond. I know he'd had a terrible shock, but honestly, so had the rest of us."

"I see," Witherspoon replied. Drat, this wasn't particularly helpful. He'd been hoping she might say something like she'd seen Glover coming out of the kitchen carrying a sugar hammer.

"I'm not usually so selfish," she said softly. "But I do need my wages."

"Not to worry, Miss Clarke. Your actions were entirely understandable." Witherspoon smiled kindly. As disappointed as he was by her information, he felt sorry for her.

"You're very kind." She smiled. "Do you think it would do any good to speak to Mr.

Glover now? Surely he's had enough time to recover."

"There's a Mr. Bingley that works at the bank and I'd have a word with him if I were you. He's a very understanding man," Barnes suggested. "I've a feeling Mr. Glover is still a bit under the weather."

CHAPTER 10

"We're not doing very well, are we?" the cook said to Mrs. Jeffries. The two women were clearing up after their morning meeting. Mrs. Jeffries had shared the facts she'd learned from Witherspoon with the others. Everyone had pretended to be very pleased with the additional information, but she could tell they were beginning to feel the way she felt, that with every new fact they learned the case was becoming even more muddled.

"I wouldn't say that," Mrs. Jeffries hedged.

"I would," the cook said bluntly. She put the last breakfast dish in the drying rack and reached for a tea towel. "Let's have a sit-down. You need to talk it out, Mrs. Jeffries. You can always think better after a good natter."

"I'm not sure it'll do much good," the housekeeper replied. She put the lid on the jam pot and tucked it into the sideboard.

"But it certainly can't hurt."

Mrs. Goodge finished drying her hands, spread the tea towel on the edge of the worktable to dry, and took her seat. "Now, why don't we start with the crime itself. Everyone hated Boyd, but hatin' doesn't necessarily mean you have to kill him. People usually kill in the heat of anger or because they'll get something they want. Who stood to gain anything from his death? That's the question."

"But that's just it." Mrs. Jeffries sat down. "It's almost impossible to tell who's going to benefit. He had no real heirs and he left all his money to various charities. No matter how desperate a charity might be for money, I can't see the trustees of the Amateur Artists Guild or the Society of Choral Singing sitting down and planning to commit murder to bring in some ready cash."

"True," Mrs. Goodge replied. "But gain isn't just money. Look at Glover: with Boyd dead, he might have thought no one would realize he'd been embezzling from the bank."

"What about Hannah Rothwell?" Mrs. Jeffries asked. "What did she gain?"

The cook thought for a moment. "Nothing. So I think we can strike her off the suspect list."

"But she hated him," Mrs. Jeffries protested. She was suddenly feeling more hopeful about the case. "And perhaps she did murder him in the heat of passion. He'd just lost all her money."

"She'd have done it the day she had the row with him if she'd done it in the heat of the moment," the cook said calmly. "And I don't think she'd have planned it all out and tried to make it look like an accident. She'd have just bashed him in the head and left him layin' in his studio. That's the real crux of the matter, you know. Why did the killer try so hard to make it look like an accident?"

Dumbfounded, Mrs. Jeffries stared at her. "Oh my stars and garters! You're right. I've been looking at this completely backwards." She wasn't surprised by the cook's analytical abilities; she'd always known that Mrs. Goodge was very intelligent. She was stunned because she'd not seen what was right under her very nose. That was the secret to unraveling this mess of a case. "That is the real question: why did the killer want it to look like an accident?"

"Because the killer didn't want a murder investigation. He or she wanted a coroner's inquest with a quick verdict of accidental death," Mrs. Goodge said. "Which makes me lean a bit towards Glover as the murderer; he might well have thought that if Boyd was the only one who was onto his thievery, then by killing him and making it look like an accident, maybe he could get away with it. It's no wonder people don't trust banks," she continued, completely oblivious to the fact that Mrs. Jeffries had gone stock still and was staring off into space with her mouth slightly agape and her eyes as wide as saucers. "Just look at the facts. Cutlip and Reese had an embezzler and so did Boyd's bank! I bet there's more embezzlin' goin' on in banks than there are tea tins in a china cupboard, but they won't tell us about it, will they? Banks don't want you to know they can't keep your money safe, do they? I'm glad my money is in a nice, secure post office account . . . Mrs. Jeffries, are you all right? You look like you've seen a ghost."

"Oh my stars and garters, I've been a fool." The housekeeper shook her head in disgust. "And you are absolutely brilliant."

"Am I?" The cook beamed proudly. "That's nice to know. I've never heard you use that particular expression before and you've used it twice now."

"I heard it in a shop last week." She leapt

to her feet and headed for the coat tree. "It's a very useful expression."

"Where are you going?" The cook got up as well. "I thought we were having a nice natter . . ."

"We were and it's made me realize something very important." She grabbed her bonnet and flopped it onto her head. "Oh blast, I've got to go upstairs and get my purse. Mrs. Goodge, can you find out something for me? It's very important."

"Of course," she replied. "What do you need to know?"

"Can you use your resources to find out exactly when the chief clerk at Cutlip and Reese was arrested?"

"What?" Mrs. Goodge wasn't sure she'd heard her correctly. "But that case was years ago."

"I know, but it's important." She started for the back stairs. "I've got to get my purse and then I'm going out. Can you have the information by our afternoon meeting? I ought to be back by then."

"I think so," Mrs. Goodge muttered. But Mrs. Jeffries had disappeared up the back stairs.

She reappeared a few minutes later with a light shawl wrapped around her shoulders and a small purse dangling from her fingers.

"If I'm not back by half past four, go ahead without me, but make sure that Luty and Hatchet don't leave before I get back. We may need their connections before this is all over." She took off down the hall toward the back door.

Mrs. Goodge was right on her heels. "I'll try to get that information, but I'm not sure I can find it out on such short notice."

"Yes you can." Mrs. Jeffries turned and gave her a confident smile. "You're very good at tracking down useful information."

"I'll do my best," the cook replied. "But where are you going?"

Mrs. Jeffries laughed and stepped outside. "To take a train ride."

"Sapington's tailor confirmed he stopped by that morning," Constable Barnes said, reading from his notebook as he and Witherspoon climbed the short flight of steps to New Scotland Yard. "But he was only there to pick up a coat he'd had them repair. The tailor, a Mr. Mowbry, says he was out of the shop by ten minutes past ten."

Witherspoon reached for the handle and pulled open the door. "How close is the shop to Boyd's?"

"It's about thirty minutes on foot." Barnes grinned. "Constable Tucker interviewed the tailor, sir, and he also timed the walk to Boyd's residence. He's very keen is that one and a great admirer of your methods."

They stepped into the lobby. Witherspoon nodded to the constable behind the counter, and Barnes, who knew the man, gave him a jaunty wave as they passed on their way to the staircase.

"It's good that we're tying up all the loose ends." Witherspoon started up the stairs. "As soon as we're finished here, I'd like to have a chat with Mr. Gibbons again, and after that, we'll have another interview with the Sapingtons."

"What about Glover?" Barnes winced as a sharp pain speared through his bad knee. He hated climbing stairs.

"We'll speak to him again, of course, and I'd also like to interview Hannah Rothwell one more time." Witherspoon paused on the landing to catch his breath. Chief Inspector Barrows' office was on the third floor.

"Did the chief inspector say why he wanted to see you, sir?" Barnes asked softly. They started climbing again. The constable was always on the alert when they were summoned to the Yard.

"I think he just wants a report on our progress." Witherspoon took another deep breath. "These stairs are a bit much but we're almost there."

Barnes knew the chief inspector wouldn't have called them in for a progress report; he received daily reports on all homicide cases. Someone was starting to apply pressure to get the case solved. The powers that be at the Home Office were very touchy about homicides. Ever since the police had failed to solve the Ripper murders, they were under constant pressure to solve cases quickly. "Should I wait outside, sir?" he asked as they reached Barrows' office.

"Certainly not." Witherspoon knocked on the door. "You're an investigating officer on the case. Your opinions are most valuable."

"Come in," Barrows called.

They went inside. Barnes stopped just inside the door and stood at attention. Barrows was sitting behind his desk, pouring over an open file. He looked up and nodded brusquely. "Come in, Inspector, Constable."

"Good day, sir," Barnes said politely.

"Good morning, sir," the inspector added.

"Sit down." He waved toward two chairs in front of his desk. The inspector took one and glanced over his shoulder at Barnes, who didn't move but continued standing by the door.

"You, too, Barnes," Barrows ordered.

"We're not the army, so take a load off those knees of yours."

"Thank you, sir." Barnes sat down.

Barrows frowned at them. "This isn't going very well, is it?" He poked a finger at the file on his desk. "Are you close to making an arrest?"

Witherspoon shook his head. "No, I'm afraid not."

"Ye gods, man, what's taking so long?" Barrows asked impatiently. "You've got someone right under your nose who had a motive and was right there when it happened. Why aren't you arresting him?"

"I take it you're referring to James Glover," Witherspoon said.

"Who else?" Barrows said sarcastically. "He was there, he had a reason to want Boyd dead, and he's an admitted thief. Why isn't he in custody?"

"I'm not certain he's guilty," Witherspoon replied honestly. "There simply isn't enough evidence to arrest him."

"Not enough evidence," Barrows repeated, his tone incredulous. "Are you serious?"

Barnes cringed inwardly. The inspector had, of course, said the wrong thing. He should have claimed they were looking at other suspects or gathering additional evidence. Instead, he'd simply blurted out the truth.

"I know it appears as if Mr. Glover is guilty," Witherspoon began, "but I've a feeling that he isn't the right person."

Barrows gaped at him for a moment and then sighed heavily. "If it were anyone but you, Witherspoon, I'd pull them off the case. The Metropolitan Police Force doesn't operate on 'feelings' but on facts."

Barnes knew that wasn't true either. The coppers he knew always operated on their instincts.

"But the fact of the matter is —" Barrows stared hard at the inspector — "your feelings often lead to the truth."

Barnes let out a silent sigh of relief.

"How much longer do you think you'll need?" Barrows continued. "We are under some pressure here. We don't want the newspapers going on one of those "incompetent police" crusades again. We've only just begun to restore public confidence and we don't want to lose it."

Barnes held his breath, praying the inspector would answer correctly.

"I'm not certain, sir," Witherspoon replied. "It's a bit of a muddle."

Barnes winced. Did the man never learn?

"Well you'd better get it unmuddled, Witherspoon," Barrows snapped. "We need an arrest and we need it quickly. Furthermore, I'm a bit annoyed that you went around behind my back to the Home Office. I've always treated you decently. There was no reason you couldn't have come directly to me with your concerns about Inspector Nivens."

Barnes drew back in surprise.

Witherspoon's jaw dropped. "I've no idea what you mean, sir," he said when he'd recovered enough to speak. "But I never complained to anyone about Inspector Nivens, and I certainly didn't go to the Home Office."

Barrows eyed him speculatively. "Someone did. I got very specific orders to reprimand Inspector Nivens for interfering in your investigation."

"I don't know what this is about." Witherspoon leaned forward in his chair. "I haven't seen or spoken to Nivens since this case began. I know we've a bit of an awkward history between us, but if I were going to complain about him, I would come to you. But I didn't because he hasn't interfered at all."

Barnes was fairly sure he knew who'd complained, and he suspected he knew why. Good for them. Maybe a good slap on the wrist would keep Nivens out of their business at least temporarily. But it also brought a whole host of other problems that Witherspoon wouldn't even acknowledge.

Barrows waved his hand dismissively. "Alright, then, you didn't complain. But do get on with solving this case."

It was clear their meeting was over. Witherspoon and Barnes both stood up.

"I'll do my best, sir," the inspector replied.

"Take another look at Glover." Barrows closed the file. "A criminal is a criminal, and Glover's already admitted to embezzlement. It's not that far a step to murder for a weak man like him."

"Yes, sir." Witherspoon backed toward the door. "I'd planned on interviewing him again this afternoon."

Barnes grabbed the door handle, pulled it open, and edged out into the hall.

"And stay away from Nivens," Barrows called. "You're not the only one with friends in high places."

Neither of them spoke as they trudged back down the stairs and crossed the foyer.

"That wasn't very pleasant," Witherspoon said as they stepped outside.

"And what's coming this way isn't very pleasant either," Barnes said.

Witherspoon spun around just as Nigel Nivens, a scowl on his face, charged across the pavement toward them. Barnes shoved himself in front of Witherspoon and rolled his hands into fists. He might be older, but he'd spent twenty-five years patrolling some of the meanest streets in London.

Two constables who'd been about to enter the building stopped and stared, their gazes fixed on Barnes.

Nivens skidded to a halt and glared at the constable. "Out of my way," he ordered.

"Don't start anything, sir," Barnes said softly. "You'll only end up damaging yourself." His gaze cut to the two policemen on the steps and then back to Nivens. If fisticuffs began, the constables would come running. Barnes knew that as Nivens was loathed by the rank and file while Witherspoon was greatly admired, Nivens would end up with the most bruises. The report about the incident wouldn't do his career aspirations any good, either.

Alarmed, Witherspoon tried to shove past Barnes. "Constable, really, let's be sensible about this. I'm sure Inspector Nivens merely wants to speak to me."

Barnes held his ground.

But Nivens was beyond listening to reason. "Get out of my way, Barnes, or I'll have you tossed off the force for threatening a superior officer. You'll not see a farthing of a pension if you're dismissed for that."

Witherspoon dodged around the constable and came almost nose to nose with Nivens. "If you try that, Inspector, I'll use every resource at my disposal to stop you," he warned. "Constable Barnes is a good and honorable officer, and I won't allow you to try and ruin him. Do you understand?"

"I understand you're both going to be sorry." Nivens began to back away.

Witherspoon stepped closer to him. "Hear me well, Inspector. I think I know why you're upset, and perhaps I'd be upset as well if the situation were reversed. But neither I nor the constable had anything to do with you being reprimanded."

"Then who did?" Niven yelled.

"I don't know and I don't care," the inspector continued calmly. "But if you try to harm either of us, I'll use my considerable resources to establish our rights and probably bankrupt you. You may not know this, but I have a great deal of money, and if need be, I'll spend every penny of it suing you."

Niven's mouth worked but no sound came out. His face was crimson and his eyes bulged. Finally, after sputtering for a few seconds, he turned on his heel and stalked off.

The two constables by the door relaxed their stance and went on inside. Barnes turned to the inspector. "I don't know what to say, sir. It was good of you to defend me like that." His feelings were a bit jumbled. He was the one who usually looked out for the inspector.

Witherspoon waved impatiently. "Don't mention it, Constable. I'm sick to death of Nivens's behavior. I'm tired of the man threatening me and running to the chief with one silly tale after another. Come along. We've much to do today." He started up the road.

"But thank you, sir." Barnes fell into step next to him. "Are we going to interview Gibbons now?"

"Yes, there's a cabstand by the bridge."

Barnes knew they'd better get the case solved quickly. Witherspoon had money, and right now, he had influence. He'd solved over twenty homicides and was the most famous detective on the force, but a failed case could cause him great harm. Nigel Nivens was a dangerous opponent, and he really did have friends in high places. Witherspoon's friends would disappear in the blink of an eye if he stopped solving murders.

"I heard some gossip that Gibbons was

seen close to the Boyd residence just about the time of the murder," Witherspoon continued.

"It'll be interesting to find out what he was doing there." Barnes waved at a hansom pulling away from the cabstand by the bridge.

"Otherwise, I'm afraid I might be forced to take another look at Glover." Witherspoon stepped into the cab and slid to the far side.

Barnes gave the driver the address and climbed in next to Witherspoon. He grabbed the handhold as the cab pulled out into traffic.

Walter Gibbons lived in a three-story townhouse in Belgravia. Witherspoon and Barnes were shown into the drawing room to wait while the butler went to see if Mr. Gibbons "was receiving."

"At least he's got some comfortable looking places for a body to sit," Barnes murmured as he surveyed the drawing room.

Witherspoon followed the constable's gaze, and a faint smile creased his lips. The room looked very much like every other upper-class drawing room he'd seen. The top half of the walls were painted pale gold and the bottom paneled in a dark-stained wood. A green velvet sofa with a tufted back and two matching parlor chairs stood in front of the fireplace, and a series of colorful woven carpets of different sizes covered the floors. "Considering Mr. Gibbons demeanor the last time we spoke with him, I don't think we'll be invited to sit down."

"That is correct, Inspector." Walter Gibbons strode into the room. "I hardly consider this a social call. What do you want?" He'd not bothered to put on either his coat or a cravat. His white shirt was unbuttoned at the throat as was the bottom button on his maroon waistcoat.

"We want to ask you some questions, Mr. Gibbons," Barnes replied sharply. "As you so aptly put it, this isn't a social call."

Witherspoon smiled faintly. "Mr. Gibbons, where were you around eleven o'clock on the day Mr. Boyd was murdered?"

Gibbons looked surprised by the question. "I've already made a statement concerning my whereabouts that day," he blustered. He jerked his head toward Barnes. "The constable interviewed me rather extensively."

"But I didn't ask that question," Barnes replied. He could tell that Gibbons was avoiding an answer so he could give himself a moment to think.

"But I'm sure you did." Gibbons walked

over to the fireplace and propped his elbow on the mantle. "However, if you want me to repeat myself, I was right here."

"No, you weren't," the inspector said softly. "You were walking on the Queens Road, and that's right behind Mr. Boyd's house. We have witnesses, Mr. Gibbons, so I suggest you tell us the truth." He was bluffing, of course. They'd no witnesses at all, only a bit of unverified gossip his coachman had heard from someone at a pub!

Gibbons straightened up and tugged at his waistcoat. "What of it? It's a free country. I'm not obliged to account for my whereabouts to you."

"That is true," the inspector replied. "You do have rights. Were you once engaged to Marianna Reese?"

Gibbons gaped at him. The color drained out of his face, leaving it virtually as white as his hair. "How dare you. How dare you ask such a personal question! I don't have to answer that."

"We can always ask Mrs. Sapington," Witherspoon said softly. "She was Marianna Reese's sister."

"This topic is none of your business," Gibbons yelled. The color had come back into his flesh and his cheeks were now bright pink.

"I'm afraid it is." Barnes wasn't sure what the inspector was about, but he'd do his part to keep the pressure on Gibbons. Witherspoon had mumbled something about gossip when they were in the hansom, but the street traffic had been so noisy he'd missed part of it. "You can either answer our questions sir, or we can ask your friends and associates."

"Marianna Reese married Lawrence Boyd," Witherspoon continued. He knew this was probably a painful memory and it wasn't in his nature to pry about such an intimate matter, but this was a murder investigation. "She publicly humiliated you by running off with the man who painted her portrait. That is a motive for murder, sir."

"For God's sake, man, why would I wait twenty years to kill the bastard?" Gibbons cried.

"Because you knew that the trustees were going to give Boyd the honorary chairmanship of the Bankers Benevolent Society," Witherpsoon replied. "I believe you're one of the trustees. Isn't that correct?"

"Yes." Gibbons shoulders sagged as some of the bluster went out of him. "I'm on a number of boards, Inspector. What of it?"

"The other trustees overruled your objections about Mr. Boyd, didn't they?"

"Most of them knew what he'd done to me," Gibbons said dully. "But they didn't care. All they were interested in was what he was going to give them."

"You resigned over the matter." Witherspoon was relieved. All of this information had come to him as gossip, but he'd discovered that quite often, the gossipmongers had their facts right. "I imagine that made you very angry."

"Don't be a fool, Inspector." Gibbons trudged to the sofa and flopped down. "I was furious. Absolutely furious. I hated Lawrence Boyd, and my colleagues on the board knew that. I made no secret of my feelings toward the man, but as I've just told you, they didn't care."

"Why did you agree to go to the luncheon if you'd already resigned?" Barnes asked.

"I do my duty, Constable."

Witherspoon suddenly recalled another tidbit he'd heard. "If you loathed Boyd so much, why did you have dinner with him a few weeks ago?"

Gibbons stared at him speculatively. "You're very well informed, Inspector. I think I shall need to reevaluate my opinion of the police."

"Just answer the question, sir," Barnes

pressed. His knee was starting to throb again.

"I had dinner with him because he had something I wanted." Gibbons shrugged. "I didn't want to invite him to my home, so I asked him to meet me at a nearby restaurant." He laughed harshly. "He only agreed to meet me because he wanted the chairmanship so badly and he knew I was on the board. Otherwise, he'd not have given me the time of day. He was like that, you know. He was a perfectly odious excuse for a man. He didn't see people as human beings. He only saw them as instruments of his own vanity. I can't imagine what Marianna possibly saw in him."

"You met at the restaurant," the inspector pressed.

"I asked him if I could buy the portrait he'd done of Marianna." Gibbons voice had dropped so low both policemen had to strain forward to hear. "I offered him a great deal of money for it, even though I knew he was rich. Of course, he refused, but I was counting on him doing that. Then I offered him the honorary chairmanship."

"What was Boyd's reaction?" the inspector asked.

"He laughed at me." Gibbons looked down at the floor for a brief moment and then back up at them. "He laughed at me and told me he already had it. At first I didn't believe him, but then I realized he was telling the truth. It was quite shocking, Inspector. I knew the board was leaning toward giving it to Sapington. He's a social-climbing martinet of a fellow, but he'd worked hard for the society over the years and had built up a lot of good will. He lobbied furiously for the position, and I was sure he had it. He was certain as well. You should have seen his face when I told him it was going to Boyd."

"You told Sapington he'd not got it?" Barnes clarified. "Why?"

"Because Boyd had invited him to the luncheon that day and I suspected he'd done it so he could enjoy watching Sapington be humiliated when he learned he'd been passed over. Sapington was certain he was going to get the honor, you see." Gibbons smiled slyly. "I didn't want Sapington to be taken by surprise by the announcement. In other words, I wanted to ruin it for Lawrence Boyd."

"Thank you, sir. This information is most helpful." Witherspoon hoped he could keep it all straight in his head. Gracious, people did do awful things to one another. "But you still need to tell us why you were on the

Queens Road that day."

"I was ruining Boyd's big surprise, Inspector." Gibbons laughed. "You see, he'd gotten the honor by agreeing to give the society a huge donation. After I resigned, I came home that night and thought about what to do. The answer was so simple. I sent the other trustees a message asking for an emergency board meeting wherein I rescinded my resignation and informed them I'd double whatever donation Boyd was prepared to make. They agreed to my terms."

Barnes looked surprised. "But hadn't they already told Boyd he had it."

"Yes, but it wasn't official," Gibbons replied. "So we took another vote, and we voted to give the honor to Arnold Sapington. That's why I was on the Queens Road that morning. The society meets at the Promenade Club."

"Which is on the Queens Road," Witherspoon muttered.

"So you see, Inspector, I had no reason to murder Lawrence Boyd." Gibbons rose to his feet, walked over to a walnut secretary by the door, and pulled an envelope out of the top drawer. He waved the envelope at the two policemen. "This was my revenge, and the sweetest part was that he had no idea. The only people who knew were me and the other trustees. For once, Lawrence Boyd wasn't going to get what he wanted, and furthermore, this time, I was going to get to watch him be humiliated."

"My feet are achin' and I ain't learned anything at all today." Luty flopped into her chair, took her bonnet off, and tossed it onto the empty seat next to her. "I hope some of you did better than me."

Mrs. Goodge glanced anxiously toward the back door. Mrs. Jeffries still hadn't returned, and she wasn't sure how long to wait before starting the meeting. Everyone else was here. "Mrs. Jeffries should be here any time now."

"It's already close to five," Betsy said. "We got a late start. Where'd she go?"

"I know I was late gittin' back," Luty apologized. "But my hansom got stuck in an awful traffic jam on the Brompton Road."

"You've no need to apologize," Betsy said quickly. "We were all late. I only got here a couple of minutes before you did, and Wiggins only arrived seconds before me."

"I was 'ere on time," Smythe said smugly.

"And I got caught in the same traffic mess as madam," Hatchet supplied. "That's why

I was tardy."

"Let's go ahead and start then." Mrs. Goodge decided to take charge of the meeting. "Mrs. Jeffries told me she might be late getting back, and as to where she's gone, I've no idea. She wouldn't say. Now, who has something to report?"

They all stared at her, their expressions glum.

"Surely one of us must have learned something," the cook exclaimed.

"I did hear a bit of gossip about Maud Sapington," Smythe said. "But I don't know that it's got anything to do with our case."

"Tell it anyways," Luty ordered. "Doesn't seem like the rest of us have much to say."

Smythe hesitated. "My source told me that Maud Sapington is spyin' on her husband. It looks like she's tryin' to catch him out." He broke off, not sure how to say what he meant.

"You mean your source thinks she's tryin' to catch him with another woman?" Wiggins asked eagerly. "Cor blimey, that'd set the cat amongst the pigeon. Does she peek in windows?"

"My source thinks that might be the case," Smythe admitted. Leave it to Wiggins to get to the heart of the matter. "So it doesn't look like her trailin' him has anything to do with Boyd's death. She started sneakin' about and watchin' him days before the murder."

"Did she follow him when he left the house in the evenings?" Betsy asked.

Smythe shrugged. "She might 'ave, but my source just said she were spotted hangin' about the bank neighborhood and trailin' him when he left during the day."

"I'll bet she did it in the evenings as well," Betsy said. She looked pointedly at the coachman. "If he was being untrue to her, she ought to leave him. Marriage should be taken seriously."

" 'Course it should, love," Smythe soothed. "But there's two sides to every story. We don't know for sure why she was following him."

"Humph," Betsy snorted delicately. "We do. She's tryin' to catch him out because he's being unfaithful."

The back door opened and Mrs. Jeffries footsteps pounded up the hallway. "I'm here," she called. "I'm so sorry to be late, but the train was late."

"A lot of trains are late these days," Wiggins observed. "Betsy ran into the same trouble the other day."

Mrs. Jeffries tossed her shawl and bonnet onto the pine sideboard as she hurried to the table. "What have I missed?" she asked as she slipped into her chair.

"Not very much." The cook put a cup of tea in front of her. "Smythe has a source that says Mrs. Sapington has taken to following her husband about without his knowledge."

Mrs. Jeffries arched her eyebrow. "Really? Did the source have any idea why she was following him?"

"He's bein' unfaithful," Wiggins snickered. "And she's tryin' to catch him out."

"We don't know that. She might be trailin' him for another reason," Smythe argued. But even to him, the words sounded weak. It was a tale as old as time: marriage vows simply didn't mean much for some people. This close to his own wedding day, he didn't want his beloved thinking all men were like Sapington. He would honor his wedding vows until the day he died.

"Sure she was," Luty added sarcastically. "Maybe she wanted to make sure he had his umbrella with him in case it rained."

"Let's move along, shall we?" The cook looked at the housekeeper. "Are you goin' to tell us where you've been?"

"Of course. I went to Slough." Mrs. Jeffries smiled at their confusion. "I'll explain in a minute. Were you able to get the information we discussed?"

"Yes, I had to send a street arab over to Ida's place with a note." Mrs. Goodge reached into her pocket and took out a slip of paper. "He came back with her answer, but Ida's handwritin' is awful." She squinted at the note. "I think it says it happened twelve years ago."

Mrs. Jeffries nodded. "That fits." She looked at Luty. "Can you find out when Arnold Sapington got the chief clerk's position at Cutlip and Reese?"

"I expect so."

"Can you do it now?"

Luty's eyes widened. "You mean right now?"

"Yes. I think I might have the answer, but it's so odd I daren't say anything until I have a few more facts at hand." Mrs. Jeffries was sure she knew the identity of the murderer, but proving it was going to be almost impossible.

Luty got up. "One of my bankers lives just up the road apiece. He ought to be able to help."

"I'll go with you, madam." Hatchet rose to his feet. "And before you protest, let me remind you that your banker probably isn't home as yet, so you may have to wait for some time. My presence will make it look much more like an eccentric social call . . ."

"Eccentric?" she protested.

"Of course, madam. Barging in late in the afternoon without so much as a calling card is considered eccentric, even by your rather loose standards. At least with me along, people will see that you're not madly rushing about the London streets all alone with the evening approaching."

"Oh, horsefeathers. Come on then. Let's go." Muttering under her breath, Luty headed for the hallway.

"We'll have the information for the meeting tomorrow," Hatchet called over his shoulder. "If madam's banker doesn't know, I've some sources of my own."

"He'll know," Luty yelled.

Mrs. Jeffries looked at Smythe. "I need you to go out as well. Do you think you can find out where Nicholas Cutlip drowned?"

"I'm not sure, but I can try," he said.

"Good, but don't stay out too late. Tomorrow is going to be a busy day for all of us."

"I'll be back as soon as I can," he promised. He dropped a quick kiss on Betsy's forehead and left.

Mrs. Jeffries waited until he was gone and then looked at Betsy. "I'll need you to go out tonight as well. Wiggins, I want you to go with her."

"Me?" Betsy smiled in delight. "What do you want me to do?"

"I want you to go to the Sapington house and have a quick word with Meg."

"The girl I went to Reading with?" Betsy looked confused.

"That's correct. When you speak with her, here's what you need to find out."

Mrs. Jeffries spent the next few minutes giving Betsy and Wiggins their instructions. When the others had all gone, Mrs. Goodge looked at the housekeeper. "Do you know who did it?"

"I'm not sure," Mrs. Jeffries admitted. "It simply doesn't make sense, but on the other hand, it's the only thing that makes sense. Let's just hope they bring me back the answers I need."

Arnold Sapington waved Barnes and Witherspoon into the two chairs in front of his desk. "I hope this won't take long, Inspector. I've a meeting in an hour."

"We'll be as brief as possible," Witherspoon said as he and the constable took their seats.

"Mr. Sapington, can you tell us if you had a meeting with Walter Gibbons prior to seeing him at Mr. Boyd's house on the day of the murder?" the inspector asked. He'd decided to verify Gibbons statement as quickly as possible. If Gibbons statement proved to be true, it would give him one less suspect.

Sapington looked surprised by the question. "I'm not sure what you're asking. I've been acquainted with Mr. Gibbons for a number of years. We've worked together on numerous committees for the Benevolent Society."

"But did you have a meeting recently wherein you discussed who was going to get the honorary chairmanship of the society?" Barnes asked.

Sapington said nothing for a moment. "I suppose you found out about it from Mr. Gibbons. It wasn't my idea. Gibbons contacted me and said we needed to meet. That he had some important information for me."

Witherspoon pushed his spectacles up his nose. "How long ago was this?"

"A week or ten days before the luncheon." Sapington shrugged. "I don't recall the exact date. We met at the Bankers Club one afternoon."

The inspector watched Sapington's face as he asked the next question. "What information did Mr. Gibbons share with you?"

"Come now, Inspector." Sapington's smile was amused. "You already know the answer to that question. Gibbons told me that Boyd was getting the honorary chairmanship of the society. He was very sorry, but there was nothing he could do. Boyd had promised the trustees a rather large donation if they'd give it to him."

"I take it you were disappointed?" Barnes looked up from his notebook.

"Very. I'd worked hard for the society, and by right, the honor should have come to me. But I wasn't surprised. Boyd had a reputation for buying his way through life." Sapington's eyes narrowed. "He's supposed to be this great artist just because he's exhibited at the Royal Academy. But he doesn't get it right. That last painting he was working on was all wrong. It's supposed to be the outside of the Bankers Club, but the color of the bricks is all wrong, the windows are out of proportion, and he's even made a mistake on the color of the cat that hangs around the place. Old Tom's a gray and white tabby, but Boyd painted him black as the ace of spades." He smiled bitterly. "But when you're as rich as Boyd was, people tend to overlook the fact that you've neither talent nor character."

It was very late by the time Mrs. Jeffries picked up the lamp from the table and went up to bed. Smythe had been the last one to come home, and he'd confirmed what she suspected. So had all the others, though Wiggins had said he was fairly sure the hansom driver hadn't believed them for an instant. Apparently, Wiggins wasn't very convincing pretending to be a private inquiry agent, but the driver had been willing to part with the shoes for a price.

Betsy had been elated to be out and about at all. She said Meg had been surprised to see her, but once she'd passed her palm with silver, Meg had told her where to find Evelyn's brother. Mrs. Jeffries sighed and stepped into her room. It was too bad they had to pay for so much information, but sometimes it was the only way. She blew out the light and went to her rocker. Sitting down, she tried to think of a way to present her suspicions to the inspector so that he would come to the same conclusion she had reached. When he'd told her about his "chat" with the chief inspector, she'd been quite alarmed. Barrows was telling him to solve this case and to do it quickly.

He'd been very tired this evening, but over a glass of sherry and a good meal, she'd managed to find out the details of his day. Nothing that she learned from him contradicted the conclusion she'd already reached, but she still had no idea how to prove any of it. Yet something he said nagged at the back of her mind, something about the Royal Academy . . . or perhaps it was the Bankers Club . . . She gave up. Perhaps she'd remember it in the morning.

Mrs. Jeffries got up and got ready for bed. She was sure she wouldn't sleep a wink, but she dozed off as soon as her head hit the pillow.

But she didn't rest easy. In her half-sleep state, images, ideas, and words drifted willy-nilly through her mind. Suddenly, she sat bolt upright. "Oh, my Lord, I've been so foolish. The proof is right there."

CHAPTER 11

Mrs. Jeffries wasn't able to go back to sleep, so she spent the wee hours of the morning going over every detail about the murder. She got up before dawn, went downstairs, and made a full pot of tea. By the time Mrs. Goodge and Samson came into the kitchen, she'd gone over the facts so many times, she knew she had to be right. Nothing else made sense. The only piece of the puzzle that was missing was the detail she'd asked Luty to confirm with her banker.

But that detail wasn't long in coming. Luty started talking about it before she even reached the kitchen. Hatchet was right on her heels. "Arnold Sapington got the chief clerk's position about twelve years ago," she said. "Now are you goin' to tell us what's goin' on or are we goin' to have to guess? You never did say why you went to Slough yesterday."

"She told us last night," Wiggins supplied

helpfully. "She went to look up the coroner's inquest."

"Coroner's inquest?" Hatchet repeated. "On who?"

"On a young boy who died accidentally in 1860. He fell and hit his head upon a patch of ice," she explained. "I do apologize for sending you off before I could give you all the details, but time was of the essence just as it is this morning." She looked at the cook. "Is the inspector's tray ready?"

"You can take it up now." Mrs. Goodge handed her a covered tray. "What do you want us to do?"

"What's goin' on?" Luty protested. "Do you know who did it?"

"Yes." Mrs. Jeffries took the tray from the cook. "But we're going to have the devil's own time proving it. Mrs. Goodge can give you the details while I take this up. But I'm going to need Hatchet, Smythe, and Wiggins to be at the ready. If I'm successful with the inspector, they'll need to leave immediately."

"Where will we be going?" Hatchet asked, his expression as eager as a schoolboy's faced with an unexpected day out.

"To the Sapington household." She started for the back stairs. "The inspector may need you if the man tries to bolt. The others will tell you everything."

"Actually, we're in a bit of a muddle ourselves," the cook admitted as Mrs. Jeffries disappeared. "She's got it all straight in her own head, but she's not really explained it properly to us."

"But she's pretty sure the killer is Arnold Sapington," Betsy added.

Upstairs, Mrs. Jeffries paused outside the dining room and took a deep breath. She was going to give the performance of her life. She pushed open the door, stepped inside, and smiled brightly at Witherspoon. "Good morning, sir. I've had Mrs. Goodge make you an especially large breakfast. Considering what you're going to be doing today, it might be hours before you have a chance to eat again."

Witherspoon, who'd been reading the *Times,* looked up at her in confusion. "That was very thoughtful of you. Er, uh, exactly what am I doing today?"

Mrs. Jeffries took the lid off the tray and put his plate in front of him. "You see, I had Mrs. Goodge cook three eggs and two extra rashers of bacon."

"Yes, uh, I see. Mrs. Jeffries, what are you talking about?"

"Come now, sir, stop teasing me." She laughed softly. "You know very well I'm on to your methods. But if you insist, I'll show you just how much I've learned from you the past few years." Still smiling, she paused for a breath. She couldn't tell from his expression whether he believed her, but he certainly looked interested. "You're going to go take a look at the painting you took into evidence from Boyd's studio, and after you've confirmed it's a likeness of the Bankers Club, you're going to take two or perhaps three constables to the Sapington home and arrest Arnold Sapington for the murder of Lawrence Boyd."

"I am?" He blinked. "Uh, er, why am I doing this?"

"Really, sir, you've such a mischievous streak! Now do stop teasing. You know very well why; you told me yourself last night over dinner. You said that Sapington described the last painting Boyd was working on when you interviewed him yesterday, and well, sir, you'd already mentioned that Boyd's staff had told you several times that Boyd never let anyone see a painting until it was exhibited. I believe you said he'd once sacked a servant for daring to take a little peek."

Understanding dawned in the Witherspoon's eyes. "Of course, of course." He forced himself to laugh. "You are very clever Mrs. Jeffries. You're onto me."

She reached for the toast rack and put it next to his plate. "And then of course, there's the other evidence. It's all very circumstantial, but I do believe you'll find enough to convince a jury. After all, you told me Sapington stopped by his tailor that morning and picked up a coat he'd had them repair."

"And the maid next door saw a man in coat climbing over Boyd's fence at the time of the murder." Witherspoon smiled happily as he began to see the pattern. He picked up his fork and attacked his eggs. "Send Constable Barnes in as soon as he gets here. We've much to do today. And do tell Mrs. Goodge the breakfast is excellent!"

"We've got other evidence as well, sir. Don't forget the shoes," Barnes reminded the inspector as they got out of a hansom in front of the Sapington house. They had discussed the case on the drive over, and Witherspoon had painstakingly gone over the evidence against Sapington. He'd been delighted when Barnes had informed him that Sapington's shoes had been turned over to the police by a good citizen who'd noticed an odd stain on the heel of the shoe and thought it might be important. The brown-paper parcel containing the shoes and the note had shown up at the Ladbroke Grove police station early this morning. Barnes was fairly certain that Mrs. Jeffries was behind it all, but he didn't care; he'd take all the evidence against Sapington that he could get.

"The shoes will be very helpful in court." Witherspoon started up the walkway. "But I'm still a bit unclear as to the man's motive."

"I expect that'll all come out in good time," Barnes replied.

"I certainly hope so. Are the constables at the ready?" Witherspoon asked. They'd reached the front door.

"There's two ready to step up here to guard the door when we go inside and an additional constable at each corner of the street." Barnes reached for the heavy door knocker. He had no doubt that Smythe, Wiggins, and probably that white-haired butler fellow who worked for Mrs. Crookshank were close by.

The second the front door opened, Barnes said, "We'd like to speak to Mr. Sapington."

The butler's eyes widened slightly. "I'll see if Mr. Sapington is receiving. You may step into the foyer and wait."

Barnes shoved past him. "This isn't a social call. Go get your master and be quick about it."

The butler gaped at the two policemen then turned on his heel and strode down the hall, muttering something under his breath. He disappeared behind a set of double-wide doors, and a moment later he stepped back out. He waved the two policemen forward. "This way. Mr. Sapington will see you in his study."

They hurried down the hall. The butler gave them a hard glare and then flung open the doors.

"Thank you," Witherspoon said to him.

"Humph," the butler snorted angrily and marched away.

Sapington, fully dressed in a brown coat, bronze cravat, and pristine white shirt, sat behind a wide mahogany desk. "What do you want, Inspector?" he said.

"We've a few more questions we need to ask you," Witherspoon replied.

"Then ask them and be on your way," he snapped. "You've invaded my office and now my home. This is getting tiresome, and if it persists, I'll have to have a word with your chief."

"That is your right, sir," Witherspoon replied. "By all means, file a complaint. But first I need you to explain something to me. Yesterday, you mentioned that Mr. Boyd's last painting wasn't very good, that the windows were out of proportion and the cat was the wrong color."

"What of it? He wasn't much of a painter despite what everyone said." Sapington drummed his fingers on the desktop.

Out of the corner of his eye, Barnes saw a door on the far side of the room open a crack. He stifled a smile. The staff must really hate Sapington if they were willing to risk getting caught eavesdropping. Whoever it was would get an earful today.

"Can you tell me, sir, when you saw this painting?" Witherspoon asked softly.

Sapington was taken aback. "What?"

"It's a simple question, Mr. Sapington. The inspector wants to know exactly when you saw the painting," Barnes said.

Sapington stopped drumming his fingers. He went very still. "I'm not sure," he finally said. "A few weeks ago, I think."

"Where did you see it?" Witherspoon pressed.

"At his studio, Inspector." Sapington sat up straighter and smiled confidently. "I'd dropped by to see him about a charity project for the society. He showed me the painting."

Witherspoon said nothing for a moment. The room was utterly silent save for the faint ticking of the clock. Finally, he said, "Mr. Sapington, I don't believe you. Lawrence Boyd never allowed anyone to see his work."

"I tell you he showed it to me," Sapington insisted.

"When did he show it to you?" Barnes asked. He noticed the crack was opening a bit wider.

"I don't recall the exact date," Sapington said defensively. "It was a few weeks ago."

"He wasn't working on that painting a few weeks ago. Mr. Boyd was a very fast painter. He only began work on the Bankers Club painting a few days before he was murdered," Witherspoon said. "So you couldn't have seen it a few weeks ago, could you?"

"I refuse to listen to any more of this nonsense." He stood up. "I suggest you leave."

"Certainly, sir." Barnes moved in closer to the desk. "But we'll have to ask you to accompany us to the station to help with our inquiries."

"Help with your inquiries." He laughed harshly. "That means you don't have enough evidence to arrest me, Inspector."

"Oh, but we do, sir." Witherspoon moved up to stand next to Barnes. Sapington was a muscular fellow, and the inspector hoped the constables in the front weren't too far away to hear him if he had to call for assistance. "You see, the only way you could have known what Boyd was painting is if you'd been there the morning he was murdered. Until we took the painting into evidence, there were only two people who had seen it. The killer and the victim. Arnold Sapington, you're under arrest for the murder of Lawrence Boyd."

"You'll never get a conviction on that sort of flimsy evidence," he sneered.

"Yes, they will." Maud Sapington marched into the room. "I'll tell them what I saw that day and they'll believe me."

Arnold Sapington stared at his wife in utter disbelief. "Maud, what are you doing? Shut up this crazy nonsense and send for our solicitor."

"Shut up yourself," she snarled. "My God, you're a monster. But I'll tell them what you did. I'll tell them what I saw. You didn't know that I was following you, did you? You killed him; you killed my Nicholas so you could marry me." Her fingers closed around a china shepherdess figurine. Suddenly, she hurled it toward her husband, but her aim was bad. It missed his head and grazed the inspector's forehead.

The distraction was enough for Sapington; he charged around the desk and hurled himself toward the door. Barnes leapt after him as did a dazed Witherspoon, but it was Maud who got to him first. She threw herself at him, throwing him off balance. She wrapped her arms around his knees as he toppled forward.

"Let go," he yelled.

But Maud recovered faster than her husband and managed to flatten him against the carpet. She then climbed onto his back, balled her hand into a fist, and began punching him in the head. "You monster. You killed him. You killed my Nicholas. I loved him; he was my only love, my one true love. You bastard! And it wasn't as if you even were in love with me. I didn't know for certain until now, until I knew for sure you murdered Boyd. That's what you've always done to get what you want. You murder people, just like you murdered my Nicholas. You pig! You monster!"

"Get off! Get off!" Sapington bucked like a wild horse, but he couldn't dislodge his wife. "You don't know what you're saying."

Witherspoon shoved his spectacles back onto his nose and leapt toward the Sapingtons. Barnes stumbled after him. They reached them at the same time, and each of them grabbed one of her arms. "Drag her off, sir." Barnes had to yell to make himself heard over Arnold Sapington's screams of pain and Maud Sapington's stream of verbal abuse.

Witherspoon hesitated for an instant. He hated treating women roughly, but he knew his duty. He yanked her backward with all his might.

"You didn't think I knew, did you?" Maud yelled. "But I've suspected for months, that you killed my Nicholas, and now I know that you did it. That's why I started following you, ever since you told me about not getting the chairmanship; I knew you'd try something. You wanted that more than anything in the world."

"Shut up, Maud!" He flopped over onto his back and glared at his wife. Both his cheeks were staring to swell and a patch of hair was missing from his temple. "For God's sake, shut up."

Just then, the study doors were flung open and two constables charged into the room. They skidded to a halt at the sight of Sapington lying on the floor while two feet away, Barnes and Witherspoon were restraining Mrs. Sapington, who was on her knees. The sleeve of her elegant lavender dress was hanging off one arm, her hair had come down, and a bruise was already forming on her forehead. Her chest heaved as she sucked in air.

"Please take Mr. Sapington to the station," Witherspoon instructed the constables. He was relieved to see they were both tall, rather burly lads.

"You'll never get a conviction," Sapington snarled. The constables helped him up and led him toward the door, which was now crowded with servants.

"Mrs. Sapington, are you alright?" Witherspoon asked.

"Yes, thank you, if you and the constable could just help me up and onto the sofa. I believe I hurt my ankle when I threw myself at Arnold."

"Oh, dear, we must get you to a physician." The inspector and Barnes helped her gently to her feet.

"Don't worry, Inspector." She smiled wearily as they helped her to the sofa across from the desk. "A sprained ankle is a small price to pay to see him hang. Do sit down, please, and I'll make a proper statement." She smiled at Barnes. "That is what you call it, isn't it?"

"That's right, ma'am." Barnes sat down next to her and took out his little brown notebook.

Witherspoon took out his handkerchief,

wiped his forehead, and took a seat opposite her. "Mrs. Sapington, you stated you followed your husband on the morning of the murder. Can you tell us why?"

"Perhaps it would be best if I told you everything," she said.

"That would be best," he agreed.

"A few weeks ago, my husband told me that Walter Gibbons had let him know he wasn't going to get the honorary chairmanship of the Bankers Benevolent Society," she began. "You have to understand my husband, Inspector; he never, ever gives up when he wants something. When I first married him, I considered that aspect of his character to be most attractive, but after living with it, I realized that with it was a terrible flaw." She stopped and took another deep breath. "He's insane. Oh, not the sort of insanity that justifies what he's done. He understood perfectly what he was doing when he murdered Lawrence, but it's a sickness nonetheless. He's obsessed with achieving any objective he sets for himself. He makes plans and draws up lists and ticks them off one by one when he's accomplished his goal." Her eyes filled with tears. "One of those goals was marrying me, but you see, I was engaged to a man named Nicholas Cutlip. I'd known him all my life and I loved him dearly. He was truly the love of my life." She dabbed at her eyes. "But he drowned in a boating accident on the Thames. Arnold was in the boat with him. The boat overturned and they fell out. Arnold claims he tried to pull Nicholas to shore, and for awhile, I believed him. I was grateful to him. He'd tried to save my beloved, so when he kept pressing me, I agreed to marry him." She sighed heavily and shook her head. "I was past thirty, my first fiancé had jilted me, and poor Nicholas was dead. Of course, I was easy pickings as the saying goes."

"From what you said to your husband, I take it you now believe that he didn't try to save your fiancé?" Witherspoon said gently.

"He killed him," she said dully. "I've suspected for some time now. That's why when I found out that he wasn't going to get the chairmanship honor, I started following him. I knew he'd do something awful, and he did." Her eyes filled with tears. "I loathed Lawrence, but as God is my witness, I'd no idea that Arnold was going to murder him that day."

Barnes glanced at the inspector and then said, "Had you followed him that morning?"

She nodded. "Yes, I knew we were going to the luncheon that afternoon and that once Gibbons made the announcement, it would be official."

"So you thought that if he were going to do something he would do it then, is that correct?" Witherspoon still couldn't believe someone would commit murder over a charity honor.

"Yes, my husband prides himself on being such a good planner, such a hard worker, but for most of his life, he's simply been lucky or persistent. He wanted that chairmanship more than anything else in the world."

"But why?" Witherspoon persisted. He desperately needed to understand.

"Because it was the first step to a knighthood." She smiled faintly. "That was his master plan. My husband was the son of a builder from Slough, but he told me once that he knew from the time he was a child that he was destined for greatness. The honorary chairmanship of the Bankers Benevolent Society was very prestigious. The next step would be a seat on one of Her Majesty's committees, and after that, he was certain to get the knighthood."

"So you followed him that day," Barnes pressed. "What did you see?"

"He left his office and went to his tailor on Bond Street. He came out carrying a parcel. I almost lost him on the Brompton Road, because he'd ducked into a mews and put on a huge, great black coat. I recognized the coat. That's how I was able to catch up with him again. I followed him to the Queens Road, and then he cut through a mews and climbed over a fence. But you see, I know the neighborhood quite well. I've spent my whole life in this part of London, and I knew he was going to Boyd's house. I hurried around the block, but it's quite a long one, Inspector, and it took me a good ten minutes to get to Boyd's garden. I got there just in time to see Arnold come out of the studio and then climb back over the fence to the mews."

"What did you do then?" Witherspoon asked.

"I ran," she admitted. "I saw the smoke start billowing out of the window and I heard a scream from inside the main house. So I ran."

"You didn't think you ought to help?" Barnes stared at her incredulously.

"Oh, no, when I heard the scream from the house, I knew someone else had seen the smoke and I assumed that they would raise the alarm. I think one part of me was still hoping that it wasn't too late, that I was wrong about Arnold, that he hadn't committed murder after murder to achieve his own ends." She smiled sadly. "But of course he had."

"Why did you wait until now to tell us what you'd seen that day?" Witherspoon asked. "You'd followed your husband; you must have suspected he'd murdered Boyd that day."

"I should have told you," she admitted. "But the truth is, I rather enjoyed watching Arnold squirm." She smiled. "When he realized you weren't going to give up and that Boyd's death wasn't going to be considered an accident, he got very upset. I've enjoyed that enormously. He can barely eat and he's not slept properly for days. My only complaint is that you caught onto him so quickly. I was hoping I'd get another good week of watching his misery."

"You were right, Mrs. Jeffries," Wiggins said as the men trooped back into the kitchen of Upper Edmonton Gardens. "It was Sapington who done it."

"Did it," Hatchet corrected. "It was Sapington who did it."

"What happened?" Betsy asked eagerly. "Mrs. Jeffries hasn't told us anything."

"I wanted to wait until everyone was here before I discussed the matter," Mrs. Jeffries protested. "Did Sapington go quietly?"

Smythe slipped into his seat and grabbed for Betsy's hand under the table. "He went quietly enough, but not before there was a bit of a dustup in the 'ouse. Maud Sapington was screamin' loud enough to wake the dead."

"I overheard one of the constables sayin' she tried to kill Mr. Sapington," Wiggins added eagerly.

"She tried to kill him?" Mrs. Goodge exclaimed. "Are you sure?"

"We're certain," Hatchet replied as he sat down next to Luty. "We don't know why, but I'm sure the inspector will enlighten us as soon as he comes home. But I, for one, would like to hear how Mrs. Jeffries figured it all out."

"So would the rest of us," Luty agreed.

Mrs. Jeffries laughed softly. "It was actually something Mrs. Goodge said that put me on the right track."

"Me?" The cook looked inordinately pleased. "That's nice to know. What did I say?"

"You mentioned that murder was usually committed in the heat of the moment," Mrs. Jeffries explained, "or because someone gained something from the act. That got me to thinking: there were a lot of people who hated Boyd, but who actually gained anything from his death?"

"But what did Sapington get from it?" Smythe smiled his thanks as Betsy handed him a cup of freshly poured tea.

"He got the honorary chairmanship of the Bankers Benevolent Society," Mrs. Jeffries reminded him. "And that was very important to him."

"Was it important enough to kill for?" Luty shook her head, her expression incredulous. "That's hard to believe."

"I know. That's one of the reasons it took me so long to understand that it was Sapington even when all the evidence pointed to him being the killer. The motive seemed so absurd. But then I realized that virtually everything Sapington had ever obtained had been because someone had died." She took a quick sip from her cup. "He got a place at the local grammar school because the lad who actually won the scholarship slipped on a patch of ice, cracked his skull, and died. That's why I went to Slough. According to the coroner's inquest, the witness to the accident was none other than young Arnold Sapington."

"You think Sapington murdered the lad?" Mrs. Goodge asked. "But he wasn't more than a child himself."

"But he was a child who knew that a grammar school education could be very useful in getting ahead in life," the housekeeper replied, "and this scholarship was his last opportunity. The other boy's death might have actually been an accident, but even so, I think it planted an idea in young Arnold's mind."

"How many other murders do you reckon he's committed?" Luty asked.

Mrs. Jeffries pursed her lips. "It's impossible to know for sure, but I think he probably murdered Nicholas Cutlip because he wanted to marry Maud Sapington."

"Why does where Cutlip drowned matter?" Smythe asked curiously.

"Because I think Sapington wanted witnesses," she smiled faintly. "I think he had it all planned. He made sure the boat tipped, and when they were chucked in the water, he made sure he got his hands on Cutlip and made it look like he was trying to save the man. In actuality, I suspect he was holding him under. But his goal was to marry Maud, and therefore, he needed witnesses so she would be grateful. From what we've heard, that's precisely what happened."

"But he was takin' a powerful risk." Luty shook her head in disbelief. "You never know what's goin' to happen when you're in the water. It all coulda gone wrong."

"But it didn't," Mrs. Jeffries said thoughtfully. "Sapington had a good run of luck."

"Why'd you want to know about when the chief clerk at Cutlip and Reese was arrested for embezzlement?" Wiggins asked. He thought he understood it all, but it was still a bit muddled.

"Because Sapington got his job." Luty grinned. "And the man protested he was innocent all the way through his trial. That's what my banker told me, and he said there was some rumors that the fella wasn't guilty."

"So Sapington got a place in grammar school because his competition for the scholarship died, got the chief clerk's position because the man who had it was conveniently arrested for embezzlement, and married the boss's daughter because her fiancé drowned and she was grateful to his would-be rescuer," Mrs. Goodge said. "And Sapington was conveniently around when all these things happened."

"That's right," Mrs. Jeffries said. "When we were chatting yesterday, I suddenly realized that Sapington was the only person who'd actually gained something from Boyd's death. All the others merely hated him, but most of our suspects had hated him for years. Why now would they suddenly take any action against him? Then I realized that every opportunity for Sapington had come at the expense of someone else. At first I couldn't credit that anyone would commit murder over a charity honor, but that was the only idea that made sense."

"Meg said that he liked to make plans and was always giving them lists of instructions on how things were to be done," Betsy murmured.

From upstairs, they heard the front door open. Mrs. Jeffries leapt to her feet. "Who can that be? It's far too early for the inspector to come home."

"Yoo-hoo, Mrs. Jeffries," Witherspoon called. They heard his footsteps tramping down the hall and onto the back stairs. "Where is everybody?"

"Goodness, sir, we didn't expect you," the housekeeper said as he came into the kitchen. "As you can see, we've visitors. Luty and Hatchet dropped by for tea."

"And the time just got away from us," Mrs. Goodge added. It was well past morning tea time.

"It's all my fault, Inspector." Luty smiled brightly. "But I heard you had an interestin' case and I wouldn't let them get up and go about their business till I heard every detail. You know how much I admire you."

"As do I, sir," Hatchet added, laying it on a bit thick. "I don't suppose we can prevail upon you to drop a few hints as to the next step in your investigation."

"You're too kind and you give me too much credit. I'm merely a humble public servant doing his duty." Witherspoon beamed with pleasure. "Luckily for you, I am at liberty to discuss the matter. We arrested Arnold Sapington this morning. He's at the station right now being processed. That's why I've come home. I'm desperate for a decent cup of tea and a slice of Mrs. Goodge's delicious brown bread."

"Gracious, sir, do sit down and tell us all about it." Mrs. Jeffries waved him into her spot at the head of the table. "I'll pour your tea."

"And I'll get you some fresh bread, sir," Betsy said. She got up and went to the counter. "Would you like a slice of seedcake as well?"

"That would be lovely," Witherspoon replied. "Of course, after our chat this morning, I'm sure this comes as no surprise to you," he said to Mrs. Jeffries. "But I must admit that even with Barnes and I confirming the subject of the painting, I still wasn't sure we'd enough evidence to arrest the man."

"Really, sir? But you said everyone connected with Boyd commented that he was somewhat obsessive about keeping his work secret until he was ready to exhibit it." She poured a fresh cup of tea from the pot on the table and placed it in front of him.

"That's true," he admitted. "But I'm not sure a jury could be convinced that was enough evidence to hang someone. Furthermore, the only motive we could think of sounded so very peculiar that I didn't think we'd much chance of bringing a case against the fellow, even though I was sure he was guilty. But luck or the Almighty was on our side."

"How so, sir?" Hatchet asked. He knew how important it was that all of them pretend to know as little as possible.

"A good citizen turned the shoes that Sapington wore when he murdered Boyd into the police this morning," Witherspoon explained. "There's a paint stain on the heel. I suspect we'll find that the paint came from the floor of Boyd's studio. Sapington tried to get rid of them by putting them in a dustbin, but one of his own servants fished them out and gave them to her brother. It was only a bit later that the girl realized the shoes might be evidence and prevailed upon her brother to turn them over to the police."

"How very fortunate," Mrs. Jeffries commented.

" 'Ow do you know the shoes are 'is?" Wiggins asked. He'd done some reading about the law recently, and he knew that evidence had to be directly linked to the crime if the Crown was to obtain a conviction. "I mean, did the servant actually see him putting the shoes in the dustbin?"

"Oh, yes, she did. But it wouldn't matter if she hadn't. Sapington's shoes are custom-made and his initials are on the inside heel. But the most important thing is Mrs. Sapington is prepared to testify not only that the shoes are his, but also that Sapington was wearing them on the day of the murder." He smiled triumphantly.

"His own wife is going to testify against him!" Luty exclaimed. "Nell's bells, she must hate his guts!"

"She does," Witherspoon replied. "Maud Sapington has been following her husband for days now. She suspected all along that he was going to do something awful." In between bites of bread and seedcake, he told them everything that had transpired at the Sapington house. When he was finished, he glanced at the carriage clock on the sideboard and said, "The real irony is that Sapington didn't have to commit the murder at all. He was actually going to get the chairmanship that he wanted so badly."

"That was a bit of bad luck for Lawrence Boyd," Wiggins commented. "Poor sod."

"Yes, he wasn't a particularly likeable fellow, but he didn't deserve to be murdered." Witherspoon got to his feet. "Goodness, I must get back to the station. We're going to have another go at interviewing Sapington."

"He isn't admitting anything?" Mrs. Jeffries probed.

Witherspoon shook his head. "No, but with Mrs. Sapington's testimony, we'll get a conviction."

"I didn't think a wife could testify against her husband," Mrs. Goodge muttered.

"He won't be her husband much longer. She told us she's going to divorce him, and she does have grounds: he did more or less marry her under false pretenses." The inspector drained his cup. "But she'll have the devil's own time proving it, I'm afraid."

"Can't she just divorce him because he's committed murder?" Wiggins asked. "Seems like that ought to be grounds for getting rid of a husband."

Witherspoon paused. "Actually, I don't think it is. But I'm sure that considering everything she suspects he's done over the years, her solicitors will find grounds. Mrs. Crookshank, Hatchet, it was lovely to see you both. I'll see you very soon, I'm sure. We've Betsy's wedding in just a few weeks."

"Good day, Inspector," Luty called.

"Good day," Hatchet echoed.

As soon as he'd gone, they breathed a collective sigh of relief.

"That was close," Smythe said. "He almost caught us."

Mrs. Jeffries said nothing. She was simply grateful that he hadn't questioned them further about why they were sitting around in the middle of the day.

"But he didn't," Betsy said. She got to her feet. "And I've got a dozen different things to do now that the case is solved." She reached into her pocket, pulled out a slip of paper, and handed it to Luty. "Here's the menu for the wedding breakfast. I finally made up my mind."

"What are we 'avin'?" Wiggins asked eagerly.

"Never you mind, lad," Luty retorted. She got up. "That's a secret. We'd best git on home as well. Like Betsy says, now that the case is solved, we've got us a weddin' to do!"

For the next few days, the household kept

their ears open for further news about the Sapington case. But they learned very little they didn't already know, and as the days passed, the case receded into the background of their lives. They all had something much more important to think about now.

Smythe and Betsy's wedding.

The guest list was complete, the banns were read, and the menu, after half a dozen last-minute changes, was finalized. Two weeks before the big day, Smythe took Wiggins to his tailor so the lad could be fitted for a nice new suit to wear when he stood up with the coachman as his best man. He also had a chat with the inspector, and both men had come away satisfied with the conversation.

Mrs. Goodge bought a new lavender dress with a nice mother-of-pearl matching jacket and a lacy jabot cravat. She bought Samson a matching ribbon, but he ran off and hid under the inspector's bed when she tried to put it on him. She made the mistake of leaving the ribbon on her bed, and the next time she saw it, it was shredded to bits.

Mrs. Jeffries decided to wear her navy blue suit with a high-necked white blouse. But she did buy herself a lovely new hat with blue veiling and two white feathers on the side.

The week before the wedding, Betsy worked up the courage to ask the inspector to walk her down the aisle. Witherspoon told her he'd be honored to give her away, and he shyly admitted he'd been hoping she'd ask him.

A few days before the wedding, Betsy's trousseau and wedding dress were finished. They were to be delivered the day before the nuptials. Betsy was superstitious; she didn't want Smythe to get so much as a glimpse of her wedding dress. There wasn't going to be any bad luck for her wedding!

Everything was going as planned except that no matter how hard she cajoled, coaxed, or complained, she couldn't get Smythe to say one word about where they were going to live or even where they were going on their honeymoon.

"Come on, give us a hint." She poked him in the arm. The wedding was two days away and they were sitting at the table having their tea.

"No hints," he said firmly. "If I say too much, you'll suss it out."

"That's because she's smart." Wiggins nodded his head wisely. "But you're even smarter because you got 'er to marry you."

"Why, Wiggins, thank you," Betsy replied. "I think."

Mrs. Jeffries smiled at her brood. She was a bit sad that things were going to change, but she knew it was for the best. These two were madly in love and they needed to be out on their own. The coachman had confided his plan to her, and she thought it had a good chance of succeeding.

There was a loud knock on the front door. Mrs. Jeffries got up. "I wonder who that can be. We're not expecting anyone."

She held her breath as she opened the door, hoping that it wasn't someone needing help with an unsolved murder. Not this close to the wedding. A plump, middle-aged woman with bright red hair stood there. She wore an emerald green day dress with a matching hat and leaned against a green-and-white striped parasol she'd propped on the top step. "Hello, hello," she smiled. "Is this the household of Inspector Witherspoon?"

"Yes, but the inspector isn't here. He's at the station."

"Then I'm at the right place." She pushed forward suddenly, causing Mrs. Jeffries to step back. "Is Smythe 'ere?"

"Smythe?" Mrs. Jeffries repeated. "Yes, he's downstairs."

"Let's go, then, I've not much time. Is it through here?" She started down the hall.

"Excuse me," Mrs. Jeffries said, "but who are you?" She had a bad feeling about this.

"I'm Georgiana Merchant," she replied. "Georgy for short. Is he down there?" They'd reached the back stairs.

"Yes, but why do you wish to see Smythe?" Mrs. Jeffries asked, keeping her voice as low as possible.

But Georgy didn't reply; she simply charged down the stairs. "Smythe, Smythe, are ya down there, darlin'? It's me, Georgy, and we've not much time."

Mrs. Jeffries knew disaster was in the making. She raced after the woman.

Georgy dashed into the kitchen, skidding to a halt as she saw the others grouped around the table. Her wide mouth creased in a smile when she spotted Smythe. "Cor blimey, Smythe, I'll bet this is a surprise for ya, isn't it?"

Smythe, his jaw hanging open, got to his feet.

"Who is that woman?" Betsy got up as well.

"It's Georgy Merchant," he mumbled. "She's a friend from Australia. Blast a Spaniard, Georgy, what are you doin' here?"

"You've got to come with me," Georgy said without preamble. She pulled a slip of yellow paper out of the jacket of her dress.

"This telegram come for me today, and we've got to get home. They're wantin' to hang Da for murder, but he's run off to the bush."

"What is she talking about?" Betsy protested. "You can't leave. We're getting married in two days."

"Betsy, let me talk to Georgy outside for a moment and see what's what," Smythe said softly. He took the red-haired woman by the arm and pulled her down the hall toward the back door.

"This can't be happening," Betsy said. But a horrid, hollow feeling settled in the pit of her stomach.

Mrs. Goodge rose from her chair and went to stand next to the maid. "Don't worry, Betsy. Let's see what this is all about before you go to frettin'."

"Cor blimey, this isn't good," Wiggins muttered. He knew something awful was going to happen. In his experience, when the women of the house wore these kinds of expressions, a man with his wits about him would do well to lie low. He wanted to sneak out and go up to his room, but he felt that might be deserting Smythe.

Betsy's eyes filled with tears, but she blinked them back.

Mrs. Jeffries saw the anguish on the

maid's face and it broke her heart. Like the others, she knew something dreadful was about to happen, but she had no idea how to stop it.

The room was quiet except for the ticking of the carriage clock and the faint sounds of the traffic from the road. Then they heard the back door open and footsteps come up the hall.

Smythe was alone. He stopped at the doorway; his face was white and there was a sheen of moisture on his forehead. "Betsy, love, can you come outside with me for a moment?"

"Is that woman out there?" Betsy demanded.

"No, she's gone." He'd sent Georgy out the garden gate with instructions to find a hansom and bring it around to the front of the house.

Betsy swallowed the lump in her throat. "You can say whatever you need to say in front of the others."

He hesitated and then gave in. "I've got to go, love. Georgy's father is accused of murder and he's taken off to the bush."

"Go where?" she yelled. But she knew.

"Back to Australia," he whispered. "Dear God, if it was anyone but him, I wouldn't leave you for all the world. But I owe him a debt I can never repay. He saved my life; he kept me from starvin' and took me in when I was half dead, I'm the only one that can 'elp him now and I've got to go."

"We're getting married in two days," she cried.

"We'll get married as soon as I get back." He moved then, coming to her and taking her by the shoulders. "I promise, love, we'll get married as soon as I'm back, but I've no choice. I've got to go."

Through her tears, she searched his face and realized that she'd lost. She pulled away from him. "Go then, but don't expect me to be waiting when you get back."

"You don't mean that, love," he cried, anguish on his own face.

"I've never been more serious in my life," she retorted. She didn't care if she was unreasonable, she didn't care if she hurt him; she knew only that she hurt more than she'd ever hurt in her life. "If you leave me now, if you put me second and humiliate me like this, I'll never forgive you."

"Betsy, no, you can't mean that," he pleaded.

But she tore away from him and ran for the stairs.

He started after her then stopped. He looked at Mrs. Jeffries. "I've got to go Mrs.

J. I've got no choice. If I don't, an innocent man is goin' to hang. There's no time to explain everything and make her understand."

"She doesn't mean what she said, Smythe," Mrs. Jeffries said softly. "She's very upset. What do you want me to do?"

He took a deep breath. "Make sure she picks up her weddin' gown and her trousseau from the dressmaker's, and don't let her do anything foolish like try to run off."

Mrs. Jeffries wasn't sure she could stop her, but she wasn't going to share that with him. "Alright. How long do you think you'll be gone?"

"I'm not certain. It's a good nine weeks out there, and God knows how long it'll take to find him. But I've got to try."

"What's 'e done?" Wiggins asked.

"He's accused of murder, so he's gone off to the bush," Smythe said. "Georgy was here in London visitin' her auntie. She got a telegram late yesterday and started lookin' for me."

"Why do you have to go find him?" Mrs. Goodge asked. She was struggling to hold back tears; watching Betsy's face had broken her heart.

"Because I'm the only one who can," Smythe replied. He started for the stairs.

"I'm going to throw a few things in a bag and then I've got to be off. The ship leaves on the evening tide."

He was back downstairs in less than ten minutes. The others, except for Betsy, were waiting to say good-bye at the front door. Mrs. Jeffries had seen a hansom pull up outside. "Your cab is here," she said. "Don't worry. I'll take care of telling the inspector."

"Thank you," Smythe glanced up toward the staircase. "I will be back."

"And I'll make sure Bow and Arrow is properly looked after." Wiggins struggled not to cry. "I promise. I know how much them silly 'orses mean to you, and I'll see that the carriage is taken out regularly." The horses and carriage belonged to Witherspoon, but Smythe had been in charge of them for so long, they felt like his own.

"You just be sure to take care," Mrs. Goodge ordered, her voice rough with suppressed emotion. "I'll not have you getting lost out amongst them heathens, and mind you get back here as quick as you can. I want to wear my new dress to your wedding."

Smythe pulled her close in a hug, embraced Mrs. Jeffries, and shook Wiggin's hand. "I'll be back as soon as I can," he promised.

He pulled open the front door and stepped outside. "Don't let her leave," he said to Mrs. Jeffries. "Promise me she'll be here when I get back."

Mrs. Jeffries hesitated. "I promise. She'll be here."

He turned and went down the stairs to the waiting hansom.

Upstairs, Betsy watched from the window. A cry of pain escaped from her lips as she saw him step into the cab. Dear God, this was her worst nightmare come true. He was going. He was leaving her, and she knew deep in her heart that despite what he said, he was never coming back.

She'd been abandoned before.

She watched the cab until it went around the corner. Betsy moved away from the window and went over to her bed. Dropping to her knees, she reached underneath and pulled out her carpet bag. She blew the light coating of dust off the frame and put it on her bed.

Then she began to pack.

EPILOGUE

Betsy stood under the tree in the communal gardens where she and Smythe had spent so many hours together. The others thought she was still upstairs, nursing her wounds. She'd slipped out when she'd heard them go downstairs for their supper. She turned and looked at the house; her packed carpetbag was at her feet.

She could see the lights from the kitchen, and she knew that they'd all be upset when they found her gone tomorrow morning, but that couldn't be helped. A strangled cry arose in her throat, but she pushed it back, determined to stay strong. She had to go. But Lord, it was so hard. She loved them all so much. They'd become her family.

"He'll die when he gets back and finds you gone," Mrs. Jeffries said softly.

Betsy whirled around as the housekeeper stepped out from behind a row of bushes. "I didn't see you come out."

"I came through the gate," she replied. "Don't leave, Betsy. If you go, you'll break all our hearts."

Betsy burst into tears. She hung her head and sobbed. Mrs. Jeffries hurried over and pulled her into her arms. "I know you've had a terrible shock, but he loves you more than life itself. You have to stay and wait for him to come back."

"But he's not coming back," Betsy cried. "I know it. He doesn't really want to marry me."

"Is that what this is all about?" Mrs. Jeffries kicked at Betsy's carpetbag. "Of course he does. That man would die for you."

"But he left me."

"Only because he had to repay a debt of honor." Mrs. Jeffries looked her directly in the eye. "If he'd refused to go and help save an innocent man, you know you'd think less of him. If you're going to marry Smythe, Betsy, then you've got to trust him." She gave her shoulders a squeeze, turned, and started for the house.

After a moment, Betsy picked up her bag and followed Mrs. Jeffries back inside.

Smythe stared at the lights of Tilbury as the SS *Oroya* pulled away from the dock. He was on the first-class deck, but he could care less about the luxurious furnishings in his quarters. All he could think of was Betsy, of her face as she'd realized he had to go. Blast and damn, this couldn't have happened at a worse time. But he had to go. He'd no choice.

He prayed that Betsy would still be waiting for him when he got back. When he'd boarded, he'd asked one of the seamen how long it would take to get to Sydney. The answer had depressed him. Nine weeks, nine ruddy weeks! If you added a month or two for him to find Tommy Merchant and settle whatever mess he'd gotten into, and then another two months back to England, blast, it would be almost Christmas before he got back.

But Betsy would be there. She had to be. He couldn't lose her now.

The employees of Thorndike Press hope you have enjoyed this Large Print book. All our Thorndike and Wheeler Large Print titles are designed for easy reading, and all our books are made to last. Other Thorndike Press Large Print books are available at your library, through selected bookstores, or directly from us.

For information about titles, please call:
(800) 223-1244

or visit our Web site at:
www.gale.com/thorndike
www.gale.com/wheeler

To share your comments, please write:
Publisher
Thorndike Press
295 Kennedy Memorial Drive
Waterville, ME 04901